Ninth Life

JANE TERESA ANDERSON

Published by Jane Teresa Anderson
JaneTeresa.com

First published 2024

© 2024 Jane Teresa Anderson

The moral right of the author has been asserted.

All rights reserved. Without limiting the rights under copyright restricted above, no part of this publication may be reproduced, stored in or introduced into a retrieval system, or transmitted, in any form or by any means (electronic, mechanical, photocopying, recording or otherwise), without the prior written permission of the copyright owner and publisher of this book.

A catalogue record for this book Is available from
the National Library of Australia.

ISBN   978 1 7635813 1 9 (pbk)
           978 1 7635813 2 6 (ebk)

Designed and typeset by Nada Backovic
Additional images from Shutterstock and rawpixel
Author photo by Michael Collins

To the random cat who appeared in our garden,
stared at me, and left this tale in her wake.

Who ever knew a solitary bee could make so much noise? Cat swipes a paw at the annoying buzz and catches the nostril-spiking perfume of spring green mixed with a musky vanilla headiness that she knows so well. Daffodils! Instantly on guard, she leaps from the scent of danger and lands on all four tippytoed paws on an old stone wall, a safe vantage point from which to consider her next move.

Come to think of it, she muses, *what was my last move? What brought me here?*

She stares blankly into mid-air. Nothing comes to mind, other than the threat of daffodils and a shameful story unravelling so fast that it flies into a million irretrievable pieces.

Cat's veins ice, and she's left with the only conclusion possible. She sinks to her belly to examine the fleshy pads on her left paw. *One, two, three, four, five*, before moving to her right paw. *Six, seven, eight*. Eight marks for eight lives lived, a smooth patch where number nine will be notched when she passes her tests and graduates from this, her final life, to become a wise spirit mentor to an earthbound being. Unless she fails.

She slumps deeper into the ancient stone beneath her belly, squeezing her eyes shut, calming her breath, looking for focus.

This is what she knows in her bones: the stone beneath her is warm. The air smells of the English countryside with a dash of salty sea on the breeze. She is beginning her ninth life and she needs to get it right this time, follow the rules, stay in line and make sure everyone else does too, or she's back to square one, and who knows how many more centuries of earthbound lives before she gets another crack at graduation.

She racks her mind for more, unable to catch any sense of her previous eight lives, yet reassured by a knowing that this oblivion is the way of things.

It's a clean start, and all she needs to do is follow her twitching nose and that beguiling line of shiny black ants marching in single file across the stone wall, intent, so it seems, on getting as far away from those wicked daffodils as possible. She hauls herself up, points her tail skywards and steps into line, a song in her heart.

Soon, the river of ants flows down the stone wall, across a patio, ascends three stone steps and enters the rose-scented hallway of an otherwise musty grand old home, before taking a sharp vertical turn up a sunshine-yellow wall covered in squiggly black lines. Unable to follow the ants up the wall, Cat sits, curls her tail around her haunches and waits, while her eyes adjust to the squiggly black lines as they settle into words:

The Serene Lotus Centre for Health and Wellbeing.

Rule one: do no harm.

Rule two: help and heal.

Rule three: support each other.

Rule four: leave your troubles at home.

Thank you, ants, she purrs, though the marching line has long gone, its task complete. Could her mission be any clearer? Get it right this time, follow the rules, stay in line and make sure everyone else does too.

Six weeks later
Irritation claws her skin. Why does everyone at the Serene Lotus Centre for Health and Wellbeing insist on calling her Amantha, the marmalade cat? She would say she's more honey than marmalade, more beehive community energy – honey for the common good – than boiled, sickly-sweet, sticky jam. She admires her front paws stretched across the plush purple velvet cushion as she lounges in the early-evening setting sun. Honey and plum purple, what a noble combination.

Noble, spiritual, wise. Self-appointed unofficial guardian and protector of the Serene Lotus Centre for Health and Wellbeing, protector of its medieval stone foundations, its twenty-first-century modifications, its practitioners and their clients. Her workplace by day, her home by night.

She spreadeagles deeper into the cushion, points her antennae ears and invites the ghosts of the afternoon's conversations into the room. Emmy the hypnotherapist's soothing voice, her client Sasha's whispered secrets, their voices clinging to the folds of the curtains and swept under the walnut-coloured coffee table, but not coming out to play tonight, it seems.

She tries three yogic breaths to find her focus: in for one meow, two meows, three meows, out for six meows. The voices in the room remain silent, but Cat's stomach growls like a red-blooded dog hungry for meat, real meat, none of this vegan biscuit with a side bowl of almond milk that she's been fed since she arrived on the scene. *No, that's not fair*, she castigates herself. *I took on this job. As a spiritually minded cat, I do no harm to any living thing. No killing of animals, no plunging of marmalade oranges into boiling water. Besides, it's the first rule of the centre.*

Her stomach growls again, and this time she smells mouse. Real, musky mouse. And strangely, mouldy cheese. Suddenly, the metallic allure of blood. She's on her feet before she can chant *Om*, face to face with the freshly mangled creature in the mousetrap under the coffee table, eyeing the baby mouse frozen to the spot inches away from her mother's bloodied body.

The baby mouse knows, Cat knows. The temptation draws her body into a tight arch, the unbearable urge to pounce quivering every muscle. Heaven knows a cat can't live on vegan food alone. She has, what, a year at most before her body will wither from a meatless diet? Can she fulfil her mission within a year, or will it take longer? Who will replace her when she's gone?

Cat sinks to her haunches, a thousand repeats of her 'do no harm' mantra done and dusted throughout a long, sleepless night prowling the perimeter of the room, one eye on the mouth-watering bloodied mouse in the mousetrap, one eye on the door waiting for Emmy to arrive, clear up the mess and put an end to temptation.

As far as the mouse is concerned, the harm is already done. Any other cat might take a quick lick and a bite, convince herself that she's helping to dispose of the dead body, a saint rather than a sinner. *But that*, Cat tells herself as she claws her nails into the rattan mat under Emmy's coffee table to firm her resolution, *is not the point*. The point is, there are rules, and Emmy broke the do-no-harm rule the moment she set the mousetrap. As guardian and protector of the Serene Lotus Centre for Health and Wellbeing, Cat's mind is clear: she must put an end to the use of mousetraps and get everyone back in line with the rules.

Cat positions herself on top of Emmy's desk and sits tall – channelling pose. She eyes the door and twitches her ears to check the rhythm of the footsteps dancing along the hallway, a distinct waltz that signals Emmy. Freya shuffles, Abby teeters in stilettos and Serenity glides almost imperceptibly except to Cat's ears, but Emmy's routine is to waltz up to her door to start her day. It's part one of her ritual, followed by part two as she opens the door to her office and sings, 'One, two, three, one, two, three, one, two, three, free!'

It's odd because most people she has observed feel free when they leave work at the end of the day, not when they begin. But this is not the time for psychoanalysing. It's time for action. Emmy is not free to disregard the centre's rules, and that poor dead mouse certainly isn't free, in this life, at least.

The feline key to successfully channelling a message is to make eye contact and hold the person's gaze for three seconds, but the stink of decaying mouse grabs Emmy's attention before she notices Cat, and she drops to her knees to peer at the mess under the coffee table. This calls for more drastic action. Cat springs from her carefully chosen position in front of the sandstone Buddha next to Emmy's laptop – she had figured a bit of backup from Buddha might not go amiss – and lands on all fours, back severely arched, eye to eye with a startled Emmy. Cat holds Emmy's gaze for the required three seconds – one meow, two meows, three meows – and begins her thought transmission: *Do no harm, do no harm, do no harm.*

Emmy's eyes widen as she clearly receives the message. 'Amantha! The perfect solution. Why didn't I think of it before? Mousetrapping is in your blood, it's in your genes, you're hard-wired to trap, and bonus, eat mice. It's authentic cat behaviour, as nature intended. And if you do this job well, you gift the mice with a nice, quick, clean death. No harm done, really, when I think of it that way.'

Every fibre in Cat's body primes to reach out and scratch Emmy's face, wake her up to her mistake, but scratching would break rule one. She slinks away to rethink her next move. For now, it's stalemate.

There's nothing sweeter, Cat thinks, as she drags her aching bones towards her feeding corner in the pokey kitchen pantry, *than a full stomach and an evening alone to lick her paws after a tough day of work.* If she's to take her job seriously – and she must if she is to graduate – she needs replenishment and time to review and plan. And a very long re-energising recovery catnap.

She hauls her tired body across the cold kitchen tiles, the two matching glazed ceramic bowls firmly in sight, each the colour of honey, one for her vegan bites, one for her almond milk. But something is amiss. She stalls, quivers her nostrils and suddenly she's wide awake, shocked, legs as straight as tentpoles propping her up to her full arched height. The smell of tinned cat meat wafts from one bowl, thick cow's cream tempts from the other. Not a vegan bite in sight.

On high alert, Cat scans the room for clues, energy imprints of the last couple of hours. Yes, there it is: the timpani of hard, dry vegan bites hitting the kitchen sink, the whoosh of water and metallic grind of the waste disposal system, the all-pervading oily, nutty aroma of almond milk clinging to the sink, the soft scream of a tin lid being rolled back and the scrape of a spoon sloshing the meat into a bowl. Emmy's bergamot-and-vanilla perfume. Cat narrows her eyes and focuses deeper, searching for Emmy's thoughts hanging in the cool kitchen air.

Aha, her tail twitches. *Got her!* She drops to the floor, exhausted. The cat's out of the bag now. Emmy's agenda is clear: if she can tempt Cat to eat meat, she might tempt her to catch mice, and if she catches mice, Emmy will not need to lay mousetraps.

Cat's body makes the decision for her.

The meat slides down her throat faster than she can argue to the contrary, and every lick of the cream follows.

Decision made, replete, feeling restored, she argues her dilemma from her new perspective. *What if*, she ponders, flicking her tail to the left, *giving vegan bites and almond milk to cats is causing them harm? What if*, she gathers confidence, flicking her tail to the right, *not eating meat is doing harm to my body and shortening my life? What if*, she concludes – though she still frames it as a question – *shortening my life is doing harm to the Serene Lotus Centre for Health and Wellbeing, its practitioners and clients, depriving them of my long-term guardianship and protection? What if*, she admires her outstretched paws, out of questions for now, but playing with the theme like a cat with a ball of wool, *what if* … But she falls asleep before she finishes her thought.

Cat startles as Abby plucks her from her snoozing place deep within the crevices of the mountainous beige canvas beanbag in the middle of the pow-wow. Or is it the Power Hour? She's not sure, but either way it must be Monday – which she knows is the name of the day after the very quiet day when she has the run of the centre to herself. Mondays start with the practitioners' pow-wow. Or is it the ow-ow, since they often seem to be comparing notes about their aches and pains, their suffering, anguishes and hurts?

Ow, that hurts, Cat hisses, as Abby digs her fingers a little too sharply into Cat's well-breakfasted stomach before settling her onto her bony lap.

'What do we think, then? Do we work Amantha into our brand or not?' All eyes turn to Serenity, chief pow-wow person, swathed in her voluminous post-yoga indigo pashmina.

Brand? Cat's already discomfited stomach wobbles at the prospect of a flaming branding iron singeing her fur and scorching into her tender skin. Could she endure the pain in return for wearing the mark of their respect, the brand badge of honour confirming her role as their guardian and protector? Abby's warm fingers smooth the tense muscles across the back of Cat's neck, and the fiery vision recedes as Cat realises they're talking about using her image in their business, not torching her skin. She shakes her head, fully awake now. Must have been a flashback to one of her previous eight lives.

'I don't know, Serenity,' Abby begins, 'we've already got quite a long, clunky name for our centre, and we've worked your name – well, a version of it – into it, so we don't really have space for more words in our title. As far as visuals go, my feeling is that we're a touch heavy on details as it is. We've incorporated the Rajpapa Foundation's logo into the lotus design to signify your yoga lineage, and well, adding a cat, what message would we be giving?' Abby kicks off her teetering, tottering heels and spreads her toes in delightful freedom.

Cat stretches her paws – claws retracted – in synchrony and

relief. What message would they be giving, indeed? She's all ears for Serenity's reply.

'Come to think of it,' Serenity bows her head to her mala necklace, passing another ten luminescent emerald beads along its silken thread, 'Guru Rajpapa tells the story of a spirit cat that guards the entrance to his ashram and ensures the safety and wellbeing of all who enter. It's why every Rajpapa Yoga class begins with cat arches moving into sphinx pose. It's tapping into protecting our wellbeing. Or something like that. I can look it up.'

Cat props herself up on her elbows and proudly lifts her head, embodying the sphinx pose she has seen Serenity teach in her pre-dawn yoga classes. Abby chuckles and points to Cat in her lap.

'Look, anyone would think Amantha knows what we're talking about.'

A burst of giggles punctuated by Serenity's 'Oh bless' boils Cat's blood. *Isn't it obvious*, she meows, *that I understand every word?* She looks around at the four adoring faces – Abby, Serenity, Emmy and Freya – four pairs of ears all deaf to meow language. She has to work out how to uplevel her communication skills if she wants to make herself understood.

'Isn't a sphinx a lion's body with a human head and eagle wings?' Emmy ventures aloud, twiddling one of her dangly but demure silver earrings. Emmy is such a stickler for detail, from her immaculately pressed jade linen pants and matching jacket over the soft glow of her chalk silk shirt, to the slick of jade eye liner giving a hint of cat eye, and the silver earrings drawing attention back to the chalk shirt. One nod for following the rules of elegant professional dressing, another nod for following the rules of language and being specific, minus a nod for her less-than-immaculate handling of yesterday's mouse problem. What would the other women say if they knew about the harm their oh-so-proper Emmy has been waging with her mousetraps?

Maybe I do have sphinx energy. Cat refines her posture. *The ruling majesty of a lion cat, a head that can understand human language and wise eagle wings that gift a higher view of any situation. Maybe I'm their guardian and protector sphinx.*

'Or, sorry, am I being a bit too academic and pedantic again?' Emmy interrupts Cat's musing. 'I'm trying to free myself up, think more laterally, be more creative.'

'We all love you just the way you are, Emmy.' Abby drops Cat into Emmy's lap. 'Amantha loves you, too, don't you, kitty?'

Kitty! Cat crash-lands from sampling her future life as an exalted lion-eagle sphinx to being everyone's darling generic little kitty. *Does kitty love Emmy?* she asks. *Yes, no, maybe, I don't know. Who am I anyway? How am I doing as guardian and protector? It's been six weeks, and Emmy's already made me break a rule, but then she's also feeding me life-affirming meat. Maybe I do love her a little bit.*

'As the least academic person in this room,' pipes up Freya, 'or at least, I feel that way these days. Somewhere in my distant past, I managed a social work degree and six years as a social worker, but it's only since I've been using my psychic gift these last ten years that I feel I've really been able to give anyone hope. Lately though, I'm feeling a bit brain-fogged. What was I saying?'

Another peal of giggles rings through the room.

'You all think I'm being funny, don't you? Truly, sometimes I feel as frayed as my name suggests. Do you think it's my age? Could I be perimenopausal?'

Ah, Cat relaxes her pose, *now we enter the ow-ow stage of the pow-wow*. But just as Cat prepares for the communal laying down of hurts and the laying on of hands, Abby restores a sense of order.

'I don't know, Freya, I'm still in my twenties, so that's unknown territory for me. And I'm not sure where you were going with your point about being the least academic person in the room, and I'm not sure where you, Emmy, were going with your point about sphinxes, but our Power Hour is almost done and we still have the question on the table: are we going to work

Amantha into our brand? Serenity has engaged me to look at our marketing materials and do a website update before the end of the month, so I need a decision and some suggestions today, please.'

'How do you do it?' Freya eyes Abby. 'Be in psychotherapist mode half the week – and I know you're really good at what you do – and then flip into this branding, marketing, writing work the other half of the week, and then do all the technical website work for us on top of that? Yes, I know that doesn't quite add up, but you know what I mean.'

'Well, I don't have as many clients as you, Freya, and I need to pay my rent, so I'm relying on the extra work until I can let it go and focus on psychotherapy. Writing and branding was a side hustle that helped support me through university, and I do quite enjoy the creative challenge and seeing something concrete come out of my work.'

'I've had a side hustle ever since I left the social work department, though that's probably the wrong word,' Freya says. 'A casual job at the post office sorting out the mail at the crack of dawn every day. My spirit-reading work still isn't quite enough to support my boys, though at fifteen and seventeen they should be off and out and earning their own keep soon.'

'Okay, everyone, back on track,' summons Serenity. 'I'm trying to get a few more clients and their money through the door for all of you, and it seems to me that Amantha's appearance on our front steps was a divine sign, especially as you've all taken to her so much, and she seems to have taken to us, too. Let's go round the circle and each say what difference you've noticed in your work since her arrival. What does she mean to us collectively, and how can we use that to attract more clients?'

Cat's ears prick up. *Use me to bring in business? Listen, people, I'm not here to bring you business! I'm here to guard and protect you all, to make sure you do the right thing and follow the rules. I'm just not sure how to convey this to you. Don't box me in.*

Emmy begins. 'People love having animals around. It settles them. People who are new to hypnotherapy can be very anxious, and it can be hard work getting them relaxed enough to surrender to hypnosis, but I've found they're more at ease when Amantha's there. So, I see her as a calming, settling presence, helping them to let go and trust.'

Freya clears her throat. 'Some clients have asked if Amantha's my familiar, which I guess means they see me as a witch, not a psychic who sees spirits. Am I a witch? If I am, I'm a white witch. The whole point of my work is to help people, give them peace and hope through messages from their departed loved ones. I don't give people spells, do I? But anyway, part of me feels like Amantha is my long-lost familiar, a spirit in cat form, keeping me safe, helping me ... oh, is she helping me to channel? Where am I going with this? Maybe I see her as my psychic assistant. Yes, that works. So, psychic assistant, or if you want to get spicy with the marketing, Abby, maybe she's a reincarnated witch's cat.'

Cat holds her breath as she looks at Abby. *Truly? Reincarnated witch's cat?*

'Emmy is right. Amantha's presence is very settling for clients. I've noticed that when my clients share difficult emotions, they often look at Amantha as if they're addressing her, not me, as if she understands, but being a cat, won't talk back. They feel she offers them unconditional love, I suppose. I hadn't seen that so clearly until now. It helps, having to verbalise things, doesn't it? In the same way that it helps my clients to verbalise their feelings and stories to a cat. They get to see their situation more clearly ...' She trails off, deep in thought for a moment. 'Oh, so she means unconditional love and is a conduit for clarity.'

As far as I was concerned, Cat remembers, *I was simply lounging in Abby's room during her consultations, mostly enjoying a spot of open-eyed daydreaming, some respite from the tension of Freya's sessions crowded with jostling human spirits, some freedom from working hard not to succumb to being hypnotised during Emmy's sessions, and time out from interacting with the yogis during Serenity's classes. A conduit for clarity, a provider of unconditional love? Who would have thought?*

Serenity shrugs the pashmina from her shoulders, pulls the eagle feather from her yoga bun, shakes her red-hennaed tresses free, and – as if to balance all that opening – crosses her legs into a tight lotus pose. 'Apart from a couple of people who have complained about Amantha because they're allergic to cat dander, most of our yoga students love having her around. I swear, she gets a bigger welcome than I do most mornings. They coo over her, tell her how darling she is and how much she's grown since their last visit. You know what? They bond over her. It's like she's the glue for their conversations, the focal point for their oohs and aahs when they don't know what else to say to each other. So, I'd say she's a welcoming spirit, makes people feel at home, brings people together. And when she sits in a spot of sunlight right next to someone when they're doing a downward dog, or when she sits on someone's tummy when they're doing *savasana*, or when she arches her back alongside someone when they're doing cat arches, they respond like they're specially chosen, or blessed, or understood, or being given a message. Perhaps they see her as divine?'

So, Cat thinks, *Serenity sees me as something between a welcoming hostess, a conversation starter and a divine messenger, when most of the time I'm just looking for somewhere to warm my freezing early-morning bones. Though the divine-messenger bit appeals. I could brush up my communication skills and work with that.*

'So,' Abby concludes, padding in her bare feet over to the whiteboard, marker in hand, 'let's make a list of what Amantha means, and vote on whether we want her to be part of our brand, and if so, how we want to portray her to attract more clients and bring us more business.'

Cat surveys the list:

1. A calming, settling presence. Helps clients let go and trust.
2. A familiar or psychic assistant.
3. A reincarnated witch's cat.
4. Unconditional love.
5. Someone to talk to who won't talk back.
6. A conduit for clarity.
7. A welcoming spirit.
8. Brings people together – bonds with communication glue.
9. A divine messenger.
10. Maybe a guardian and protector of the centre like Guru Rajpapa's sphinx.

She could live a very comfortable life in any of these roles, well fed, loved, looked after, looked up to, but only number ten fits with what she's here to accomplish in her ninth life. Guardian, protector, keeper of the rules. On reflection, roles one to nine do not necessarily involve making sure people do the right thing. It boils down to accepting a life of comfort and ease but having to reincarnate and go through another nine lives, versus finding a way to communicate her destined role, get it right this time and graduate from her ninth life.

'Okay, beautiful people,' Serenity surveys the whiteboard one last time, 'none of us would be in this business if we weren't wonderfully intuitive, so let's take a quick vote. Do we want to include Amantha in our branding? Show of hands for *yes*.'

All hands shoot up.

'Abby will need just one of the attributes to focus on. What's the one message we want to give about Amantha? What will bring more people through our doors?'

Cat can't listen to the final discussion as they whittle it down.

She covers her ears with her paws and shakes, until Abby reaches down and lifts her into a communal hug. 'Welcome, Amantha, divine messenger,' they chant, almost squeezing the life out of her in their jubilant embrace.

Cat's heart momentarily swells with pride and possibility, before the cold, hard truth hits home. They're using her, misrepresenting her to get more clients, more accolades, more income. In using her, they're hurting her and breaking their most precious first rule.

Abby scrubs the whiteboard clean and swings it around to display the rules permanently inked on the reverse:

Rule one: do no harm.

Rule two: help and heal.

Rule three: support each other.

Rule four: leave your troubles at home.

Cat thumps her tail, anchoring her resolve. Time to show them who she is and what she's here for. First, let off some steam – perhaps catch a mouse or two to support Emmy and build her own strength for the job ahead – and then retire for a quiet evening of licking her wounds and a good sleep before a fresh start in the morning. *Right, that's the plan*, she decides, sniffing the air for a mouse.

Cat leaps from Freya's well-worn burnt-umber leather chair onto the stone windowsill, stretches her legs until the tips of her paws tingle and sinks her belly into the cat-shaped hollow in the aged stone. It's the perfect vantage point to watch Freya's clients as they perch, hopefully yet nervously, on the green velour armchair opposite Freya's leather throne, and to watch their faces as they receive messages from their departed loved ones.

Talking of departed loved ones, some don't know the meaning of the word *depart*, do they? Cat jostles every day with at least ten earthbound spirit cats whose bodies have carved this hollow over the centuries and believe it's still theirs to occupy, but Cat, being physically in the world, gets first dibs. The human spirits prefer to hover near the office door, not sure whether to stay or go, sometimes suspiciously eyeing each other, cautious of what secrets they may intend to expose about one another. Cat counts three human spirits waiting for Freya's first client of the morning.

She watches as Freya enters the room and dumps a pile of inky-smelling flyers on the windowsill, right under her nose. 'Fresh off the printer, Amantha. Fast work, eh? I hope you're impressed. "Freya the psychic, accompanied by her faithful cat, Amantha." And look, there you are in all your slinky, witchy cat glory. It's one of my favourite photos of you. What do you think? I'm planning on posting them around the neighbourhood this afternoon and leaving some at reception.'

Cat feels nothing. Numb from heart to paw. The freeze frame before the storm.

Suddenly Freya is all whirlwind, pulling off her emerald-green woollen jumper, throwing it onto her chair and whipping a paper fan from her handbag. A new ritual, maybe? Freya frantically fans her reddening face, a river of sweat cascading down her neck and visibly splotching her crisp white linen blouse. 'No, please no, not now,' she whimpers.

But it is now, and Cat watches as the first client, clearly a hassled young mum with the telltale smear of baby vomit on her shoulder, enters the room and settles into her chair. Freya begins her reading.

'I'm just an ordinary middle-aged woman, but Amantha is my link to the spirit world, my conduit,' she says, pointing at Cat. 'Please nod to Amantha to acknowledge her presence.'

Cat's numbness fast recedes and a soaring irritation claws at her skin. Did Freya ever ask if she could refer to Cat as her psychic conduit? Did she ever ask if she could use Cat's image in her new marketing materials? She stills her twitching, seething tail and reminds herself of her true calling as guardian and protector of the centre, its practitioners and clients. Wise guardian, not symbolic sidekick. She slithers over to the flyers while Freya is busy with her client, backs up against the window, positions herself to take aim, sprays her scent to her deep satisfaction, then finishes the job by crouching and pee-flooding Freya's entire batch of flyers into sodden oblivion.

'One pee, just one pee to make my mark, sign my name, spell with the smell, teach her that I'm Cat, not Amantha, and what do I get for my effort? Grabbed by my neck and tossed out the window into a patch of stinging nettles. Is that the way to treat your "faithful cat, Amantha"? I don't think so.'

Cat paws at a black stag beetle, her captive audience, flips it into the air and watches it land on its back, legs flaying. It feels good to talk to someone. She nudges the beetle back on its feet. The mighty little creature signals good over evil, right over wrong. And Cat feels so very wronged.

'That Freya, so skilled in receiving messages from spirit people, but she can't understand my very plain, simple message about the way she uses me and how she does me harm. She has no idea how much I can help her, guide her, share my wisdom, if only she'd listen! And how can I do that when she tosses me out here?'

The beetle listens as it glistens in the mid-May sunshine.

'There will be no "out here" when I graduate from this life. No animal body for people to photograph for flyers, toss out the window, trip over when they walk down the hall, overlook when they're consumed by their own thoughts, disregard as being a lower form of life, or misrepresent as their divine messenger, all in the name of making more money. If it wasn't for this body, I wouldn't be stuck out here, stinging with nettled rage. I'd be at Freya's side in a flash, another spirit whispering in her ear, only I'd be sharing my wisdom, none of the "It's Harry, I want you to know that I love you, and that's all I have to say" kind of message that seems to be all the spirit people can muster. Or all that Freya can hear.'

Cat drops to her belly, eye to eye with the silently steadfast, attentive beetle.

'Good over evil. Right over wrong. I don't know how long I've got. How many sunsets, full moons and hot summers to do what I need to do to graduate. To complete this mission. Because that's what it is, isn't it? My mission. And if I fail, how many sunsets, full moons and hot summers will I face in a new cat body, plunged back into another cycle, hauling myself over the coals through another eight lives, before I get to this position again? And that's not counting the possibly vast number of earthbound years between lives spent as a disembodied spirit awaiting reincarnation.'

The beetle's job is done.

Cat wraps up the conversation. 'No. It's now or never. Time for a different approach, a message that Freya cannot miss. But first, I need to get back into the building and gather some ammunition – I mean, ramp up my communication style.'

She turns around to head back inside, but the usual door is nowhere to be seen.

'There you are, Amantha,' a gravelly, kindly voice drawls. 'I've heard all about you, and caught glimpses of you out the front, but I've never seen you round this side of the building.'

Ah, thinks Cat, meeting Briar, the gnarly, muscled gardener, up close for the first time. She looks around, eyes focusing beyond the nettle patch and the muddy bark where the black stag beetle had held her gaze. *How do I get back inside from here?*

Here, it turns out, looks very different to the front of the building, where Cat only pops out long enough to pee or poop or stargaze before heading back inside. She likes to stay close to home, close to her duties, and besides, she's not entirely convinced that those ominous, vile-smelling daffodils won't suddenly reappear if she ventures over in their direction. But here she is, thanks to Freya, wondering if there's a way back into the building that doesn't involve traversing the old daffodil patch or launching herself at Freya's high first-storey window next time it's open. Which it isn't, right now.

'What do you think of our masterpiece?' Briar waves his topiary shears at a towering box hedge. 'Our Reclining Woman with Child.'

A blackbird swoops down and lands delicately on an outreach of the hedge that Cat sees is the reclining woman's open palm. In a flash, her eyes accommodate to the vast scale of the hedge sculpture, and there, where once there was a boundary hedge, is a voluptuous woman cradling a baby in one arm, gazing at the serenading blackbird in her outstretched hand. The hedge canvas is too enormous for the blackbird to see anything other than a good bit of hedge from which to call for his mate.

The more Cat looks, widening her vision, she sees the reclining woman is one of several, all regally dressed in the style of a bygone century, all sunbathing – or rainbathing, or moonbathing, or frostbathing with equal comfort, according to the season and time of day. How long have they been here?

As if he can read her thoughts, Briar slides his shears into his leather toolbelt and crouches beside Cat, enveloping her in the sweet aroma of freshly cut hedge. 'In all honesty, Amantha, I can't really call her our masterpiece. She's been lounging here since Henry Gable first wielded his shears back in sixteen ninety-eight. Fortunately, Henry had the foresight to make drawings of his early work and records of his plans for their evolution and longevity. I am one of a long line of garden artists who have kept her in check over the last three and a half centuries, and I'm proud of my work.'

We share a mission, Briar and I, Cat thinks, *keeping our ladies in check and in alignment with the original vision of their purpose.*

'Oh, hello, Snowy,' Briar greets a sleek white cat who appears and sinuously curls its body around his legs. 'Where did you come from?'

'Pearl,' Snowy meows to Cat. 'It's Pearl, not Snowy. Humans aren't good with subtleties of colour. Or gender. I'm non-binary, by the way.'

'Cat,' Cat replies. 'Not Amantha. Female.'

'I know.' Pearl winks. 'Now, about this reclining-woman-masterpiece thing ...'

'It's an extraordinary work of art, isn't it?' Cat meows. 'Beautifully kept in check by following Henry Gable's rules and vision to a tee. I'm impressed and inspired.'

'But didn't Henry break nature's rules about how the box plant grows?' Pearl says. 'What would you say to Mr Henry Gable if you were around back then, when he first took his shears to the box? Would you argue in favour of the box plant or the artistic vision? In favour of nature's rules or the artist's rules?'

Briar interrupts their feline philosophical wonderings. 'Let me show you something I've just started, over here, behind the vegetable garden.' He leads them to a pile of freshly chopped twigs and leaves, which he sweeps aside with a spindly bamboo rake, revealing a box hedge as high as his chest. 'It's just a beginning. Can you see, Amantha? It's you, or your topiary cousin.' He laughs. 'A few chops in, but the cat shape will be more recognisable in a few days.'

Pearl flashes Cat a sideways glance. 'Nature's rules or the artist's rules? Nature's vision or the artist's vision? Following Henry Gable's rulebook or pioneering a whole new approach? Look at Briar's work, it's different, see?'

A shaft of sunlight reveals a couple of wire struts below the surface and something resembling an interior watering system, or perhaps the basis for a fountain, poked into the emerging Amantha shape.

'I'm experimenting with the interior structure,' Briar says, 'at the cutting edge, you might say, of a new topiary art form.'

Cat squirms as Briar wanders off. Breaking the rules of the ancient art of topiary or breaking nature's rules, she's not comfortable either way. Which are the correct rules? What is the right thing to do?

Pearl speaks the elephant in the garden into being: 'Briar's creating a topiary Amantha, divine messenger. How are you feeling about that, Cat?'

'Misrepresented. Confused. Getting a bit shaky on my role and purpose.'

'Look, you're following your nose, and that's the right thing to do for a cat in her ninth life,' Pearl meows. 'Sometimes your nose knows what your head and heart don't, so it can feel like working in the dark. Your heart might throw you some tricky emotions, your head might question or over-analyse your situation, but your nose asks you to step courageously into the unknown for reasons that will become clear to you later. It can be very scary.'

'I've been following my nose since I arrived at this place, and it's telling me to sniff out people who break the rules, and correct them, put them back on track,' Cat says. 'I'm just a bit wobbly now on which rules to endorse: nature's rules, centuries-old human rules, new rules for a new world …'

Pearl tumbles Cat to the ground, breaking the serious mood. 'Get back inside, Cat. You'll find all the keys to your graduation there, not out here.'

'But, Pearl,' Cat quivers, 'those daffodils lurk under the earth between here and the front door. How do I get past that scary place?'

'Just follow your nose,' Pearl says, delivering one last playful swipe at Cat's whiskers, before running off into the receding evening light.

Cat blinks. Evening light? How the day has flown.

A whiff of bergamot and vanilla catches Cat's attention.

Emmy's unmistakeable signature perfume. She turns to follow her nose, prowls eleven paces, finds Emmy looking up at the moon and wraps herself, purringly, around her legs. 'What are you doing out here, Amantha? You missed your lunch. Or did you find a tasty mouse? Come on, darling, let's take you in before I lock up the place and go home for the night.'

And with that, Cat's immediate problem is solved. Emmy whisks her up into her arms, carries her past the patch where the daffodils sleep beneath the earth, up the stone steps and into the kitchen, where her tinned meat and full-fat cream dinner awaits. Sustenance, Cat reassures herself as she dives in for a feed, for what she needs to do next.

In the early-morning light, Cat climbs the old oaken staircase to the yoga studio on the first floor and audaciously positions herself on top of the stone altar beside the gilt-framed picture of Guru Rajpapa. She sits tall, Buddha-style, and practises a warm, benevolent gaze. Welcoming pose. What was it Serenity had said about her? A welcoming spirit, a bonding glue for the students? And that bit about how students feel she's giving them messages. If she's to brush up on her communication skills, the yoga class is a good place to start. Begin where it's working, where people feel a connection, where they're interested in what she can offer. From there, she can step more firmly into her role.

In the last peaceful moments before Serenity lets the students in, Cat surveys the offerings laid upon the altar around her. Feathers, crystals, sprigs of herbs, a couple of black-and-white photos of parents or grandparents who have passed, maybe, a smudge of tears, a hint of unburdened despair, and an assortment of sweets and lollipops, all veiled in the ashy remains of the incense that had burned throughout the night to cleanse the air after the last students had left the class. In the centre of the altar sits the black leather box inset with tiny mirror fragments, its lid open, ready to receive the written messages each student delivers before surrendering to the class. What messages will they bring today, what questions for the universe, intentions for the day, prayers, wish lists, confessions or pleas for divine forgiveness?

The whiff of hot, milky morning coffee in paper takeaway cups ascends the stairs ahead of the first students.

'Oh, darling Amantha,' the tall one with a halo of dark curls escaping her indigo headband coos. 'You gorgeous being. The answer to my morning prayer, and you'll never know why. Thank you.' She fishes into her purse and extracts her folded piece of paper. 'I guess I'll still post it. Can't do any harm to ask for further confirmation.' She pops it into the black box. 'First in, first served, maybe.' She laughs, peeling off her raincoat and slipping out of her boots, before walking barefoot onto the sacred yoga floor.

Well, that was easy. Cat has no idea what the student was talking about, but she hopes the answer she received was a good one. She intensifies her welcoming pose and makes eye contact with the pixie-haircut woman next in line. *Hold the gaze, that's it.* One meow, two meows, three meows – transmit ... She decides on a test message: *Press your hands together in prayer and delight.* Pixie woman responds immediately, adding a sumptuous smile. 'One glance and you light up my day, Amantha, bless you,' she sings, folding her umbrella before extracting her message and dropping it into the box.

This is good. When people are open and curious, when they hold her gaze, when her message is easy to follow, it works.

Blonde ponytail is next to reach the landing, closely followed by a cheeky elfin face peeking out from under a leaf-green corduroy beret. Cat senses Ponytail's uncertainty as Elfin skips past her, drops her note into the box and beams at Cat. 'Speak up for me, please, Amantha, when my message reaches the heavens.'

Cat holds her gaze for the requisite three meows and transmits her reply, *Slow down, step mindfully, and all will be well.* In an instant, Elfin's skip morphs into a slow tread, accompanied by a more relaxed heartbeat audible only to Cat, but deeply embraced by Elfin's spirit. Cat mentally high-fives; another win for her communication skills, and a much-needed piece of universal wisdom delivered.

Ponytail hovers nervously. 'I'm new. Do I need to put something in the box before class?' she asks Elfin.

'Oh, welcome. I'm Anna, what's your name?'

'Hello, Anna, I'm Clary. Lovely to meet you.'

'And this,' Anna gestures towards Cat, 'is Amantha, our divine messenger. Or friendly Serene Lotus Centre kitty, whichever way you want to look at it. Or at her, I should say. Sorry, Amantha.'

'Hello, Amantha.' Clary steps closer. 'I love cats. My beloved tabby, Tabs, died last month. I think she was heartbroken when I started to pack up the house, ready for the move down here from London. I don't think she wanted to come with us. So, she didn't.' Clary looks from Amantha to Anna. 'Sorry, I'm not sure which one of you I'm talking to here.' She laughs, an escaped tear glinting on her cheek.

Anna wins Clary's gaze, leaving Cat as a silent witness.

'It's a ritual. Serenity encourages us to drop a message into the box before class. It can be anything. It's totally private and no-one ever reads it. They all get burned as an offering to the universe at the end of the day. It's part of the Rajpapa system, but you'll hear more about that in class. There's a notepad and some pencils over there if you want to jot something down and post it before coming in. See you inside. Maybe you'd like to join us for a coffee downstairs afterwards so you can meet the others?'

'Thank you,' Clary blushes, 'that's very kind.' Cat watches as she tears a sheet of paper from the notepad and pauses before writing. She writes slowly enough for Cat to decipher the soft, gliding sounds of the pen strokes: *This is for you, Mum, wherever you are in Heaven. I miss you, and little Benji still cries himself to sleep. Give us a sign to let us know you're okay. Love, Clary.* She folds her message into quarters, kisses it and drops it into the box.

'Have you done a Rajpapa Yoga class before?' Serenity asks, as Clary rolls out her yoga mat, almost knocking Cat off her paws. Cat prances back a step but stays close, ready to curl up near Clary's feet to make her feel a little more at home.

'No. I've been to lots of different yoga classes, but I've never tried this style. I've just moved into the village, and this place is so beautiful I thought I'd give it a try. I'm Clary.'

'Welcome, Clary. You'll find a lot of the individual poses familiar to those you've done in other classes, but we put them together according to Guru Rajpapa's teachings about the nature of the universe.'

Serenity takes her place at the top of the room, pausing for a moment at the expansive picture window behind her to admire the vividly luminescent rainbow arching across the sky. 'Sunshine after the rain,' she announces, 'which fits beautifully with today's theme.' She bends to press 'record' on the laptop in front of her. 'Welcome to all our worldwide students joining us by Zoom. We have eight hundred and thirty-three of you here online today, plus twenty-two beautiful souls in the room. Let's start by lying on our backs for the invocation.' She lights a stick of incense, and the class begins.

Contrary to her intention to stand guard over Clary, Cat falls into an immediate, deep slumber and remains there until Serenity rings the bell to end the class.

'Before you all go,' Serenity says, 'a reminder that there's no class for the next two days as I'm going up to London for the annual Rajpapa Yoga Teachers' Convention. Catching the train before lunch today, so I must dash. Watch my social media. I'll keep you in touch.'

'Eight hundred and thirty-three students by Zoom!' Clary exclaims to Anna.

'Oh, that's nothing compared to the number of people who access the recording after the live class.' Anna shakes her silver-streaked russet locks from her yoga bun and showers Cat's sensitive nose with the lingering rose-petal scent of her shampoo. 'You don't know our Serenity. Tell you more over coffee. Are you coming?'

This is news. Other students? Hundreds of them? Maybe more? As guardian and protector of the centre, its practitioners and students, Cat's remit is so much bigger than she realised. She trots after the small group of students, refreshed from her sleep, ears set to antennae mode to gather the information she needs if she is to do her job well.

Four students gather around the table in the corner of the softly lit café on the ground floor, the smell of hot fig toast and peanut butter momentarily masking the background coffee-bean aroma underscored by a touch of mouse that only Cat notices. They relax back into the Moroccan-inspired cushions of the bench seating, cradling their swiftly delivered coffees, while Cat hops onto a nearby shelf and points her ears in their direction.

'I'm Milly,' Indigo Headband Woman announces to Clary. 'Pleased to meet you.'

'And I'm Pixie,' Pixie-cut Woman adds, much to Cat's surprise. 'I was behind you in class. You've obviously done a lot of yoga before. You're very flexible.'

'I'm Clary. I taught yoga for a couple of years before my son, Benji, was born five years ago, but I prefer being a student these days. I've just moved down from London, and I thought I'd join a class to get to know a few people, settle in.'

'Did you go to Rajpapa classes in London?' Anna asks.

'No. I'd heard of the style, but I don't know much about it. I was more attracted to this beautiful building, to be honest, and the topiary gardens. Intriguing. And the timing of the class works well with dropping Benji off at his new school.'

'What do you think, then, about the Rajpapa style?' Milly spreads a thick slab of peanut butter onto her toast. 'It makes you hungry, doesn't it, or is that just me?'

'It's certainly energetic,' Clary says. 'What was it that Serenity said? Something about building heat and alchemising our spirit?'

'Guru Rajpapa designed the system to cleanse us, physically, emotionally, mentally and spiritually,' Milly says, chewing her toast. 'That's why we start by writing our messages and offering them up to him on the altar. Well, not to him as a person, but to him as a symbol of the divine. The idea is to surrender the message, or your question or your intention or whatever, to the divine, to release your burden and lighten your load, before stepping onto your yoga mat. Let the physical poses and the heat they build in your body do the magic. When Serenity burns our messages, it symbolises the completion of the process. I don't know how much of that I believe, but writing a message and letting it go works for me, regardless of whether Guru Rajpapa or the universe has anything to do with it.' She looks around at the others, somewhat sheepishly. 'I've never shared that before, have I? Am I a heretic?'

Their laughter floats up to Cat. Heretic? Rule breaker?

'The class we did today, Clary, was number six from the Rajpapa system,' Pixie continues. 'There are a hundred and eight classes altogether, each designed to fit a specific theme. Today's theme was "sunshine after the rain", and we had that lovely synchronicity with the rainbow that Serenity mentioned.' Pixie pauses for reflection. 'Or maybe Serenity picked number six because it was raining this morning, and the rainbow was a surprise bonus. Or a sign from the universe or from Rajpapa himself. Anyway, it's a system of set classes that the yoga teacher can select from to suit whatever she thinks we need.'

'I'm not usually a fan of set classes,' Clary says. 'I enjoyed the creative challenge of designing sequences as a yoga teacher, and having the flexibility to change a plan to adapt to how the students are going and what they need. As a student, I like unpredictability. I like to be kept on my toes, to be surprised, not knowing what's ahead of me, but it sounds like these classes provide quite a lot of variety. And I did enjoy today's, very much.'

Cat tilts her head to one side, thinking about Clary's written message and the tear she'd witnessed. Sunshine after the rain was what Clary needed. Sunshine after the rain of her mother's death, sunshine after the rain for little Benji, still missing his grandmother. Possibly some sunshine after the rain of London, or of leaving London for a better life, too. And judging by Clary's smile, there's some sunshine going on for her right now. Yes, number six was exactly the right thing for Clary, and perhaps a lesson about the benefits of following the Rajpapa rules, as well.

She's staggered by the realisation that Serenity's yoga classes abide by strict rules, and how beautifully this fits her mission. Her exponentially expanding mission, given today's bombshell about the enormous number of students doing classes at the centre. She must sharpen her attention to make sure Serenity's students all follow the Rajpapa Yoga rules.

Cat repoints her antennae ears and tunes back in to the animated, caffeinated conversation.

'Eight hundred and thirty-three students by Zoom,' Clary continues, 'is that a record?'

'I think it reached well beyond a thousand per class during the pandemic lockdowns,' Milly says. 'Of course, it was COVID that got online yoga classes started, and Serenity was one of the first yoga teachers to jump on that, and then to build the library of classes that students could access later to suit their time zones. It was all free for a few months, an act of kindness for us all stuck at home, but then she started charging fees, as, of course, she should, and her business went through the roof.'

A business guru, then.

Clary catches Cat's eyes for long enough. 'A business guru, then,' she repeats aloud. 'Building an empire from right here in this village, who would've thought? But Rajpapa is a worldwide movement, so aren't there other Rajpapa Yoga teachers offering their classes online, too?'

Anna stops scrolling and puts down her phone. An hour's yoga had nudged her into mindfulness mode, Cat notes, but the post-yoga coffee had launched her back into high-speed multitasking. 'Other teachers aren't allowed to teach on Zoom or record classes. It's in their contracts. Serenity may be only twenty-eight, but next to Guru Rajpapa she's the big name in Rajpapa Yoga. I can't believe you don't know all this.'

Cat can't believe she doesn't know this, either. Would she have made the commitment when she first arrived if she had known the scale of her mission, or would she have followed her nose out of there as fast as her paws could carry her?

'Google her,' Milly pipes up. 'The long and short of it is that she studied yoga with Rajpapa at his ashram in India when she was eighteen. He was known only as Rajpapa back then. It changed her life. She brought his methods back to London, got a clever marketing person involved, and invited Rajpapa – Guru Rajpapa, they decided to call him because it sounded better – over for a media junket and the rest is history.'

'I'm a devotee.' Pixie presses her hands together in *namaste*. 'It works for me.'

'Serenity documented his classes, their solicitors drew up contracts, and they launched the teacher-training and accreditation courses,' Milly says. 'I believe they're both quite rich now. How else would she be able to afford to rent this whole place?'

'Guru Rajpapa comes over to London once a year for the annual Rajpapa Yoga Teachers' Convention. He's just a figurehead these days, in his seventies now, I think,' Pixie says. 'Check out

Serenity's social media. She'll be posting loads over the next couple of days. She's got a gazillion followers online.'

A gazillion! Cat's eyes widen. *Am I the guardian and protector of a gazillion students?*

'She's a good soul,' Milly adds. 'Don't get us wrong, Clary. She's an excellent teacher, she holds our best interests at heart and we all have stories we can share about what her classes have done for us. I can't imagine that she needs to teach these days, but it seems she enjoys having her bare feet on the yoga floor and staying in touch with village life. It must be quite anchoring for her to have a personal home base.'

Clary begins to gather her things. 'I'm definitely coming back for more yoga when Serenity returns. And I'm booked in to see Freya tomorrow morning. My old neighbour in London recommended her when she discovered we were moving here. She's got quite a reputation, I hear.'

Cat's heart misses a beat. This intel work is time-consuming, but she needs to be in place for Freya's next appointment so she can make amends after the brochure-peeing debacle. Cat needs to be on the right side of everyone if she is to be effective. And to begin with, the right side of Freya is inside her room. If Freya will have her back.

Cat settles into her hollow on Freya's windowsill and tries to quell the anxious heartbeat thumping at her chest by reviewing the centre's rules. In retrospect, peeing on the flyers broke all four rules. It may have harmed her relationship with Freya, it was potentially more damaging than helpful, it wasn't supportive of Freya, and she should have dealt with her personal irritation and troubles back in the safety of her after-hours rooms, not let it rip in one big pee in Freya's office. But it did feel good, she squirms, allowing herself one wickedly satisfying flick of her tail.

NINTH LIFE

The door bursts open and Freya shuffles in, juggling a bulging yellow supermarket bag over her arm while clutching a pile of fresh flyers to her chest. 'I am so very sorry, Amantha, dear one,' she splutters, spilling the flyers onto her coffee table and fishing a large beige plastic storage cube from her bag. 'Dear soul, please forgive me for yesterday. I was so hot and tired, and I know you didn't mean to pee on our flyers. I should have let you out for a break earlier, or maybe I should get you a kitty tray. You did your best, looking for something to soak up the pee. You weren't to know they were valuable. You're only a cat, after all. Albeit a gorgeous cat, our official divine messenger and my psychic assistant.'

Cat purrs, an offering, a fresh start. She'll let off steam about being 'only a cat, after all' later. One step at a time.

'Anyway, Amantha, I procured this storage cube from the post-office sorting room during my shift this morning. They don't need it anymore and it's the perfect size to stack and display the flyers. It can sit right here, on my table, see? You can have the whole windowsill to yourself.'

Next out of Freya's bag is her paper fan, not a moment too soon. She waves it frantically in front of her reddening face and plops down heavily into her chair to take some deep breaths while checking her diary. 'Bobby is next, Amantha. Right now, all I seem to be able to channel is a river of sweat, but once it subsides, I'll be able to get my head in the right space for channelling spirits.'

She leans forward, dripping, and reaches deeper into her bag. 'What's this, then? Oh no,' she groans, 'not again. Looks like I've popped the last parcel into my bag instead of into the local delivery pigeonhole. I'll get sacked from that job if I don't watch out. These damn hot flushes, this damn brain fog.'

She examines the parcel more closely, tosses her head back and laughs. 'Amantha, this one's for you, I think. It's from Barts Health Urology up in London, Professor Kat P. Flyer. You think I'm joking, don't you? You can't make this stuff up sometimes. Synchronicity with a capital S. But what does it mean?' She flips the parcel over. 'Oh, it gets even spookier. It's addressed to a Bobby Smith.' She turns to face Amantha. 'Bobby, the name of my next client?'

As if I'm that stupid, Cat thinks, relieved by the hilarious banter. Friends again.

Bobby enters the room and settles into the green velour armchair, confident, silent, appraising. *All Pearl energy*, Cat thinks, clearly a they/them Bobby.

'I'm just an ordinary middle-aged woman,' Freya begins, 'but Amantha is my link to the spirit world. Please nod to Amantha to acknowledge her presence.'

Cat holds steady. She can get past this for now by focusing on the mission.

Bobby obediently nods at Amantha then stares at Freya, clearly not wishing to speak or give any clues about their life or their questions.

'I've got a Paul here in spirit, Bobby,' Freya says.

Cat looks over to the huddle of spirits at the door. The one at the front, eyebrows arched high in surprise as if he didn't expect to be heard, must be Paul. He looks about forty.

'Paul wants you to know that he's surprised you're here, and that he's been watching over you since he passed. Does this make sense?'

Bobby's lips quiver, but they remain silent. *They want more*, Cat thinks, *before they're willing to endorse what Freya says. Paul is a common name, after all.*

'He passed quite young,' Freya continues. 'Yes, Paul is nodding his head. I think he's saying he died at age forty-three. Can you relate?'

Bobby sheds a single tear and burps a sob. 'Is he my dad? What else can he tell you to confirm who he is?'

Cat looks over at Paul, who mimes taking a pee then clutches his belly and mimes slitting his throat. This peeing theme is taking synchronicity to the nth degree. She puzzles over the message, but Freya is quick at the mark, clearly accustomed to interpreting spirit messages.

'It's tragic news, and I'm worried about sharing it. How much do you want to know, Bobby?'

Bobby shifts forward in their seat, clasping their hands under their shaking chin. 'Everything, I'm ready.'

'I'm getting the feeling that he died from a urinary infection, or bladder cancer, I can't be more precise. But I need to ask Paul another question. Please, be patient for a moment.' She then addresses the spirit: 'Paul, can you be clearer about the throat thing?'

Paul takes a moment to compute, then shakes his head, violently.

'Paul,' Freya says, 'are you saying you didn't speak, that you kept silent about your illness, or are you saying …?' She lets the question hang in the air. Cat realises what she's asking. Did he top himself because of his diagnosis, or did the finger-across-his-throat sign mean he stopped talking?

Enthralled, Cat studies Paul for his response. He thinks for a moment and then clamps his lips together with his fingers.

Freya lets out an audible sigh of relief. 'Bobby,' she says, 'Paul didn't tell anyone about his diagnosis. He could never find the words to tell anyone. I don't know why.'

'He didn't believe in medical intervention,' Bobby says. 'He was quite vocal about it, thought all illness was God-given, that illness is an opportunity to atone before death.'

'He's saying now,' Freya continues, 'he's saying … thank you.'

Bobby sits upright, chin-tucked, puzzled.

A torrential river of sweat breaks its banks as Freya scrambles for her fan and a thick fog descends between her and the spirit world. *Brain fog*, Cat thinks, *this is what Freya has been talking about.* The sharp scent of high anxiety assails Cat's nostrils. She jumps from the windowsill and sits in front of Freya, up close, eye to eye, holding her gaze. One meow, two meows, three meows – transmit: *Breathe, Freya, this too shall pass.*

Freya breathes, the river of sweat begins to subside and the fog lifts. Cat carefully sidesteps the dreaded storage cube of flyers and leaps back up onto the windowsill.

Bobby looks on, mesmerised.

Freya returns to her spirit-channelling senses.

'Bobby, your father is thanking you and he's fading away, which means he has delivered his message. It means he's free to go, no longer tethered to this earth.'

Bobby's face falls. 'But we've just made contact, why would he go now? I don't understand why he's thanking me. What I've done is contrary to everything he believed in. I've broken all his rules.'

Cat's ears prick, her head spinning. She knows that Paul is now free. Surely, Freya's work is done. None of the remaining spirits in the room are moving. They must be waiting for other clients, or just here for the show – *or for the learning*, she thinks, reprimanding herself for being so judgemental.

'Why is he thanking me?' Bobby repeats, a flicker of suspicion in their eyes. 'It doesn't ring true. All the information you've given me, you could've researched before I arrived. I haven't learned anything new. And he certainly wouldn't be thanking me.'

'Does Professor Kat P. Flyer mean anything to you?' Freya asks. Cat can see her straining to hold back a giggle, rushing through the P part of the name to give it less emphasis.

Bobby blanches. 'Kat's my PhD supervisor,' they say. 'How could you possibly know that unless you looked me up beforehand?'

'I'm not one of England's top psychics for nothing,' Freya says. 'And I do have Amantha, my psychic assistant, helping me, as you witnessed earlier when she visited me for a little tête-à-tête.'

Bobby leans forward, challenge biting the air. 'Have I passed my doctorate, then?' they ask.

'I can't tell you that,' Freya says, 'but I can tell you that Paul thanked you for studying medicine, and for specialising in urology. For helping others less rigid than himself, helping others who are open to medical intervention, helping to save lives. More than that, he thanked you for researching new ways of healing urological conditions.'

Cat counts the silent seconds, smells the advancing tsunami of withheld pain and watches as it breaks shore.

'He's thanking me for breaking his rules,' Bobby says, shaking in grief. 'He approves of what I'm doing.' They sob for a full five minutes. Freya hands them a box of tissues and glances up at Cat.

Undeniably, Freya has helped Bobby. She has given them relief and release. But to do this, she stepped beyond channelling spirit and used her human knowledge of the parcel that she had inadvertently slipped into her bag. She cheated. But if she hadn't taken the intuitive leap of connecting Paul's diagnosis with the parcel from Bart's Health Urology, Bobby would have been left angry, thinking Freya was a fraud. Did she break the rules of honest and ethical channelling? Yes. Did she break the centre's first rule? No, she did no harm. Did she uphold rule two? Yes, she helped and healed. But Cat's stomach is as queasy and uneasy as a vegan cat that's swallowed a mouse.

Freya shows Bobby to the door, closes it behind them and collapses onto her leather throne. 'Amantha,' she howls, snuffling and snorting, pulling fistfuls of tissues from the box. 'What have I done?'

Cat licks her honey paws, intently grooming her whiskers. What can she say?

'I used to be so sharp, but this brain fog is killing my ability to channel. What am I going to do? I can't just suddenly go blank in the middle of a reading, and these sweats and fogs only seem to be increasing. Am I losing my psychic ability? When

I get through peri – ha, if I get through peri – will I be a wise old crone with infinitely restored psychic powers, or will I be a shrivelled has-been, a dead end as far as spirit channelling is concerned, if you pardon the pun? Should I leave while I'm at the top of my career? But what would I do? I need to earn money. Move to full-time sorting of mail at the post office? That won't pay my bills.'

Cat watches Freya slip into imagining possible undesired futures, before shaking herself back to the present.

'But I have to thank you, Amantha. If you hadn't peed on my flyers yesterday, Professor Kat P. Flyer's name would never have jumped out in the way that it did from that parcel, and I wouldn't have remembered that it was from Bart's Health Urology. I see a thousand parcels and letters, a thousand addresses and names every morning at the post office. Nothing ever sticks. Until this one. You and your peeing saved me, and you saved Bobby. Here I am talking to you like you're more than just a cat, and I know that's all you are, but you really do fit the bill as my psychic assistant, even though you know nothing about it!'

Freya laughs, wanders over to the windowsill, lovingly strokes Cat's back and lifts her to her cheek. Cat boils but holds herself steady, once more.

I'll show you, Freya. You may be one of England's top psychics, but your abilities pale compared to mine.

And with that, she leaps from Freya's arms and slinks out of the room to lick her wounds and decide on her next move.

😼

Cat polishes off her morning mouse with a whole bowl of cat meat and more cream than any normal cat might manage, but *normal* is not a word that applies to a cat in her last life, a cat on a mission. She's halfway up the stairs before she remembers that there's no yoga class today or tomorrow, but it's here where she spies Abby laying a bunch of forget-me-nots the colour of a deep lazy summer sky on the altar. And it's Abby she wants to snuggle up with before braving another session with Freya. She bounds up the rest of the steps and enticingly curves her body around Abby's invitingly warm legs.

'Amantha,' purrs Abby, because although Abby isn't a cat, she does have a way of purring her love and attention. 'Amantha, my muse. Let me show you what I've been working on.' She scoops Cat up and carries her over to the nest of yoga bolsters she has made, where Serenity would normally sit. 'My secret early-morning office when there's no yoga,' she confides. 'When the cat's away, the mouse will play. Oh.' She laughs, clapping her hand over her mouth. 'Where did that come from? I didn't mean to offend, Amantha, I don't see you – or Serenity – as predators. But am I a mouse? Yes, as in timid sometimes, easily intimidated by more powerful people – and that includes Serenity – no matter how assertive I sound in Power Hour or with my clients.' She looks down at her hands, rippling her long, slender fingers. 'Or not so much a mouse, maybe a shy ugly duckling waiting to grow and unfold magnificent, confident swan wings and bring whatever I am meant to be fully into the world. In the meantime, I prefer my own space away from people, freedom to play, imagine, create, be myself, be inspired, which brings me back to you, my muse.'

Cat's heart misses a beat as Abby holds her eye to eye, eyes the same deep, lazy summer-sky forget-me-not colour as her altar offering, and drops Cat into her lap in a cloud of citrusy amber perfume. *Forget-me-not*, Cat thinks, Abby's request to the universe, or her intention to remember to look after herself and her needs. Or to remember her waiting swan wings.

Abby leans over Cat and lifts her laptop from the floor, balancing it on her knees. Cat extends a curious paw to the keyboard, but Abby bats it away. 'Look, I've been busy on the branding, playing with working you into our website header to start with. After that, we'll move on to a sign for the front of the building, and who knows, maybe some billboard advertising if Serenity wants to go that way. She's all about making a big splash.'

Three drawings flash up on the laptop screen.

'Look, Amantha. In this one, I've got you rather cheekily holding the Rajpapa lotus in the palm of your paw. I probably won't show this one to Serenity. It was the first idea that came to me and it made me giggle. People love cats, but what is this message really saying? That you have Guru Rajpapa in the palm of your hand? Serenity would probably see that as blasphemy. Now, if it was you holding a plain lotus, it would make sense since the lotus represents spiritual enlightenment, but the Rajpapa lotus symbol shifts the meaning somewhat.'

Cat squints at the screen, a fragmented picture made up of thousands of tiny boxes, like all screen images she has seen. What is it with people and their screens, when pencil and paper or paints on canvas would make everything clear? She blinks, looking up at Abby, perplexed.

'Anyway, moving on to number two,' she says, scrolling down to reveal another picture built from tiny boxes. 'In this one, I've made some of the letters into honey-coloured cats, representing you. Here you are as an "n" doing a nice cat arch, and here as a capital L with your belly on the floor, front paws outstretched and your tail held vertical. And over here, see? A capital H, standing still sideways on, tail up vertical, head up vertical, more comical than natural, though. But this one's cute: curled up in a tight ball for an "o" with a beatific expression on your face. Just an idea at this stage, something we could refine. What do you think?'

Cat tries curling into a tight ball, and puzzles over the instructions for being a capital H, but she gets the gist. What would this design symbolise? That she's an important part of the structure of the centre, in their mind as their divine messenger, in her mind as their guardian and protector? She's wondering how to contort her body into a capital G and P, when Abby scrolls down to number three.

'I'm still playing with this one. There you are, see? In sphinx pose at our entrance doors, one door ajar, like Guru Rajpapa's spirit cat that Serenity mentioned. It's a nod to Rajpapa, but see the way that I've drawn your face? It's portraying you as an all-knowing, welcoming divine presence. I can't work the Rajpapa lotus in, though, without it being overly busy. What do you think?'

The pixelated image claws at Cat's eyes. Vision is not a cat's strong point, unless we're talking inner vision. She employs her inner eye. Sphinx pose guarding the entrance is more accurate to her mission, and if Abby can manage a more psychic expression on her face, it might draw attention to her communication skills. Not for her ego, she reprimands herself, but for getting people to listen to her, to take her seriously, so she can do her job.

'Anyway, that's enough work for now. Let's see what Serenity's up to in London,' Abby says, exchanging her laptop for her phone and pulling Cat closer into her citrus-amber cloud.

Cat's head spins and her stomach somersaults as Abby scrolls her phone at speed, millions of tumbling pixels punctuated by occasional, shocking ear-ripping blasts of rapid-fire noise and discombobulated speech. She closes her eyes but can't block out the sounds. Abby chats on regardless.

'She's all over Instagram, her own posts, other people's posts, photos of Guru Rajpapa and her sharing the stage ... Oh look, one with Guru Rajpapa's arm around her shoulder – three hundred and fifty-seven thousand likes already ... And here she is wearing those rainbow crystal pins in her hair, shining like a tiara. Serenity, queen of the Rajpapa Yoga empire.'

Is there a hint of disdain in Abby's voice?

'Oh my Buddha!' Abby's suddenly booming voice makes Cat jump. 'Why didn't I think of this before? Cat videos! Cat videos flood everyone's social media – look at them flooding mine! People love cat videos. I can make videos of you with our yoga students and edit them to make it look like you're doing cute yoga poses. I can make videos of you with Freya, and with ... my mind is buzzing, buzzing, buzzing. This is absolutely what we need to do, and I can't wait to get onto it. Serenity's got the Rajpapa Yoga side of things covered in her social media, but adding videos of you into our marketing will pump up attention to everything that we do at the centre, as well.'

At the mention of Freya, Cat squeezes her way out of Abby's lap and races off to monitor Clary's appointment with Freya. Something's not right, she can feel it in her bones and sniff it on the air.

'Do I take that as an energetic yes for the cat videos, or as a run-for-your-life message?'

Abby's lovely laughter trails after Cat. Too hard basket for now.

※

Clary nods to Amantha, as directed by Freya, and carefully pulls the sleeves of her voluminous forest-green woollen coat over her hands. *To hide her jewellery and fastidiously scrubbed fingernails*, Cat thinks, cautious of giving Freya any physical clues. The smell of oil paint and clay – an odd combination – while potent to Cat's nostrils is probably well beyond Freya's odour detection, but hands can give away so much, and an artist's hands are notoriously readable. A psychic might not set out to gather physical clues, but what is seen cannot be unseen. *Body language, too*, Cat thinks, *subtly or not so subtly informs us, and a psychic is no less immune to picking up such clues as any other person.* Clary's body language is hungry for genuine spirit connection beneath her careful attention to withhold revealing information about her daily life.

Five spirits are gathered at the door today, four observers and one recently passed grandmotherly type. The recently passed still carry an aura of shock and move more clumsily than those accustomed to being bodiless, and even the most comfortable older women generally choose a younger disposition when they learn the art of flexible presentation. Yes, Cat cocks her head from side to side, this must be Clary's mother, the one she mentioned in the message she placed on the altar yesterday. And that is a perfect example of how easily a good psychic such as herself can be led astray with prior knowledge and preconceived notions.

Freya is unusually quiet. Cat smells the burning tension building in the room as Freya's face turns red and she fumbles for her paper fan, fingers shaking as the fog thickens around her. Cat readies herself to jump onto Freya's coffee table and talk her through her breathing, before deliciously and wickedly changing her mind and sinking to her belly. *Let her fry, let her stumble. Let's see who's the great psychic guru now.*

Clary's mother's spirit waves her arms, shouts out and looks to the other spirits for guidance before fading away, unheard. That's another thing about the recently passed – they need a lot of practice to channel their energy into earthly communication and stay visible to a good psychic, not to mention a psychic trapped in a hot-flush brain fog. Some of the spirit onlookers must have several hundred years' experience in the field, going by their clothing, and a reason to linger in this plane. What is it about this place that keeps them here?

'Superman,' Freya splutters, her throat parched, the paper fan folded and replaced on the table. The brain fog has thinned, and apart from the onlookers, there's nothing but high anxiety in the room tickling Cat's nostrils. Freya's perimenopausal hot-flush wave has stranded her, high and dry, with no spirit message for Clary. Other than 'Superman', which makes no sense whatsoever to Cat.

But Clary's eyelids flicker just enough for Freya to take the cue and follow through.

'I see a little boy in a Superman cape, an energy around you, not in spirit, but an earthling angel. Does this make any sense to you?'

Clary stays mute.

'There was an incident, a ... was it a heart murmur, I'm not sure. I'm getting a picture of his hand on his heart. No, wait, it's not his heart, it's his lungs, his breathing.'

Clary starts to shake. 'Asthma. He was rushed into hospital. We got there just in time. He stayed in for a few days, they gave him a Superman cape when he came through.' She retracts her hands into her coat sleeves again, thinking she's given too much away, but she is visibly moved.

'Think of him as an earthling angel,' Freya says, 'because he chose to stay here with you.'

Cat's body takes over from her observant mind, arches her back and tingles her spine. She manages to hold back the urge to hiss at Freya. Something is very wrong. Where is Freya getting this information from? There's no spirit in the room relaying it, and Cat's psychic eye sees nothing other than Freya's alarm. She needs to guard and protect, but whom? Clary? Freya? Herself?

Clary sobs.

'Wait,' Freya says, 'I have more. Let me tune in. Yes, I have a spirit here with me.'

Cat looks around. *You do not!*

'She has a motherly energy, I'm not getting a name, but she is recently passed, and she's telling me Tabs is with her. Who is Tabs? I'm not clear. Is this making sense to you, Clary?'

Clary lets her heavy coat fall from her shoulders and leans forward, her long, lanky frame exposed, her hand reaching for the box of tissues. Freya's eyes clamp on her bare wedding-ring finger and the flecks of yellow paint around her nails. Cat watches the whole scene as if in freeze frame, knowing what is coming next.

Clary cannot talk about Tabs. She can't utter a single word.

'Your mother wants you to know the move from London is good. And that yellow is a good choice. What does that mean? A yellow dress, a yellow room, a yellow painting?'

Cat winces. Freya is going too far now. Too much detail. She's beginning to sound fraudulent. And she is. Cat decides to stay silent, observe as much as she can before working out what to do.

'I'm painting a picture of Tabs, in our new place, in a yellow room, all sunlight and promise,' Clary says. 'Tabs is our gorgeous tabby cat. Was our gorgeous tabby cat.'

'Your mother is speaking again,' Freya lies. 'She says Tabs urges you to get a new cat for Benji.'

Suddenly enlightened, Cat springs from her windowsill, and in two furious jumps, lands on Clary's lap just in time to hold her frozen gaze long enough. One meow, two meows, three meows – transmit: *Freya has read your message, the one you put on the altar yesterday.*

Clary looks from Cat to her shaking hands, sees the slick of yellow paint around a cuticle and springs to her feet.

'You're right about Superman, right about Benji's asthma, and that's incredible, but the rest. I can't ... I have to go now.' She grabs her bag and gathers enough decorum to walk to the door and close it gently behind her.

Cat glares at Freya, tries to hold her gaze, but Freya's eyes shift away. Cat jumps at her, claws her cheek, draws blood, hisses.

'Some psychic assistant you are, Amantha,' Freya snarls. 'We're supposed to be a team, you and I, and this is how it works: you do your job and I'll do mine. Right?'

Too right, thinks Cat, *only your vision of me doing my job is rather different to mine: making sure you follow the rules, do the right thing, guide and protect you and your clients.* She seethes as she prowls, thrashing her tail left and right, as if swiping a cloud of invisible swarming pests, before walking, like Clary but with a tenth of her decorum, out the door.

🐾

A sphinx, Cat thinks, sinking her overfull belly onto the stone terrace to one side of the entrance doors, fresh mouse blood deliciously coating her tongue. She props herself up onto her elbows, holds her head high, fury abated, coolly refocusing on her mission. As sphinx, guardian and protector of the Serene Lotus Centre for Health and Wellbeing.

'I like your energy, and your style's not bad, either, for a honey-coloured cat. But don't sphinxes usually come in pairs flanking an entrance?' Pearl appears on the far side of the doors and copycats the pose. 'No, on second thoughts, we look odd. You need to be pearly white, or I need to be honey. Sphinxes come in matching pairs.'

'Guru Rajpapa finds one sphinx is all he needs to guard the entrance of his ashram and ensure the safety and wellbeing of everyone inside,' Cat retorts. 'And I do believe that I am that sphinx, not you.'

'You! And what are you going to do in nine months' time when the daffodils raise their heads right in front of you? Scaredy-cat Cat.'

'I won't be here in nine months. I'll have done my duty, passed my tests and graduated my ninth life well before then.'

'Not possible,' Pearl jousts. 'Storms approach. You think you've seen it all, but you've seen nothing yet. Anyway, there's no graduation until you confront the dreaded daffodils.'

'It's called motivation,' Cat spars. 'You told me to follow my nose, and there's no way my nose is going to change its mind. Me and daffodils, no deal. I've no idea why they freeze my bones, but I trust my nose, and my nose knows what's good for me and what's not. And it's not daffodils.'

Pearl languidly peels themself from the terrace and wanders over to the honey sphinx, placing their paw on Cat's shoulder. 'What do you picture for yourself once you've graduated?'

'What I really, truly want, in my heart of hearts?'

'Apart from graduation and being as far away from these daffodils as you can possibly be, yes. Has your heart of hearts spoken to you yet?'

Cat hesitates, gathering courage, not wanting to big-note herself. She tucks her chin to her chest and purrs, almost inaudibly, 'I want to be a spirit mentor to an earthbound being.'

Pearl gently strokes Cat's shoulder. 'That's wonderful, Cat. An earthbound being, hey? Plant or animal?'

Cat bats Pearl's paw away, rolling onto her back and squirming in delight. 'You're wicked, Pearl. Don't even go there. I will not be a spirit mentor to a daffodil, no matter how wise and enlightened I become when I graduate.'

'Wicked, am I?' Pearl jumps to their feet and rockets off in the direction of the topiary garden. 'Catch me if you can! And when you do, there's something I want to show you.'

'Well, nose, what do you think?' Cat grins to herself. 'Ah, okay, I hear you. Follow that cat.' And she bounds off, astonishing herself with her bravery as she takes the shortcut across the patch of earth where next year's daffodils are sleeping, and finds herself, unharmed, a few paces away from Reclining Woman with Child.

'Over here,' Pearl's voice summons, and Cat sees them standing, tail switching, in front of Briar's emerging topiary of Amantha now sporting an add-on feature, a topiary blackbird in the palm of her paw. 'I don't think he's implying that you're a cat about to eat a bird,' Pearl teases. 'That would be against rule one, wouldn't it?'

Cat lowers her eyes.

'I think Briar means that as a divine messenger you protect all creatures, including birds. That you're not really an earthly cat,' Pearl says.

'But I am an earthly cat. And I'm sure your twitching nose knows that this cat ate a mouse this morning.'

'I know, Cat, and I understand your predicament. You've acted to save Emmy from doing no harm with her mousetraps, and you've acted to protect this beautiful ancient building from being overrun and undermined by hordes of mice, and you're nourishing yourself properly to ensure that you're here long enough, and healthily enough, to complete your mission. It's an inside job. Just don't eat any birds, right? They're an outside job.'

'How do you know about Emmy and the mousetraps?'

'I'm a cat, Cat. Give me some credit.'

Cat examines Briar's topiary sculpture more closely. 'At least I can see it.' She laughs. 'It's not an artwork made of thousands of tiny boxes like the pictures Abby showed me on her laptop this morning.'

'How are their branding plans going?' Pearl swipes at a bee buzzing too close to their ear.

'Abby sees me as a sphinx, recalling Guru Rajpapa's guardian and protector spirit. So far, that one appeals the most to me. Fits with my mission. She had some other good ideas, too, nothing obnoxious, unlike Freya's vision of me.'

'Obnoxious?' Pearl drops to their belly in half-sphinx pose, and turns to lick their raised back leg. A touch of grooming over a good piece of gossip.

'She tells all her clients I'm her psychic assistant, but does she believe that? No way! She has no idea about my powers. She tells me I'm just a cat, and she's using me to further her business or give her some kind of witchy aura, I don't know. But that's not the worst of it, Pearl.' Cat pauses to see if Pearl is paying attention.

Pearl turns to face her, back leg left hanging in the air, mid-wash. 'And …?'

Cat shifts from paw to paw, looks this way and that and swallows the warm, mousy flux tossed up into her throat by her queasy stomach. 'I hate to say it. She's a good psychic. I've seen the way she communicates with spirits, listening, watching, and she's the queen of interpretation when they perform their charades, I give her that. She's patient with the spirits when they have little of substance to say, but I can see that her clients are moved by their messages and the way she delivers them. They leave the room with renewed faith in the afterlife, inspired, healed, forgiving and forgiven, while their spirit relative is released from this earth. But lately ...' Cat rasps, her throat running completely dry.

'Lately?' Pearl releases their back leg, looking Cat square in the face.

Cat swallows, lowering her purr. 'Something's not right, Pearl. She's started breaking out in sweats, and when she does, a fog appears, and the spirits are lost to her. She loses all connection until the fog lifts.'

Pearl relaxes and licks a paw to resume their grooming. 'So, she waits, then, for the fog to lift? Chats about something else to the client, fills the gap, tells them what's happening until she can reconnect?'

'That would be honest, wouldn't it? But no.' Cat sits taller, her voice gaining momentum. 'She cheats.'

'How so?' Pearl is all erect, pointy ears.

Cat explains what happened yesterday with Bobby.

Pearl raises their eyebrows. 'An unlikely story, Cat, even if I could understand it. A talking parcel in her shopping bag?'

'It's complicated.' Cat shakes her head. 'Today's a bit easier to explain.' Cat tells Pearl what happened with Clary.'

'Serenity,' they meow in chorus. 'You go first, Cat,' Pearl says.

'Serenity was up in London. She wasn't here to burn the altar messages.'

'Am I correct in thinking,' Pearl enunciates slowly, 'that following her success with the fluke parcel, Freya decided to actively seek information about Clary so she'd be prepared if the fog descended again? Or did she just happen to read the message when she burned it for Serenity and then used it in desperation during the session?'

'I was in a quandary this morning,' Cat continues, oblivious to the subtlety of Pearl's distinction, 'with rule three. Should I support Freya, or support Clary? And with rule one, should I do no harm to Freya's reputation and business, or protect Clary from harm? And rule two: should I help Freya through her fog, help

Freya in her quest to make Clary feel comforted about her spirit mother, or help Clary see that she is being cheated?'

'That's more than one quandary. What did you do?'

'Let's just say that Clary knows about Freya and the altar message now.'

They each turn their gaze to Briar's topiary statue. A moment to reflect in silence. A late-afternoon crescent moon cradles the topiary blackbird in Amantha's palm, a luminescent silver bird's nest, a sign that Cat should be getting back inside before the doors are closed and she's locked out.

'The Silver Crescent Nest,' Pearl purrs, lifting a paw to point at the moon, though Cat's eyes are already entranced by the ethereal vision. 'They say there's a Silver Crescent Nest somewhere around here, which holds a secret. My nose tells me it's a secret for you to find, a solution to your quandary, and a key to graduating your ninth life.'

'Now who's the psychic?' Cat chuckles, but deep down in her bones something of what Pearl says rings true. 'A prophecy, hey?'

'Do a little research for me, Cat,' Pearl whispers. 'The key to that of which I speak is inside a building. I'm an outside cat, I can't go in there. You can.'

The moment passes. Pearl shakes their head as if emerging from a trance. 'What was I saying?'

'That it's time for me to go back inside, but thank you, Pearl.'
'For what?'
'The way you listen to me. How you make me feel.'
'How do I make you feel?'
'Heard. A bit less confused.'

'You can find me anytime you need to chat, here in the topiary garden. Cut across the daffodil bed if you dare.' Pearl reaches out to swat Cat one last time, but Cat is already running towards the door, arriving just in time to slink in before Emmy clunks the key in the lock.

NINTH LIFE

🐾

Serenity stands by the altar at the top of the stairwell, hair aglow in the morning light, still sparkling with the rainbow crystal pins she bought for her annual photoshoot with Guru Rajpapa at last week's Rajpapa Yoga Teachers' Convention. Like an angel. The angel gracefully lifts her arms, like wings, and brings her palms to meet in front of her third eye, a slight bow in Cat's direction, a deeper bow to the altar.

'There's a big queue outside, Amantha. Must be due to the cover story about us in the *Weekend Magazine*. We may have to turn people away. Best be prepared.' She selects a white-tailed eagle feather from the altar and gracefully threads it into her hair – like a bird in a rainbow crystal nest. 'Eagle feather for eagle pose. What do you think, Amantha, divine messenger? Are you ready? Shall I open the doors?'

A whirlwind of students ascends the stairs and bottlenecks in a cluster around Serenity as she checks each one in on her tablet. The cacophony of new student business – the *cha-ching, cha-ching* of pinging phones as they pay for their class, the hurried instructions to write a message to place on the altar, the tearing of paper, the scratching of pencils, the jostling, the discarding of shoes – prickles Cat's cool. She lowers her haunches, prepares to jump from the altar, to run, to hide, to find somewhere quiet, when the earthy clay perfume of Clary's warm hands lifts her up and away and into the stillness of the far corner of the yoga room.

'Stay with me today,' Clary coos, 'you gorgeous, divine creature. I'll look after you.' She rolls out her yoga mat and lies down, placing Cat on her chest, their heartbeats mingling. *Reclining Woman with Cat*, Cat thinks, every fibre of her body melting in grateful repose.

'Welcome,' Serenity's singsong summons Cat from her peaceful drifting. 'We have a packed class here, so please be aware of your neighbours as we move. It's lovely to see some new faces in the room and,' she jabs at her laptop keyboard, 'hundreds of new faces joining our live class by Zoom. Um, looks like the numbers are jumping as I speak. Close on two thousand joining us from all over the UK and around the world. A record number of students for a live early-morning class. I'm Serenity, for those of you who are new. Welcome to Rajpapa Yoga.' She bows a graceful *namaste* and takes a few silent steps towards her mat, a conductor bringing her charges into stillness. 'We'll start lying on our backs, eyes closed, tuning into our breathing. Don't try to change it, just observe its rhythm as it is right here, right now.'

Cat feels the rise of her abdomen on her in-breath, floats on her out-breath, paws weightless, and drops back deeply down into Clary's earthy clay perfume, stirring only briefly, minutes later, when Clary lifts her from her chest and places her on the floor beside her mat.

🐾

'Holding eagle pose,' Cat's ears flicker as she emerges from her nap, 'what can you see from your high vantage point when you look down at the land below you? The Earth, its peoples, animals, plants, its past, present and possible futures. What do you see for the world, what do you see for yourself? Which path will you choose?' Serenity pauses. 'And open your wings – spread your arms to your sides. That's it, hold the pose – feel your chest expand, your heart open, your vision clear. You know what you need to do.'

A sob, a sigh, a sharp intake of breath, a muffled giggle, as the students refold their eagle wings and move through the last poses before settling onto their mats for the final pose, *savasana*, a full five minutes on their backs in stillness, dedicated to absorbing all the goodness from their efforts and insights. Cat climbs back up onto Clary's chest and surveys the energy patterns in the room. Their bodies may look relaxed, and according to yoga their minds

NINTH LIFE

should be still, but all Cat can see is the command rippling around the room: 'You know what you need to do.'

😺

'Coffee?' says Anna, rolling her yoga mat into her carry bag. 'I know exactly what I need to do. Coffee, coffee, maybe another coffee, a croissant. To start with, anyway. You coming?'

Cat follows Clary, Anna, Pixie and Milly down to the café, hoping to prompt Clary to share her story about Freya's cheating and get some action going in that direction. *Oh yes*, Cat thinks, *I know what I need to do.*

'Watch out, Amantha.' Pixie draws her chair up to the table. 'We're four powerful eagles here, and we're hungry.'

'Ha,' Anna says, 'more like a cat amongst the eagles, wouldn't you say? Should we be scared?'

'Trust,' bellows Milly. 'It's all about trust, isn't it? She trusts us not to pounce on her, and we trust her not to pounce on us. Do no harm, the number-one rule of this place.'

'I'm going to do some serious harm to this croissant.' Clary breaks off the end of her flaky crescent pastry and slathers it in both butter and honey.

'In need of some sweetness in your life today, honey?' says Pixie. 'Or calorie-loading ready for your eagle flight?'

'I've had a bit of tough weekend.' Clary plucks Cat from her perch on the bookshelf, drops her into her lap and inadvertently sprinkles her with almond croissant flakes. Cat licks her paws and sets about grooming the crumbs from her honeyed fur. Nowhere near as tasty as mouse and cream, but a cat's got to stay clean and alluring.

'We're here if you want to talk,' Pixie says, 'at any time. It's not easy moving into a small village like ours. We're a tight-knit group, and we help each other out. Just saying.'

'Thank you. I'm missing Tabs, my cat. She passed away just

before we left London. She was a city cat. I think she knew we were on the move and died of a broken heart. But it's more than that. Something happened last week, and I will tell you about it, but first up, I'm curious. What was it that Serenity said about a cover story in the *Weekend Magazine*?'

Milly delves into her yoga bag and draws out the *Observer Weekend Magazine*. 'This.' She unrolls it and smooths it flat with her palm in the middle of the table. 'Stunning cover picture, Guru Rajpapa laying a lotus garland around Serenity's shoulders, Serenity's hair all lit up in the shaft of sunlight cascading through the window behind them. Yet, look closely. She's no innocent angel, is she? There's something about the way she's looking at the camera that's like the cat that ate the cream – sorry, Amantha.'

Four heads crane forward to examine the picture, piqued by Milly's observations.

'Well,' says Pixie, 'she is the cat that ate the cream really, isn't she, and well done to her, I say. She's worked hard to build her empire, and it's all for the good. She's made – and is still making – a wonderful contribution to the world, and to yoga.'

'And she's creamed a squillion pounds, or whatever Rajpapa Yoga is worth,' adds Anna, pulling her ochre cat-eye reading glasses from her bag to take a closer look. 'But she lives a life here in the village much like the rest of us, and cherishes the centre and our small community. What does she do with her money? Investments? Houses? Buildings? Charity? Does anyone know?'

Milly points to the cover again, an exquisitely manicured fingernail tapping the header, 'The Truth Will Set You Free'. Then she leans back, catching Cat's eye. 'Have any of you read the article, or would you like to have a guess at what it means?'

'The money would set me free,' laughs Pixie, 'but I'm guessing Serenity's got her material wealth covered so she can dedicate her life to truth, living her truth, being authentic, I don't know. Enlighten us.'

'It's a four-page article.' Milly thumbs the magazine open to the start of the piece. 'Over eight hundred thousand readers of the hard copy, and who knows how many people have read the online version. A nice bit of PR for the business, but she doesn't really need it. She's well known on the international circuit and in the heady business-empire realms.'

'Oh, that's right,' Anna pipes up, 'this is all up your old street, isn't it?' She turns to Clary. 'Milly was a big-name investigative journalist in London before she moved here a few years ago. Print, radio, television, the lot.'

'Ah,' Clary claps her thigh close to Cat's surprised ear, 'that's where I know you from. The TV. You seemed so familiar, but I couldn't work it out.'

'And being a media show pony,' Anna continues, 'she's not answering her own question about the truth setting whoever free. She's fobbing us off with numbers to give us time to get curious, to really, really, really want to know. So, Milly, you've got something on your mind around this truth thing. What is it?'

Cat watches them all closely, not sure where this conversation is going, but curious, yes indeed. She catches Milly's bloodhound scent. Milly's onto something, she knows, but she can't quite put a paw on anything that makes sense yet.

Milly's eyes meet Clary's. 'I left journalism behind me, but I've still got an instinct for a good story, and an instinct for reading between the lines that something's not quite right. I've read and reread this article, and I still don't know what it is. But time will tell.'

'So do tell, Milly,' Anna says, 'about the truth thing. Why that title?'

Milly points to one of the photos on the first page of the article. 'This photo was taken when Serenity – or Serena, as she was known back then – stayed at Rajpapa's ashram near Rishikesh. She was doing her gap year before going to university, or at least that was the plan, according to the article. She was going to do an ashram crawl – my words, not theirs – notching up as many ashrams and spiritual insights as she could gather before returning to London to do a business degree, but she ended up spending the whole year at Rajpapa's.'

'She met Rajpapa and saw the light?' Pixie says, one eyebrow raised.

'Not quite, not at first. See this photo?' Milly holds up the page showing a smart, corporate-looking guy, superior tilt of his balding head, defiant glint in his eyes. 'Serenity's father, a hot-shot lawyer arrested when she was fifteen, for fraud and embezzlement.'

Cat extends a paw and triumphantly traps an imaginary mouse trying to skitter away. *Got you! Rule breaker!*

'Jailed for ... let me check,' Milly runs her finger down the page, 'three years, so he was due for release around the time Serenity finished school.'

'So,' Anna says, 'she didn't want to face him and she hopped off for her gap year to somewhere she couldn't be disturbed?'

'Pretty much,' Milly says, 'and I probably would have done the same at eighteen, in the circumstances. After his arrest, she, her sister and mother moved to Chichester – chosen by dropping a pin onto a map, apparently – changed their family name and vowed never to mention him again.'

'No love lost there, then.' Pixie drains the last drop of her coffee.

'The article doesn't elucidate,' says Milly, 'but I'm guessing the relationship between her parents was already hanging by the smallest of threads, and her mother needed to cut them all free.'

'But it was a freedom based on hiding the truth, if they had to change their family name and move to an incognito life in another city,' says Anna.

'Long story short, Serenity says it was in the loving embrace of Rajpapa's ashram that she felt able to talk about her father, and the relief in telling the truth set her free. She changed her name to Serenity to celebrate her newfound sense of peace.'

'Is it just me, or am I looking too deeply into this?' Pixie peers into her empty coffee cup as if looking for an answer. 'But his name, "Raj" for king, "papa" for father. It strikes me as some kind of exalted father-figure name. Especially when she markets him as a guru. And the Rajpapa style of yoga is so tightly defined, with our set classes, no creative flexibility for teachers, as far as I can see. It's kind of rule-bound, isn't it? Fits with someone whose father was jailed for breaking the law, wouldn't you say?'

'It's just you,' Anna laughs, 'reading meaning into words. Although, there may be some truth in the father-figure thing, and you're probably onto something with the classes.' She pauses and takes a breath long enough for Cat to grasp the moment with a deeply resonant purr designed to catch Anna's eye.

One meow, two meows, three meows – Cat feels her heart pumping hard as she begins transmission: *Clary's story?*

'Anyway,' Anna resumes, 'Clary, have we answered your question? What was it you wanted to tell us? I'm all ears.'

Cat preens her whiskers, communication successful. Time for Clary to expose Freya's fraudulent activity and see some justice done.

'You have,' Clary smiles, looking down at Cat for reassurance, 'and the whole thing about the truth setting you free gives me courage.'

Excitement tinged with a small yet delicious surge of power thumps through Cat's body.

'I had my reading with Freya last week. Have any of you consulted her before?'

Heads shake; Cat holds her breath.

'She's supposed to be good,' Pixie says. 'I don't know why I've never consulted her. Haven't needed to, I guess.'

'I don't know if I needed to,' Clary says, 'but I wanted to. I told you that Tabs, my cat, died, but so did my mum. It was just hard to say that to you earlier. And with moving here – I want to raise Benji in the country – I wanted some guidance about what to do next. I booked the session on a whim, not too seriously invested, but curious and hoping for some insight.'

'Sorry about your mum,' Anna says. Pixie and Milly nod in silent communion.

'Thank you.'

Oh, get on with it, Cat squirms. Clary's mum's spirit rests her arm on Clary's chair, winks at Cat and offers a *namaste. She's looking younger now, must be getting the hang of spirit manifestation*, Cat thinks, then does her best imitation of a human rolling her eyes and almost loses her balance in the ensuing dizziness. She squeezes her eyes tight and pulls herself together.

'So, how did it go?' Pixie asks.

'She spooked me straightaway, saying "Superman", then talking about a little boy wearing a Superman cape, and that he was an earthling angel, not a spirit. I knew she was talking about Benji, but I was struck mute for a moment. Then she started talking about his lungs, and I knew she was seeing Benji and his asthma. He ended up in emergency with a bad attack before we left London, and the nurse gave him a Superman cape when he pulled through.

'I started to tell Freya about it, but – and I know this is going to sound weird – it was like Amantha was trying to stop me. I can't describe it any more than that. Freya had said Amantha was her psychic assistant, and I thought that was Freya just being playful, setting the mood or something, but the whole room seemed to shake, and I couldn't say anything. I just sobbed and felt this beam of love coming from Amantha.'

Cat feels all eyes upon her, and a glow of satisfaction learning that Clary had picked up on her so early in the session.

'Then Freya says there's a motherly spirit in the room telling me Tabs is with her. And that was it, I was all tears, you can imagine. I knew it was Mum.'

'That's spooky, alright,' Anna says, unable, as usual, to let a quiet moment go without filling it with words. 'Freya must be the real deal.'

Exasperation swishes Cat's tail. She stares at Anna, turns around and gazes into Clary's eyes. *Go on, Clary*, she transmits. *Let's do this.*

'Well, that's the thing,' says Clary. 'It sounds like it, and she gave more accurate details, but I could feel my body shrinking away from her. That's the only way I can describe it. She told me Mum was saying to get a new cat for Benji, and that's not something Mum would have said. We only found out recently that Benji's asthma can be triggered by cat dander, so Mum just wouldn't suggest that.'

Cat pokes her head up and looks around inquisitively, expectantly.

'Oh, Amantha,' Clary soothes, 'you're just too lovely not to cuddle. I brush myself down before I go home to Benji. Please don't be offended.'

Clary looks up at the others. 'So, my mind finally caught up with my body's suspicion, but I didn't know how to explain Freya's knowledge. Then something else weird happened. At least, I think it was weird.' She looks at Cat. 'Maybe it wasn't. Maybe there's more to Amantha than meets the eye. Anyway, Amantha jumped down from her windowsill onto my lap and glared at me like she was trying to tell me something important, and that's when it happened. I realised Freya must have seen the message I put on the yoga altar the day before. I don't know how or when she read it, but I wrote about Tabs, and about Benji missing Mum, and about Mum being in Heaven.'

Milly gasps, eyes popping, and drums her fingers on the table. 'What did you do?'

'My hands were shaking – so much rage! I looked down, willing them to stop, trying to regain my composure. I don't know how I managed to contain myself. It's all a haze, but I think I might have told her that she was right about Superman and Benji's asthma, and that I didn't know how she knew that, but then I was speechless and got myself out the door before I did any damage.'

Anna reaches out to touch Clary's hand, signalling the waiter for another round of coffees and a jug of water.

'What's your surname?' Milly says, all business-like, fingers poised over her phone.

'Vernon. Clary Vernon.' Clary looks confused.

'Good, an unusual name,' Milly says, and in less than the time it takes Cat to almost dislocate her jaw in the biggest yawn of relief she's released in days, Milly passes her phone to Clary. 'Your Instagram page, one child wearing a Superman cape. You haven't posted much since then, have you?'

'But how did she know my full name?'

'Did you pay by credit card when you booked?'

Clary nods. 'She's that wicked?'

'It explains Superman,' Anna says, 'but the altar message?'

'I think I put my name on the altar message to Mum. "Love, Clary", probably.'

'So, are we surmising,' Pixie leans forward in her chair, 'that Serenity asked Freya to burn the altar messages because she was in London, and Freya read them before offering them up to the sacred flame?'

'Yes, though probably out of curiosity or nosiness more than anything else, I imagine,' Anna says. 'But a name like Clary – and Tabs – would have stuck in her mind.'

'And I'll just go on and say it,' adds Milly, 'a message to someone in Heaven would have stood out to Freya, given her line of work. When she saw Clary's name on her client list for the next day, she must have hung around and looked up her credit-card details after everyone had gone home.'

'I don't know if the truth has set me free,' Clary lifts Cat from her lap and settles her onto the cool flagstone floor, 'but I feel better for sharing it, thank you. I'm left wondering about other people being diddled. Should I say something?'

Cat weaves herself provocatively around Milly's legs, purring loudly until Milly reaches down and scoops her up onto her shoulder. 'Clever girl, Amantha. Your message has been heard, divine or otherwise, and it's time for action.'

'Uh-oh.' Pixie's grin lights up her face. 'Let me guess. Investigative journalist is back in action. You're going to set Freya up, carry a hidden camera?'

'I'm going to book a session, pay by cash and give my name as Delta Jones, living in Southampton.'

'Delta Jones?' Pixie screws up her face. 'How's that going to help?'

'Because back in the day as an investigative journalist, I had a Facebook account under the name of Delta Jones from Southampton. Used it to become Facebook friends with story leads, inveigle myself in the personal lives of those we were investigating. Believe me, you don't want to know more than that. I haven't posted to the account since I left the job, but I know a trick or two to add a few recent months to Delta's timeline, some juicy stuff Freya can "channel" from Delta's spirit relatives. What do you say?'

'Might she recognise you from around here, though?' Clary asks.

'You really don't know much about an investigative journalist's skills, do you?' Milly laughs. 'I'll use a good old-fashioned disguise.'

One meow, two meows, three meows – Cat holds Milly's gaze and transmits: *Paint Amantha.*

'Right, that's it, then,' Milly says. 'I'm off home to make a booking and get some cash out on the way to cover the fee. Oh, and one more thing, Clary. You wanted some insight and direction from Freya. She failed, but I have an idea: why don't you paint a picture of Amantha after you've finished the one of Tabs? Have you noticed the art hanging on the walls here, all for sale?'

'You don't know if I'm any good, but I love that idea, thank you.'

'I don't,' says Milly, 'but I feel it in my bones.' She looks momentarily surprised.

My words exactly, Cat thinks, another mission complete.

∴

Cat positions herself in sphinx pose beside the pristine whiteboard at beige beanbag central, her new name for the bland pow-wow room. *Over there*, she thinks, *right above where Serenity usually sits for meetings, is the perfect place to hang Clary's portrait of me.* An indigo background to show off her honey fur. Or no, forget-me-not blue, like Abby's eyes. Or one of each, or a range of portraits against different-coloured backgrounds. Presiding over their meetings, reminding them to follow the rules, to listen to what she has to say. *More than that*, she thinks, rolling onto her back to examine the fleshy pad of her right paw and the smooth patch where mark number nine will be notched as she departs this life, *Clary's portraits will be a legacy, an enduring testimony to my excellence as guardian and protector of …*

'There you are, Amantha.' Serenity glides into the room, breaking Cat's daydream. 'Such a punctual cat. Anyone would think you can tell the time.'

Oh, the innocence of her! Cat resorts to her inner eyeroll since emulating the human version still gives her dizzy spells.

Serenity looks different today. No yoga tights, no feathers, crystal hairpins or shawls, no beads, no bare feet. Breathing a little hitched and looking like … *What is it*, Cat thinks, before Milly's words come to her: 'the cat that ate the cream', but this time a cat wearing a figure-hugging navy cashmere dress matched with navy knee-height boots. Dressed more like Emmy than Serenity.

'Wow, so smart.' Emmy enters the room. 'Sorry, Serenity, didn't mean to be quite so personal, but I'm accustomed to seeing you in your yoga attire.'

'That's okay, and thank you.' Serenity smiles, no trace of the cream on her lips now. The old Serenity, just wearing different clothes.

Emmy and her bergamot-vanilla cloud settle into a beanbag at the back of the room. Typical Emmy, likes to see the big picture from a distance, watch everyone's body language, check their faces, judge her next best move.

Forget-me-not blue peering through amber citrus heralds Abby's entrance. Immediately kicking off her heels, she chooses a beanbag closer to Cat. 'Big day for you today, Amantha,' she says, 'the big reveal of the branding ideas. And something to surprise you, just you wait.' She tickles Cat under her chin, sits back and stares at Serenity, an audible gasp at the vision in navy.

'Hi there, Abby.' Serenity chuckles at her response. 'I'm so looking forward to seeing what you've come up with today.'

Just breathe, Cat tells herself, *act like everything is normal, don't let on. Freya mustn't suspect anything, stay cool.* A moment later, her stomach lurches as Freya enters the room. *Stay cool, stay cool, stay cool and breathe out.* She finds her equilibrium.

Freya casts a glance in Cat's direction, drops her eyes, fumbles in her roomy pockets and extracts a nutbrown biscuit. 'Baked it myself, a special treat for my psychic assistant,' she announces to the room, bending down to whisper into Cat's ear, 'a peace offering, darling.'

One sniff and Cat knows it's safe; no witch's poison, no evil herbal spells, Freya suspects nothing. Gone in one gulp.

'Oh.' Freya sees Serenity and takes a moment to absorb the clothing. 'Good morning ... lunchtime, I mean. Sorry I'm a tad late.'

'Thanks, everyone, for accommodating the change of time for this week's Power Hour,' Serenity begins. 'I know it's not always easy to juggle your appointments, so I'm very grateful to you all. As you can see from my dress, I had to be somewhere else this morning. I'll come to that, but I have to say, look at Amantha. Now, how did she know what time to turn up for her special day? There's something about her, there really is.'

Cat beams, realises she's now the one looking like the cat

that ate the cream and tries to pull her features into a humbler expression.

'Because it's kind of relevant to Abby's presentation today,' Serenity continues, 'I have some news to share.' She lets a heartbeat or two hang in the silence. 'Well, it's not public news until tomorrow, but I'd like you to hear it first.'

Cat moves closer to Abby, paws a little shaky. *It's to do with the cream*, she thinks, and Milly doesn't feel good about that.

'I've just come back from the city,' Serenity says, 'drove fast, no time to change. Yes, there is another side of me apart from yoga chick – or is that yoga chic,' she jokes. 'Although, I'm sure you know that, already.'

Cat switches to radar mode, checking the vibes. Emmy, anxious. Abby, curious. Freya, silently channelling an elderly, moustachioed spirit hovering near her ear.

'I've been sitting on this news since the Rajpapa Yoga Teachers' Convention last weekend,' Serenity says. 'Had to keep quiet about it there, too, had to wait until I signed the contract, which I did early this morning, up in London.'

Kept quiet about it except for the look on your face in the magazine photo, Cat thinks.

'Have you heard of the Winsor one-o-eight Health and Wellbeing chain?' Serenity asks.

'International, high-end retreats, resorts, that chain?' asks Emmy.

'Yes.' Serenity arches her eyebrows. 'I've just bought the New York arm.'

'All the New York venues?' Emmy again.

'Yes!' Serenity claps her hand to her mouth, eyes wide. 'I saw one-o-eight as a sign from the universe. Like our one-o-eight Rajpapa classes. And one-o-eight, you all know, I'm sure, is the symbol for unity, the wholeness of the universe, spiritual completion. Related to the Fibonacci Sequence. And Winsor, I see as Win and Soar.'

Serenity looks around at the shocked faces. 'I did consult my financial advisors and accountants. The one-o-eight thing is something I'm sharing only with you.' She laughs.

'Congratulations,' Emmy says. 'Wow!'

'Yes, congratulations, Serenity.' Abby shakes her head.

'Is it too late?' Freya says. 'Sorry, Serenity, but I have a spirit here who is …' she stumbles to a halt. 'Sorry, excuse me, not my place. Congratulations, Serenity.'

Okay, thinks Cat, ignoring Freya for the moment, *my role as guardian and protector has expanded by a factor of an unfathomable number if this all comes under the roof of the Serene Lotus Centre for Health and Wellbeing. This is either going to be more gold stars for me if I do my job well, or I'll be forced to come back for another nine lives if it's beyond my capacity.* She slumps into her beanbag, heavy with the newfound enormity of her mission.

'You're probably all wondering how it will affect us here in the village,' Serenity says. 'For a while, at least, I'm going to let the New York businesses remain as they are, then I'll gradually introduce Rajpapa Yoga into the offerings and possibly negotiate a change of branding in alignment with us further down the track. I've got leeway for that in the contract. Your jobs are safe. I lease this place, but it's so dear to my heart, a kind of spiritual home, that I'll keep it going or buy it if it ever comes up for sale. I've made enquiries, but the owner's not budging. It's been in their family for a couple of centuries or more, and that's the way they want to keep it.'

That explains some of the ancient spirits around the place, Cat thinks, *people and cats.* It's not just the current owners who have an emotional attachment to the building, but why are they hanging around instead of departing for their next life? *What's unresolved*, she ponders, so deeply in thought she almost misses Serenity's next announcement.

'One more thing before we move on to Abby's presentation

on our branding. Guru Rajpapa is stepping back from the public side of his role in Rajpapa Yoga. That magazine story was his last public gig. He's getting tired, wants to step out of the limelight. Nothing will change on the yoga front. The classes will remain the same and the annual Rajpapa Yoga Teachers' Convention will continue – though maybe in New York as well as in London. His legacy will live on in the classes.'

'Ah,' Freya utters. All eyes look her way. 'Good to know,' she adds, looking wary.

'Moving along, then.' Serenity claps her hands in delight then rests them in prayerful *namaste*. 'Over to you, Abby.'

Abby springs up from her beanbag and walks to the front of the room. More graceful-swan than ugly-duckling waddle.

'I've got three ideas worked up for our website header to start with.' She flashes the first graphic up on the pow-wow room's screen. Cat tries to focus on the tiny boxes that mist the picture she knows the others can see, judged by their oohs and aahs, but it's too hard. She closes her eyes to focus on what they are saying instead, but drifts into her overdue morning nap.

She's still floating in the land of nap when Abby lifts her up and holds her to her cheek. 'Wake up, Amantha, it's time for your surprise.'

A coffee aroma twitches Cat's nostrils. Must have been a long nap and a long chat. She blinks herself wide awake, relishing Abby's caress, wondering what she missed.

'Imagine this,' Abby addresses the others, 'you're scrolling through your social media and you see …' she taps her keyboard and the pow-wow screen lights up with a photo of Cat. *Oh, not a photo*, Cat thinks, *this is the video idea Abby told me about.* She strains her eyes as her image flashes across the screen, rolling around on the yoga floor with the students, being picked up and cuddled by Clary, dozing on Milly's lap in the café, luxuriating under many a student's fingers lovingly stroking her back, her chin. *When did all this happen, and how is it I didn't know about it?* There's music and there's writing across the screen, words too boxy for Cat to understand, but luckily Serenity reads them aloud, 'Leave your troubles at home.'

'Oh, that's just gorgeous, Abby, well done,' Serenity says, as everyone claps and Emmy hurriedly wipes a tear from her eye.

Cat's ears prick to attention. Abby has portrayed her, in the guise of Amantha, teaching and upholding rule four. *Yes, there I am, guardian and protector of the centre, doing my job, playing my part, with Abby's assistance.* Her chest puffs, just a little, before she self-consciously pulls it back in.

'You're a woman of endless talents, Abby,' Freya says. 'I know you're building your psychotherapy business, but you should feed your creative gifts, too. That's just me speaking, by the way, no spirit channelling.' She laughs.

'Let's do it,' Serenity says. 'Post it to all our social media channels today, Abby. You've got access to my account, haven't you? Make sure you post it there, too, under my name. We'll measure how viral it gets and work out how to proceed from there.'

Seems I need Abby, Cat thinks, *to help me do my job and graduate my ninth life.* She purrs resonantly and stands up to arch her spine and stretch her long, honeyed limbs, the taste of nutbrown biscuit still on her tongue, along with, she smirks, perhaps a dab of cream.

'Must fly,' says Freya. 'Another client awaits.'

Cat jumps into action, racing Freya to her office, hoping to settle into place before Milly, in Delta disguise, arrives for her reading. She doesn't want to miss a moment of the showdown.

Video queen of the day, Cat purrs, finding another nutbrown peace offering on her windowsill in Freya's office. She arranges her body in prime position, nibbles at the biscuit and salivates at the prospect of catching Freya out once and for all. *Rules are rules*, she reminds herself, and rules are not to be broken.

She looks across to the vacant green velour chair, soon to be the seat of the crime ... she stops herself, mid-thought. Seat of the crime? No, it's not Milly who's committing the crime. She may have booked in under a false name, but that's not fraud. That's all in a day's work for an investigative journalist intent on uncovering the truth. It's a lie for a truth. Rules are rules, and Milly surely follows rules for working undercover to expose the truth. *As I do*, Cat thinks, batting away a vision of Pearl questioning her: '*Are you upholding the rules, Cat? Are you intending to do no harm? Are you supporting Freya as a practitioner?*'

A sudden sweet camphor aroma spins Cat's nose to the left, where an elegant bunch of tall lavender stalks communes with delicate pink rosebuds in a clay vase on Freya's coffee table. That's new. She widens her gaze as the rest of the coffee table comes into focus. The carton of flyers is still there, and a box of tissues, but the tissues are now in a bright-pink dispenser matching the roses, and the previously bare table is now adorned with a pale-purple silk cloth. Two lavender-blue glasses and a silver jug – containing water, Cat guesses – and two glowing crystals, amethyst and ... she's not sure what the other one is. Gone is the slightly fuzzy smell of Freya's office, the overlay of stale coffee and the harsh ceiling lighting. There, behind Freya's chair, is a tall oaken lampstand with a cream silk shade, basking the room in a gentler hue.

'There you are, Amantha, darling.' Freya enters the room, swathed in tangerine-perfumed mist. 'I see you found your extra nutbrown treat.'

She sits down in her consulting chair, gently places her paper fan on the coffee table and picks up the two crystals. 'A fresh start, a new day, Amantha. Did you notice the changes? I was here until late last night setting everything up for a smooth day. Moonstone for my left hand and amethyst for my right.' She places the crystals in her hands. 'Prescribed for hot flushes ... Oh, not to bring them on, to stop them. It's so good to talk about this to you, Amantha. I know you're only a cat and you've no idea what I'm saying, but that's what's so healing for me, hearing myself speak out loud, voice my feelings and worries. I've got no-one else to talk to that I can trust. I'm committed to doing everything I can to stay connected with the spirits, and – just to be on the safe side – I'm prepared with a little backup information. Knowing I have it on hand should alleviate the anxiety that shoots those hot flushes into stratospheric proportions and veils me in brain fog. That's the plan, anyway. Thanks for listening, Amantha. It's hard to speak about this aloud, even to myself, but I feel so much better.'

Freya closes her eyes, breathes slowly and deeply, holding her crystals, then hums. Like a bumble bee.

It's Milly who looks like a bumble bee, dressed in a yellow-and-black-striped jumper, looking rather larger than usual, possibly a cushion tied to her belly. And straight blonde hair; a wig. Nothing like Milly at all except for her musky perfume, a dead giveaway for a cat, but not for Freya, who doesn't know Milly, anyway.

Milly offers the required nod to Amantha, lifts a bulky rhinestone-encrusted handbag onto her lap and fishes inside for ... Ah, a pen and notebook, Cat sees. 'Is it okay if I take notes? I don't want to miss anything.'

'I can record your session for an extra ten pounds if you like, Delta.'

'Yes, that will be wonderful, thank you.' Milly props her notebook against her fake bulging tummy and fiddles with her pen as if she's nervous.

The tiniest of clicks reaches Cat's ears, the faintest of hums, the kind that only a cat can hear. Ah, the camera is in the notebook, the lens probably poking through one of the eyes of the cat's face on the cover. *Oh, Milly, you are so funny.*

Cat checks the spirits gathered at the door, all but one appearing in bygone-era clothing. Though she knows they can change their clothing, their ages, their looks, in an instant, this bunch have been looking much the same for the past few weeks. Although, today they all have an extra sparkle, a slight phosphorescence even, a sense of anticipation that frissons Cat's fur. *Here for the showdown, too*, she purrs, stretching her legs forward, flicking and then retracting her claws, before settling in for the entertainment. *Not entertainment*, she admonishes herself, *the reckoning, the correction, a step in the right direction for my graduation.*

The spirit appearing in modern-day garb, denim dungarees, thick jade bracelet, emanating a female vibe, floats to the front of the little group and starts swinging her arms in circles, pursing her lips and blowing.

'I have a spirit here, Delta,' Freya begins. 'She's showing me a windmill, or wind ... no, I'm sure it's a windmill. I don't know why. I'm asking for more information.'

Milly switches the cross of her ankles, *trying to hold back a giggle*, Cat thinks.

'She's showing me a jade bracelet, says you'll know what it means.'

Milly shakes her head, says nothing.

'Jade, it's Jade,' she's saying. 'Who's Jade, Delta?'

Milly's face pales, her lips trembling. 'Jade is my sister. She died four years ago.'

Very convincing acting, high five, Milly. You've got Freya on a string now. Keep pulling. Cat cocks her head to one side. But who is this Jade spirit? Is she a player for the spirit world, helping us to catch Freya out?

'She's showing me denim dungarees and holding up a finger on each hand. Usually, that means twins. Did you have twins, did she have twins, or are you twins?'

Why oh why are spirits so vague? They need to practise some communication skills. They need a good teacher. Like me, perhaps. I could teach them the tried-and-trusted 'one meow, two meows, three meows, transmit' technique. Or does that only work for cats? Or does it only work when they are in earthly bodies, able to hold eye contact? Life would be so much easier if they could give detailed information, or custodial advice, something beyond proof of an afterlife. As I will do when I become a wise spirit mentor to an earthbound being, she thinks, jolting back into the present. *Focus, Cat, you have a mission to complete.*

'Jade was my identical twin, is my twin, was my twin,' Milly whispers. 'The only time we dressed the same was when we wore our denim dungarees. No-one could tell us apart then.'

'She's saying there are two of you today, not twins, but two different names, but it's like wearing dungarees.' Freya looks confused. 'I don't quite understand, it's not something she's showing me, it's something I feel, or hear. It's hard to describe, but that's the message I need to tell you.'

An icy shiver touches Cat's paws, creeps into her deepest bones and chatters her jaw. Two names, Delta and Milly. Windmill meaning mill – Milly. This channelling is genuine, pure Freya on a roll, but what's surprising, Cat shivers again, is Freya's complete trust that Milly is Delta, even while she's giving information to the contrary. She's a genuine spirit medium, a brilliant channel when she's not gushing in sweat and swathed in fog, but she can't function without spirits. No reading the vibes. No deep intuition. *Not like me, or like cats in general. Or like cats in their ninth life, anyway. Focus.* She pulls herself together again, glancing at Milly.

'Dungarees,' mutters Milly.

'What else do dungarees mean to you, Delta?'

'Not having to dress up corporate.'

'Do you wear dungarees?'

Milly looks down at her hands, staying mute.

No more corporate clothes for Milly, not since she left her television journalism career behind, not since she moved to the village; no need for suits here.

'She has one more message for you. She's showing me digging. I think she means get digging, or start digging. Is this making any sense to you?'

Milly remains quiet.

Cat sees a kerfuffle at the door, one of the other spirits appearing as a male energy in – Cat guesses – Victorian-era clothes, brandishing a giant fountain pen. These spirits do go overboard sometimes.

'I now have another spirit, Delta, a man, looks like he's from the late nineteenth century. He's showing me a pen. I'm getting the message that he wants you to write something. Yes, he's nodding his head and pointing to Jade's dungarees. Hang on, it's coming to me. He wants you – no, they want you to do some digging and write about it. Does that make sense? Is it gardening or something, a book about gardening?'

Cat practises her inner eyeroll again. *Slow, Freya, so slow*. But there's nothing for Milly to write about so far. Just the opposite. So far, Freya has been deadly accurate, and by the look on Milly's face, Milly knows it, too.

'There's more. They're saying to dig into history, dig back in time, something for you to find ... No, it's gone.' Freya looks at her watch. Cat knows she's only halfway through the reading.

In the pin-drop silence that follows, Cat sniffs a whiff of anxiety – Freya's distinctive anxiety. Excitement crawls through Cat's fur, tingling her neck hairs erect. *Now for the cheating*, she predicts, as Freya's skin glistens in sweat, a wisp of brain fog fast thickening around her head as she reaches for her paper fan.

'I'm seeing the number sixty-eight, or a hundred and sixty-eight. Someone wearing a uniform, no, they're showing me a badge with the number one-six-eight on it. Green with gold lettering.'

Milly leans forward, subtly checks the orientation of her notebook and clicks her pen twice. *Clever girl*, thinks Cat, *camera still rolling*.

'Something to do with sport, lawn bowls,' Freya says, watching Milly closely. 'Does this mean anything to you?'

'My father, he plays lawn bowls. That may be his team

number,' Milly says. Cat can detect Milly's switch to Delta mode, a very subtle change in voice tone that only a cat would distinguish.

'I've got a male spirit, a friend of your father's, name begins with a J, James, no, Jim. He says tell your father to take care, watch his heart. Is this making sense, Delta?'

'Jim was Dad's best mate. He died last year. Dad had a heart attack shortly after, but he's feeling much better now,' Delta replies.

'Jim says to tell your father he's enjoying feeling younger, and he wants you to know that your puppy, Lora, is happy in spirit. That's all I have for you today, Delta.'

Cat looks from Freya to Milly, from Milly to Freya. *Now, Milly, attack now, spill the beans.*

'I have to be honest with you, Freya,' Delta says. 'Jade's message about there being two of me here today, I'll explain that in a minute, but it's like there are two of you here today, one of you that's amazing and spookily accurate, and one of you – the one that talked about my father, Jim, and my puppy, that's ... quite frankly, a con.'

Freya steams bright red, says nothing, then slowly gets up, walks over to Cat and lifts her onto her lap. 'What's the matter, Amantha?' she says, tears cascading down her cheeks and onto Cat's neck. 'Are you feeling unwell?' She turns to Milly. 'I'm sorry, Delta, it seems my psychic assistant has let me down. She can get her wires crossed sometimes. I must have been reading for my next client. Amantha is such a treasure, an invaluable support and link to the spirit world, but sometimes I guess she's only human, um, feline ... you know what I mean.'

Cat's blood boils, her back uncontrollably thrusts into a tight, high arch, and her claws protrude and dig into Freya's thighs. A second's indecision, then she jumps from Freya's lap and leaps onto Milly's, remembering at the last moment to sit to one side of the hidden camera lens.

'No,' Milly says, removing her blonde wig and relaxing into

her normal voice. 'I'm Milly. There is no Delta Jones. I created Delta Jones's Facebook page and it's a total fiction. I posted the photos of the badge and the photos of the two men playing lawn bowls. The puppy, too. Got them off the internet. I made up their names and their stories. And why would I do that? Because one of your recent clients felt scammed and asked me to test you out. I'm an investigative journalist. And I've caught you red-handed, haven't I? It's nothing to do with Amantha. You had my name, you looked for me on social media, found what you needed and fed it back to me, pretending that it came from spirit.'

Cat watches as the fog clears around Freya's head and she reaches for her amethyst and moonstone, breathing deeply, tears streaming down her cheeks, the tissues long forgotten.

'I don't know what to say,' Freya croaks.

'But you know what?' Milly says. 'Freya, you blew me away with the information you gave me earlier. I wasn't expecting that. Everything you told me about Jade was true. And everything you relayed from Jade was true. There were two of me here today, you know that now, two names, Delta and Milly. You communicated that, but you didn't realise what she really meant. The dungarees felt like a message from Jade to go back to my "digging" work – my investigative journalism work – but not in a corporate way. To do it from here, in the village, in my own skin, in my home clothes, by myself, freelance. I haven't worked since I left London, just after Jade died. I needed time out to work out how to be in the world without her, to work out what I wanted to do with my life.'

Milly runs out of breath and examines her hands again. Cat examines Freya's face.

'The windmill: she was using that as a sign that she had a message for Milly.' Freya brings the moonstone to her cheek. 'And the Victorian gentleman with the pen was telling you to write, to pick up your journalism again?'

'Maybe,' Milly says, 'but his message was about history, writing about history, and that doesn't make sense to me. I'm more interested in what's happening today. Was he real or did you make him up before you turned to Delta's Facebook information?'

'He was real. And I know that's an admission that the later stuff was fake. And if you're the real deal, I imagine you've got a hidden camera somewhere, have you?'

'On second thoughts,' Milly says, ignoring Freya's question, 'I'm not sure how this works, but do you really see spirits, or are you reading my mind? Apart from the information about writing history – which I can't relate to – you haven't told me anything I didn't already know. I had been toying with the idea of doing freelance work from home. You could be a genuinely gifted mind-reader, but what can you say to convince me that you're talking with spirits?'

'I'm a hopeless mind-reader, no idea what's on people's minds. I only speak with spirits, and I only do that when a client gives me permission – unless the spirit's message is urgent. I'm not constantly nattering away with the departed. They're all over the place, and it would be overwhelming. I tune in when asked to do so, with the intention of helping people with my gift.'

Freya pauses a moment, and Cat wonders if she heard the other part of Milly's question.

'I can't convince you that I'm talking with spirits, but I can convince you that I'm not mind-reading. If I was mind-reading, I would have known your game, known you were Milly, because that would have been top of your mind. But about that Victorian spirit, his message will prove to be all the convincing you need, but you will have to wait for time to unfold. He said you were to dig into history because there was something for you to find. That probably sounds vague to you now, but the day will come when that makes sense, your skin will tingle, you will remember your reading and something meaningful will fall into place. People always question the messages they can't relate to, but that's because they're about the future. It can be very frustrating working as a psychic sometimes.'

I know the feeling, Cat squirms.

'So, what are you going to do, Milly? Is this the end of my career, my reputation down the plughole?'

'I'm torn because I'm confused. If you have a gift – and clearly you do, you have proved that to me, much to my surprise – why cheat?'

'Cheating's a strong word, Milly. I was trying to console you about your father, your puppy, give you hope, a sense of meaning and purpose, faith in life and in the afterlife. Make you feel better than you did when you came in.'

'Sorry, not making sense,' Milly says, removing the skullcap she had been wearing beneath her wig and shaking her dark curls free. 'You gave me all of that with the genuine part of your reading. Did the spirits leave you? Was their work done? Did you feel you had to give me my full hour, justify your full fee, so you added the rest?'

'I'm embarrassed to tell you the reason. But I'm in so deep already, I'll try. Nothing to lose. You probably won't believe me, but I've only been collecting information from social media for a couple of weeks, three weeks tops. I didn't need to before that. I always had a full hour's chitchat to convey from the spirits until something happened last month.'

Milly folds her hands in front of her notebook, careful not to obscure the cat's-eye camera lens, making sure Cat doesn't get too close to it.

'I'm forty-eight. Last month, out of the blue, I started experiencing hot flushes, and I can tell you, you may have heard other women talk about perimenopause and hot flushes, but nothing, absolutely nothing can prepare you for the devastation they bring. One day everything is normal, and the next you're a walking, talking, erupting volcano. It starts with a dizziness in your feet – only way I can describe it, like you're disconnected from the ground, like you're standing on a wave, like you might fall, like you don't know up from down – then a little fire starts in your chest and you think it's nothing, it's going to be okay. But it's not okay, and it escalates into a river of hot, molten iron that explodes up into your head and all through your torso, and you don't know where to put yourself. You're hotter than you've ever felt in your entire life and you're getting hotter by the second. You try to grab at your clothes, pull off a cardigan, but there are toes in place of your fingers, so you lift your shirt away from your chest and blow down on your skin, but now, as the heat reaches its max, your skin prickles and an ocean of sweat cascades from every pore of your body. You try to think, but all you can think about is escape, and there's nowhere to escape to. If you're indoors you panic, feel claustrophobic, wish for open windows, but you can't figure out how to open them. And there's more. When it happens, you're so engulfed by the physicality of it all that you can't think in a straight line. They call it brain fog, apparently. Eventually, after what seems like half an hour but is probably five minutes, you cool down and start to shiver. Unfortunately, the foggy thinking can last longer. Oh, and then guess what? In twenty minutes or so, it all begins again. And does it stop while you try to sleep? No. It goes on and on through the night, and you end up lying wide awake on soaking-wet sheets. And you know what, it's all about to start again right now, so you can watch if you like. Catch it on that camera that I'm sure you've got hidden somewhere. I should add, in case it's not already obvious, that it makes you moody and a tad irritable, too.'

Freya grabs her paper fan and adds a further torrent of tears to the ocean of running sweat.

Milly tilts her notebook to focus the camera on Freya's face. All Cat sees is an intense fog, but she knows Freya is in there somewhere.

They all wait for the flush to pass.

Cat ponders the new information she has learned. Words can add a lot to understanding.

'And the cheating?' Milly asks.

'When I have a hot flush, I lose connection with the spirits.'

'And you don't want to leave your clients high and dry – excuse me, no pun intended – so you do a little homework so that you have something up your sleeve. Sorry again, didn't mean to compare you to a magician.' Milly smiles.

Homework! So, are we calling cheating and rule breaking nothing but a little homework now? Do a little homework to do no harm, is that what Freya thinks? Is that what Milly thinks? But what about Clary being told her mum advised her to get a new cat, when her mum would have known that Benji had just been diagnosed with asthma and is allergic to cat dander. Do no harm? I don't think so. Indignation spikes the hairs along Cat's spine, fuelling a low, moody purr.

'I'm sorry, but you've got me spouting now,' says Freya, 'and I need to get this off my chest. It's this bad and it's only been happening for two or three weeks. Google tells me this can go on for months, years, and no-one understands what I'm going through. I'm exhausted with anxiety and lack of solid sleep.'

'I understand,' says Milly. 'More than you think. It happened to me last year. I'm the same age as you, and it was so disruptive that I saw my doctor and decided to go the hormone-replacement route, so I'm feeling more balanced now, but hormone therapy isn't for everyone. I know women who've resigned from work, retired even, because they just couldn't cope with the sweats, let alone the brain fog and the lack of understanding from their colleagues.'

'Your media story will be the end of my career. I can see that. I could promise not to do it again, but the cat is out of the bag now.' They both turn to look at Cat.

'I need to sleep on this.' Milly gathers her notebook and pen into her bag. 'Garish, isn't it,' she says, nodding at the rhinestone handbag. 'Delta's choice, not mine.'

Both women laugh. Cat's head spins.

'Look,' Milly says, standing up, 'thank you from the bottom

of my heart for your messages from Jade, for opening my eyes to your skills and – who knows – starting me on some kind of mystery history writing adventure, but promise me this. Don't cheat again, Freya. Just be honest. Say you've lost touch temporarily with the spirit. The idea I'm going to sleep on is to do an exposé on the challenges women face dealing with perimenopause at work, dealing with brain fog, but mostly dealing with other people's ignorance about a natural process that should be supported.'

Freya sobs.

'And no more blaming that gorgeous cat.' Milly scoops the discarded blonde wig into the loud, sparkly bag and heads for the door.

As the door closes, Freya lifts Cat and cradles her in the crook of her elbow. 'I am so, so sorry, Amantha. I know you're just a cat and have no idea what I'm saying, but that's exactly why I love you. Do you think Milly will still write about my little homework safeguard? Can I handle the lulls in my reading in a different way? I have a nub of an idea. It involves you. I'll sleep on it. You'll find out tomorrow. This could work out well for both of us.'

A silent scream electrifies Cat's body, projects her from Freya's embrace, propels her to the windowsill and leaps her through the open window, where she lands on all fours, shaking, face to face with Pearl.

🐾

'That's one way to bypass the daffodil patch,' Pearl purrs.

'I wasn't even thinking about the daffodils.' Cat relishes the peppermint fragrance of newly cut grass sticking to her paws, cooling her fire. 'Just had to get out of there.'

'Prowl with me, Cat. Let's hunt some mice, or chase those butterflies over by the roses, unwind, have a chat.'

'It's so good to talk purr language,' Cat says. 'To tell you exactly what's going on, instead of trying to communicate with people using charades and the occasional successful transmission of a few words or a brief concept.'

'So, you're getting some messages across to them, then?'

'One or two. Not enough. One paw forward, six paws back. And it's weird, being able to understand everything they say and not being able to communicate back on the same level. And that Freya, she still thinks I'm "just a cat". I'm so much more, and she needs to listen to me. It's driving me crazy.'

'Like jumping out of the window kind of crazy?'

Cat prances and dances, slinks and arches, pirouettes on her hind paws, tilts her head to the left and opens her jaws wide enough to gulp a monster mouse. 'That kind of crazy,' she says, slightly breathless. 'Exorcised now.'

'That thing you said,' Pearl muses, 'about not being able to communicate on the same level, I imagine that's what being a spirit mentor would be like. You'd understand everything your mentee said, everything they thought, everything they planned, everything they felt, and, unless they were really attuned, they wouldn't know you existed, let alone listen to you. How are you going to handle that? More charades, arranging to place perplexing symbols on their path – feathers, animals, riddles for them to solve?'

'Good point, Pearl. But won't I have better communication skills when I leave this earthly body?'

'If those human spirits Freya talks to are anything to go by, no.'

'How do you know what Freya's spirits say?'

'We cats have our ways, Cat. Maybe I'm a little more evolved than you.' Pearl nudges Cat off her paws, pushing her into a bed of heavenly honeyed rose perfume.

'Ouch,' Cat growls.

'Didn't mean to hurt your feelings, just joking.'

'No, ouch because you pushed me onto a thorn.'

'On which subject, tell me about the thorns you encountered

today. You flew out of that window covered in hackles. How are you feeling now?'

A blackbird flies past, singing to the breeze. A bumble of bees swarms over the roses. Petals unfold and fall. A large blue butterfly emerges from a chrysalis and lifts into her maiden voyage. The June sun journeys across its zenith and begins its dance into the west. And Cat reaches the end of her story.

'I see,' Pearl purrs.

'Thank you for listening. It's so good to talk about this to you. It's so healing for me, hearing myself speak out loud. I'm committed to doing everything I can to fulfil my mission, and it's not as easy as I had imagined. It's hard to speak about this aloud, even to myself, but I feel so much better.'

'That's almost verbatim what Freya said to you. Did you realise that?'

Cat replays her memory of the earlier conversation, a spikey niggle of recognition sparking through her.

'And,' Pearl flicks their tail, 'stop me if you don't want to hear this. You were as prickly and thorny as these roses when you flew out of the window. Much the same as Freya has her prickly, thorny moments that make her do crazy things when things don't go to plan, wouldn't you say?'

'Watch out.' Cat bats a paw at Pearl, and tumbles them to their belly, giggling. 'I've got a hot flush coming on and a brain fog so thick you won't see me for days.'

'Before you disappear completely, then, remind me of the rules you're trying to enforce.'

'Rule one: do no harm,' Cat begins. 'It does no harm for Freya to talk to me, to get things off her chest, to feel better. It does no harm for me to listen. But Freya does harm when she tells lies, even though we might understand why. Milly can put an end to this by exposing Freya, but Milly may harm Freya's career, and Freya is very good at what she does when she acts truthfully. It's complicated.'

'Keep going.'

'Rule two: help and heal. As ambiguous as the first rule when it comes to Freya.'

'Helping and healing is Freya's heartfelt intention,' Pearl says.

'Rule three: support each other. Milly supported Freya when she listened to her and shared her own hot-flushes experience. Whether she still supports her when she decides what to write, we'll see. I supported Freya when I ...'

'When you? You didn't, did you?'

'No, but what was I supposed to do? Support her lying?'

'Maybe there's another way to support her so she can offer her helping and healing gifts to people who need them without resorting to cheating.' Pearl holds Cat's gaze for ... *Could that be one meow, two meows, three meows, transmit? But we cats don't need to use the old one-two-three thought implant, do we?*

'That way, you could bring her back in line with the rules,' Pearl says, their voice a little distant and fuzzy to Cat's discombobulated ear.

Cat shakes her head, dismissing the heady, distorted weirdness. 'Rule four: leave your troubles at home. I can see that's hard for Freya when her troubles come with her. Oh, there's one thing I haven't told you. Abby made a video about me, called "Leave Your Troubles at Home" and ...'

Cat looks around. Pearl has disappeared. Off home to their troubles, maybe. Cat laughs. Either that or one of them has indeed caught Freya's brain fog and is invisible!

She trots off in the direction of Freya's window just as Freya leans out and slams it closed.

😺

'Way to go, Amantha!' A sturdy, grass-stained hand scoops Cat skywards and brings her eye to eye with a ginger nest of a beard, essence of Briar tingling her nose. 'I hear you're trending, climbing towards cat-video stardom.'

'What, already?' Clary's crisp tones announce her presence as Briar's heart jumps a resounding octave in Cat's ear. 'Serenity only gave Abby the go-ahead to post that at lunchtime, so that's, what, four hours?'

'Oh, I didn't see you there. Sorry to disturb you. I'm not one for social media, but Abby mentioned it to me when she was out here for a breath of fresh air a couple of hours ago. I think she said two hundred thousand likes and soaring. I'm Briar, by the way, the landscape artist and gardener for these grounds.'

'I'm Clary, yoga student here, new to the village. Pleased to meet you, Briar,' she says, fiddling with the straps on the well-worn leather satchel slung over her shoulder.

'I saw you sitting over by the topiary earlier. Looked like you were drawing. I didn't want to interrupt you, a fellow artist at work and all that.'

'Just working on some ideas and soaking up the June sunshine.' Clary meets Cat's gaze.

'Sketching our Reclining Woman with Child?'

'No. I mean, she's beautiful, it's beautiful, your topiary is beautiful.' Clary flushes bright red. 'I was sketching some ideas for a painting I want to do, a portrait of Amantha. I took some photos of her, but photos on their own aren't enough. I needed to work on her essence, what I want to portray, and was drawn to this spot.'

'That's exciting, Clary.' Briar's beard tickles Cat's cheek as he holds her closer. 'I've been making a topiary statue of her, but I don't think I've caught her essence at all. And, I should correct you, the Reclining Woman with Child, the topiary you commended me on, is not mine. I tend it and trim it, keep it in shape and keep it healthy, but the artist who created her was Henry Gable back in sixteen ninety-eight.'

'You're not telling me it's the same as it was then, surely? That would make it over three hundred years old.'

Thank goodness for that, Cat thinks. *Words I can handle, numbers beyond nine hundred and ninety-nine not so much. Three hundred years I can picture. It's roughly three cat lives. No, three hundred cat lives. Or thirty cat lives?* Annoyance flicks her tail. *It's a long time.*

'It's much the same as it was in sixteen ninety-eight. I've got all the logbooks at home, passed from generation to generation, beginning with one of my ancestors.'

'Hang on,' Clary gasps, 'are you saying this work has remained in your family for over three hundred years? You're from a long line of topiary artists?'

'More like a long line of gardeners charged with keeping the topiary in shape.' Briar's words are still a little too close to Cat's ear for comfort. 'I'm the first one who went to university, studied landscape architecture. One day I might open a landscape-design business, but to be honest, these gardens are enough for me now. My heart is here. Pull of family history.'

'My head's reeling.' A slight frown crinkles Clary's forehead. 'You've got three-hundred-year-old documents at home? A whole continuous history of gardening? Shouldn't they be in a museum or something? Oh, sorry, my big mouth. I didn't mean it like that ...'

'No, you're right, they should be, but I can't let them go. I've got them stored in a dehumidifier inside an innocent-looking cabinet, and I wear white gloves when I look at them. You're not some kind of archivist detective, are you?'

Cat studies Clary's face for her reaction. *Is she here in the village on a mission, like me, making sure people keep to the rules?*

'Hardly.' Clary laughs. 'But have you thought about getting some advice, maybe get them stored at a museum where you can access them at any time, and keep copies at home that you can thumb through without worrying about them deteriorating?'

'Well, Clary,' Briar lowers Cat to the grass, setting her free, 'you're right, of course. That would be sensible. But sensible doesn't cover how I feel about diaries written in my forebears' hands. And it's more than that, you know. I can't describe it, but it's like I'm charged with keeping a secret. And here I am telling you all about it!'

'I won't say anything about them,' Clary says, 'but what can you tell me about Reclining Woman with Child? What's public knowledge about her?'

The late-afternoon breeze carries the scent of rose petals, prickling Cat's skin with the memory of the thorn. She slinks over to Clary and curves her body around her legs, Clary's lovely, earthy essence smoothing her fur and soothing her heart.

'She's possibly one of the oldest continuous topiaries in England. The oldest still in existence is in Cumbria, designed by Guillaume Beaumont in sixteen ninety-four. The artform itself goes back to Roman times, forty-four BC, I think. Pliny the Younger wrote about the ones in his Tuscan villa garden.'

'Fascinating! I had no idea it was such an ancient art. Was she modelled after any woman in particular?'

'She's wrapped in mystery, Clary. People say she goes back to a time when this land had something to do with witchcraft, or healing, whichever way you want to look at it. Was our reclining woman someone tended by the – let's call them healers – or was she representative of their healing arts? There's plenty of conjecture, lots of wild imaginings, but no-one knows for sure.'

'Nothing in the diaries?'

'Not unless it's hidden in code.'

'Really?' Clary bends to tickle Cat under her chin.

'I was joking.' Briar laughs. 'But you never know.'

'Here kitty, kitty! Puss-puss! Amantha!' Emmy's call floats across the garden.

Cat unfurls from Clary and sprints off, carefully skirting the bed where the daffodils sleep, eager to get inside the building before Emmy locks up for the night.

Kitty, puss, my bones, Cat thinks, her irritation slightly lessened at the prospect of a bowl of cream and a cosy cushion to wile away her evening reclining in contemplation.

❧

Morning sunlight instantly flashes Cat awake, Emmy's 'Here kitty, kitty! Puss-puss!' still ringing in her ears. Not in the mood for yoga, she whips and flips her tail, then bats her paws at an invisible cloud of squealing bugs closing in around her head. Not in the mood for sitting still, not in the mood for curling up, not in the mood for being patient, not in the mood for work. She leaps up, bolts into Emmy's office, pounces on a startled mouse, gulps it down and licks her bloodied lips. Not in the mood for licking her paws, not in the mood for being inside. She bounds down the front steps and runs rings around the sleeping daffodils, sweat flying. *See if I care, go on, shake me up, scare me to death, relieve me of my duties, I'm over it, totally over it all.*

Nothing happens.

She slows down, comes to a halt, head lowered, chin grazing the quiet earth. Her bones begin to chill, sweat evaporating faster than the morning dew glistening across the distant lawn.

She stalks her way over to the topiary garden, switching her eyes from left to right, on the lookout for friends or foes. Most likely, foes.

A solitary butterfly crosses her path before changing direction and flying towards Reclining Woman with Child. Cat follows her; nothing better to do.

She squints into the distance. *Yes. I knew it!* Not one but many rows of Reclining Women with Children. The butterfly turns and slowly descends onto her nose, Cat's eyes crossing as she tries to keep focus on the tiny sparkling wings. A long, slow moment. Mesmerised. Calmed. Restored. The call of a blackbird, and the butterfly lifts up and away, flying across the multitude of Reclining Women, except they are gone. In their place, one solitary Reclining Woman with Child.

Curious but grounded, Cat's heart beats squarely in the present moment. She turns her tail and heads back to the café in time to catch Milly reporting back to the others about her session with Freya.

🐾

A bamboozling mix of food, cacophonous chatter and high hopes catches Cat's attention as she approaches the café. People are queued at the entrance, waiting for seats since the place is crowded inside, spilling out, she can now see, through French doors onto the patio, where more people clamour for tables and chairs, some sitting on the grass sipping their coffees, soaking up the sun.

What has happened? Where have all these people come from? Where's Milly? Cat stands stock still. *Don't panic. Focus.* And there they are, not at their usual table, which is currently occupied by a twittering teenage foursome, heads bent over their phones, but over there, closer to the kitchen. She begins to weave her way between abandoned bags, rolled yoga mats and legs, as a waiter dances through the mayhem carrying a tray of coffees above the heads of the crowd. She sticks to the floor. It's too risky, too busy, to jump onto chairbacks, her preferred way of negotiating the café. She spies a long sideboard, leaps up onto it and wends her way between vases, piles of shiny magazines and towers of boxed puzzles, until she is close enough to drop into Clary's lap.

'There you are. Surprised you made it this far without anyone recognising you.' Clary laughs. 'Hashtag video star, hashtag cat video, hashtag leave your troubles at home.'

'Over a million views and still trending,' says Pixie. 'You know how much money Serenity could make on YouTube with a million views? About four thousand pounds, according to Google. And probably a lot more through sales for her Zoom classes on the back of the publicity. And it's nowhere near the top of its stratospheric climb yet. Probably will be a stayer, too.'

'I hope she'll share some of that with Abby, after all the work she put into creating it.' Anna catches the eye of a waiter to order more coffees.

'Excuse me,' Milly addresses a gaggle of girls at the adjacent table, 'can you put your phones away, please, to give us some privacy?'

'Sorry,' says the one wearing metallic bracelets that tingle and offend Cat's ears. 'But Amantha's famous. Can we just grab one photo?'

'Sorry, not in here, not with us in the picture. Try to catch her outside later if you wish. Thank you for understanding.'

The girl scowls at Milly and winks at Cat. 'See you later, gorgeous divine messenger.'

Clary strokes Cat's back, gently guiding her hackles to settle.

'So anyway,' Milly relaxes back in her chair, 'now that you've heard the whole story, what do you think?'

'I can empathise with Freya,' Pixie says. 'Been through it myself, out the other side now that I'm fifty-nine. Doesn't excuse cheating, but if she's telling the truth, and she's only been experiencing this for a few weeks, maybe we should exercise kindness and compassion, not throw her to the dogs without giving her a chance to redeem herself.'

Cat catches her claws in the act of extending and pulls them back in. *Well done. Don't waste energy. Hold back, make your actions count. Do no harm*, she adds, puzzling over what that would look like in this context.

'I'm only forty,' Anna says. 'Although, if you'd asked me last week I would have said, oh my God, I'm forty, I'm feeling old. I dread to think what lies ahead for me given your experiences, but perhaps I'll be better prepared, now that I've learned a little more about what perimenopause can be like. I can't believe I'm talking about this, already.'

'I'm sure there will be more options available for you when it's your turn,' Pixie says, 'medically and culturally. If Milly tells Freya's story in a way that draws attention to the predicament and women's challenges within the workplace, within society, she can help build a different world.'

'My vote, considering Serenity's message about compassion and forgiveness this morning,' says Anna, 'is for us to be compassionate towards Freya and extend forgiveness for her cheating. From what you say, Milly, she's unlikely to do it again.'

No! Cat's every muscle twitches. She turns to face Clary and holds her gaze: one meow, two meows, three meows – transmit: *Freya needs to follow the rules.*

'But what do you think, Clary?' Milly asks. 'She cheated you, and you were as keen as the rest of us to expose her to protect others.'

'Freya needs to follow the rules.' Clary claps her hand over her mouth as soon as the words are out. 'I don't know where that came from. Do I really mean that? I don't know. What rules?'

'Rules of ethics, maybe,' Pixie says. 'Or psychic-reading rules, if there are such things. Rules of human decency.'

'Or the rules of the Serene Lotus Centre for Health and Wellbeing.' Clary twirls the dainty ruby ring on her pinkie finger. 'Maybe that's what I mean. Do no harm and all that. Leave your troubles at home.'

All four pairs of eyes sweep to Cat, crinkly smile lines beaming their affection, Cat senses, for her, their leave-your-troubles-at-home poster child.

'Though, I can't imagine what she's going through,' Clary continues, 'and, at thirty-five, my view might be rather short-sighted.'

Milly and Pixie nod.

'But really,' Clary says, 'I'm swayed by the synchronicity, the Rajpapa message of compassion and forgiveness, so my vote would be for an article that focuses on Freya's predicament if it helps pave the way for better understanding of perimenopause in the workplace.'

'If I'm going to be true to my training and make this article work,' Milly bites her lip, 'I'm going to have to write about Freya's temptation to cheat – and the couple of times when she did – to give emotional depth to her predicament. But if I can do it in a way that embraces her intention to work authentically from now on, it will help highlight the challenges we have to face, the pivots in how we approach our work, maybe.'

'Where do you think your article will have most impact?' Pixie asks. 'Have you still got good contacts in the media?'

'Digital media, because I think it's the kind of story people will share, and we want word to get around. I'm still friends with a digital editor for the BBC news website. More than that, I phoned her and ran the idea past her last night, and she's ready to run with whatever version of the story I file.'

'Fast work, Milly.' Anna's face lights up. 'You haven't lost your touch over the last four years, then.'

'Truth be told,' Milly flushes, 'I'm very excited about this. Ready to get back on the horse, but with my own stories, in a way that counts, to me, at least. And I must admit, Freya's spirit message about doing some digging and writing a history of the place has energised me, even though I have no idea what it means or where to start.'

'On that note,' Clary leans forward, 'have a chat to Briar, the gardener-slash-landscape-artist for this place. His family has been tending the garden here for over three hundred years. He's your man for history. And "digging", you know, maybe it's a link to gardening as well as digging for information. It could be a start, anyway.'

'I'm all goosebumps.' Milly smiles, gathering her bag and yoga roll and bidding them farewell. 'Watch this space.'

'And I, Amantha,' Clary lifts Cat off her lap and into the

radiance of her emerald gaze, 'am off home to begin work on my portrait of you. But first, let me rescue you from all your fans.'

Cat's heart thuds as Clary carries her through the throng, out into the garden and stoops to free her near the roses.

The truth of the matter slowly dawns. Those people, those unruly crowds, were here to see Cat, video queen and what? Divine messenger? She rolls on her back, mindful of the thorns, and paws at the overhead butterflies, playfully, doing no harm, engaging her thoughts. Milly intends to use the media to help and heal. Help and heal women in Freya's predicament, get the message across. *So, if I ...* She rolls onto her belly and assumes the sphinx pose. *If I have the media at my paw-tips through the videos Abby is making of me, can I use those to get my messages across and get people back in line? Is fame my path to graduation from my ninth life so I can become a spirit mentor to an earthbound being, a being I can assist to help and heal the world?*

🐾

Cat prowls the hallway, one more mouse cleanly despatched, looking for a sunny spot to spruce up her whiskers and plan her next move, when the distinct Clary aroma of earth and paint begs her twitching nose to follow. It leads her to the mysterious room beyond the cornflower-blue door, next to the café's kitchen, which has always been locked, until now. A room not so mysterious now that she pokes her head around the jamb and sees Clary standing at a sink filling a jug of water. A musty tang of a room with four long trestle tables arranged as the four sides of a square, each facing a central nest of brightly coloured cushions suspended in what looks like a tree, its boughs draped in shiny tinkling bells, twists of fraying silk, and fine threads bearing fishy biscuits and other mouth-watering titbits. One leap, and Cat's ensconced on the purple velvet cushion at the very centre, eyeing a biscuit that she wishes she could eat, if it were not for her bulging, mouse-filled belly. A perfect place to wile away the morning and make plans.

'Just in time.' Clary squeezes between the tables to stroke Cat under her chin before *click-click-clicking* her phone. 'This way, Amantha, up here, look this way. Gorgeous!' She stops, jabs at the screen and sighs in satisfaction.

'You, my dear, are the star of the show today, about to be immortalised in pencil, charcoal, paint and beautiful memories. Are you ready?'

Ready? I don't know. Curious, yes, but isn't that the nature of a cat? Not that I'm any old cat, certainly not Freya's 'just a cat', and Clary knows that. Already immortalised in Abby's viral video. And now what? Star of video screen, pencil, charcoal and paint, guardian and protector of Serenity's international megastar empire, its practitioners, its clients, its fame and fortunes. All eyes and ears on me and what I can do to help them. Not long to go now, graduation here I come. Shed my skin, my flesh, my bones, ascend to my true mission.

She feels her body lift, her wings spread, a butterfly aflutter, as she falls deeply down into sleep for what feels like eons but is only the time it takes for the room to fill with excited chatter and startle her awake.

'I've been so looking forward to this.' Pixie drapes her buttercup-yellow summer cardi over the back of a chair and dons a long-sleeved smock over her white T-shirt. 'What do you think? Appropriate?' She spins a dainty pirouette, appealing to Clary.

'Totally.' Clary laughs. 'Picasso's most celebrated works immortalised in fabric. Where did you find that?'

'Trip to London, years ago, Tate Modern. Couldn't decide whether it was trashy or quirky, and it's been hiding at the bottom of a drawer ever since. Perfect as a painting apron, though. And you know, I've never tried painting since I was a teenager at school, so I'm not expecting much of myself beyond a few cubist lines. I'm going for quirky, but we'll see.'

'There's an artist in everyone, Pixie, and it's my job today to locate her.' Clary's eyes crinkle warmly.

'Even in me?' says Milly. 'I think my inner artist is practised in writing. I'm not so sure that she can turn her hand with any success to a paintbrush. I'm nervous and excited, a child faced with a sandpit, or paint-pit maybe.'

'Thank you, everyone, for booking in for a paint playtime,' Clary says, now that all sixteen seats are occupied. Sixteen pairs of eyes flick between Clary and Cat. 'Let's call it that, a paint playtime, so that you're all at ease, but I know you're all in for a big surprise.'

'Just glad you took Serenity's prodding seriously,' Anna says. 'She's been thinking of leasing out this room for workshops, and this is a lovely way to bless the space. When I saw the painting you did of Amantha – her portrait, I should say – I mentioned possible classes to Serenity and she ...'

'So, you're to blame,' Pixie elbows Anna, 'for whatever I produce today. And for digging out this eccentricity to wear.'

'Okay, everyone.' Clary steps into the centre as silence descends. 'How many of you think you're going to go home with a painting of a cat looking a bit like our Amantha?'

Cat sits to attention, adopting the pose she imagines they'll be interested in painting. Honeyed, regal, wise, guardian, protector, eyes forward to meet the onlooker's gaze. The talented ones might be able to do that thing she's seen in stately homes – she pauses to question the memory. Must be from an earlier life. That thing, where the eyes look straight at you wherever you are in relation to the portrait. Now, that would be powerful.

'Not me, not really,' says a newcomer, though Cat feels she's seen her at yoga once or twice. Essence of primrose with a hint of hawthorn, a nest of red ringlets framing a pale face. 'Might be more like a cartoon cat, or a dog, or guinea pig, if my past attempts at drawing are anything to go by.'

'So, Hazel,' says Clary, 'probably like everyone else in this room, you're thinking of trying to paint – or draw – what Amantha looks like, yes?'

'Er, yes.' Hazel looks around at the other hopeful students. 'I went to one of those paint-and-sip classes a few years ago, where we all sipped wine and followed the teacher's step-by-step instructions. The others did quite passable replicas of the teacher's painting, a vase of daisies reflected in a mirror. Mine was, well, let's just say I probably drank too much of the wine.'

'No step-by-step instructions today, Hazel,' Clary says. 'Or no paint-by-number approach is what I should say. You'll each have something quite unique by the end of our day.'

'And in place of wine, thankfully,' Abby slides into the room, 'here are your hot drinks, as per your orders. Plus, complementary blueberry-pecan muffins from Serenity in the café.'

Dear Abby, forget-me-not Abby. Who could ever forget Abby, her swan wingtips protruding from her too-corporate-looking tailored shirt, her stilettos lifting her to her tippytoes, ready to fly.

'Abby!' cries Clary. 'I almost forgot you were joining us. See that chair over by the sink? Pull it up here. Shuffle over a bit, Anna. Grab your coffees, everyone, and let's get started.

'There are rulebooks for painting and drawing. Rules to follow if you want to produce a perfect portrait. Rules to get the hang of some basics. Drawing rules. Painting rules. Washing-out-your-paintbrush rules. Following-the-steps-at-a-paint-and-sip-class rules.'

Excellent. Clary's easy. No problems with Clary: she understands the importance of following rules, doing the right thing, seeing the big picture ... Oh, I think I just made a joke. She loves me, she painted a portrait of me, she's helping to put me on the path to fame and graduation. And she's a teacher, too, passing on the message. Full marks, Clary.

'I could teach you by the rulebook,' Clary continues, 'but rules are meant to be broken.'

Every single hair on Cat's body stands to frozen attention, her claws flick from their sheathes unbidden, her lips retract beyond her control, and she can see from the look on Milly's face that her exposed fangs are signalling their worst intent. *No, Clary. No!*

'Well, some rules are meant to be broken, and today's all about exploring and being curious about your inner artist and trusting her to guide you. You'll see you've got charcoal, paints, pencils, brushes, a small canvas and other paraphernalia in front of you, and you'll also see a notepad and pen. We're going to start with the notepad and pen, and a bit of fun.'

Cat settles back into information-gathering mode. What can she learn about Clary's attitude to rules, and is she just playing everyone along, a plan in mind, an outcome, secret rules?

'What's Amantha's social media handle?' Clary says. 'Play with me here. You've got five minutes to watch Amantha, imagine how she's feeling, what she's thinking, how she sees herself, her personality, what name she would pick. There are some rules ...'

Thank goodness.

'You can't have @marmalade_cat, or @ginger, or @honey, or @puss, or @kitty, or @cat.'

Huh, if only she knew, Cat swats at a playfully hovering cream butterfly. *Naturally, I would choose Cat, that being my name.*

'You're looking for something that personifies her, something you think she would want to project about herself. Maybe try to get inside her head and heart, close your eyes and feel what it would be like to be her. What name would you choose if you were her?'

I'd choose @Cat_guardian. No, too plain. Maybe @Cat_on_a_mission. No ... @Ninth_life_Cat ... @Viral_video_Cat ... @Psychic_Cat ... I quite like that one. The butterfly lands on her nose, now graced with splendiferous pink wings. *I've got it: @Spirit_mentor. That's the one.*

'Time's up,' Clary calls. 'What have you all got?'

Anna starts: 'I have @Paws_a_moment.'

'And @Forever_feline,' says Pixie.

Milly wrestles with her pen, laughing, and says, 'And I've got @Follow_my_nose.'

'I chose @Animal_instinct,' adds Hazel.

'Seventeen names for you to choose from, Amantha, if ever you wish to be online,' says Clary, as she writes the last student's offering on the whiteboard. 'You've all created something evocative, using a scrubby old pen and piece of notepaper, and your fabulous imagination. Now, look through the pencils and papers in front of you and choose beautiful tools more worthy of your imaginative art. That's it, keep it simple, reach out for what attracts you.'

'This charcoal pencil and this bright-yellow sunshine paper,' Pixie says.

'Same yellow as your cardi.' Milly sorts through the choices. 'Super-sharp lead pencil and this cream vellum for me.'

'Archival? Investigative, Milly?' Pixie says.

'Enough with the analysis, guys.' Clary takes control. 'Don't do anything until I get to the end of my instruction: write down the social media handle you've chosen BUT don't use words. Draw it in pictures, or squiggles, anything but words. Don't be too logical about it. The key word today is *play*. Okay, do it now.'

Cat bounds from her tree nest onto the tabletop and slowly walks the perimeter, an intense scrutiny of each drawing disguised as a casual, noncommittal gaze. They all seem to be following the instruction Clary gave them.

'You've just produced your first portrait of Amantha,' Clary announces. 'Not what she looks like on the outside, but your feeling for what she looks like on the inside. Essence of Amantha, you might say. Would you like to take it a step further?'

Nods all round, accompanied by a shuffle of sharing as the portraits are passed around the table.

'All so different,' says Hazel, 'a far cry from the paint-and-sip approach.'

'We're going to do the paint-and-sip approach next week, but coffee not wine, we want to keep it meditative. This way, you'll learn the basic rules of how to paint cats, and you'll each have a conventional portrait of Amantha to hang on your wall at home. Then on the third week, the last session for this course, you're going to use the technical skills you learn next week to paint your own unique vision of her, guided by the playful work you're doing today. You'll capture her as a cat in her essence. As you see her. That's just to give you an idea where we're headed.'

'Throw away the rules, learn the rules, combine the best of both worlds?' asks Milly.

Cat belly-slithers her way along the table to the best jumping-off point and launches herself at her velvet cushion. Throw away the rules, learn the rules, combine them? Best of both worlds, or brand-new rules? Her head spins. She paws a hanging fishy biscuit into her mouth and curls her body into a comforting ball. *If I am to escape being forever_feline and graduate to become a spirit_mentor, I need to follow_my_nose, my animal_instinct, and paws_a_moment to puzzle out this rule conundrum. Signed @Spirit_Mentor_Cat.*

'Choose your tools, paints, canvas, charcoal, paper, use your first portrait as a muse and boldly go ahead. No more rules. Only the rule to abandon any concern about the right way to do things ...'

Clary's voice trails off as Cat's eyes close. Not to shut out the terrifying thought of not doing the right thing, but because a cat's overloaded mind needs to sleep.

🐾

And sleep, and sleep, until the murmur of voices in the room nudges at her ears and uncurls her body into a stiff-limbed stretch, a throaty yowl of a purr. She blinks her eyes. *Where was I? That's right. Painting class.*

'I've just realised the irony,' Anna says. 'People always tell me I talk too much, rush to fill in the gaps in a conversation, and when I'm honest with myself, I can see that's sometimes true. Yet, I've painted Amantha's essence as @paws_a_moment. It's what came to me when I looked at her. Is she telling me to pause a moment before opening my mouth?'

'They say she's a divine messenger,' Pixie adds. 'Look at her now, yawn after jaw-breaking yawn. Is she mocking us, that exaggerated opening of her mouth?'

'I thought I was being droll yet obvious,' says Milly, 'choosing @follow_my_nose as her name, because that's what I did as an investigative journalist and I still do it, don't I? But perhaps Amantha spoke to me, reinforcing the spirit messages Freya gave me about digging something up. Following my nose, basically. And following MY nose, as a freelancer, not following the leads an editor assigns me.'

Leads. Are leads rules? Is Milly breaking rules when she decides she doesn't want a job following leads, wants to follow her own ... Hang on, that's what I do. And that's what Pearl advised me to do. Follow my nose. It's what cats do. Is it a rule for cats? This is getting so complicated.

'Fess-up time, then,' Pixie says. 'I got the @forever_feline feeling watching Amantha, and it felt powerful and freeing and fun, and I don't know, a kind of permission to express sensuality. So I ran with it, but when I started the painting version, I felt a deep sense of permission to age with grace and agility, to be forever myself, no matter how many wrinkles I gather, or whatever my body looks like to others. Forever_feline feels like a powerful mantra I can take with me as I enter my sixties in a few weeks' time. Did Amantha consciously awaken that in me? Did I see something of myself in her – an innocent cat – a sense of promise that I had overlooked? Or did she give me a divine message?'

Cat seizes the moment. Time to demonstrate her skills. She jumps across the divide and lands squarely eye to eye with an astonished Hazel. One meow, two meows, three meows – transmit: *Rose, rosemary, crushed woodlice.*

'Rose, rosemary, crushed woodlice,' says Hazel in a soft, entranced voice.

Cat still has Hazel's attention. One meow, two meows, three meows – transmit: *Medicine.*

'Medicine,' Hazel murmurs.

'Crushed woodlice, did you say?' asks Milly. 'Medicine?'

'The words spoke themselves. I felt they came from Amantha, but I must have got it slightly wrong.'

'I'm going with this,' Pixie says, prodding at her phone. 'Okay, this is interesting. Crushed woodlice was a medieval medicine for fertility. What about rose and rosemary, let's see.'

'I'm not saying anything, but I really want to,' Anna says. 'Pause a moment, Anna.'

'Got it,' Pixie says, eyebrows dancing, eyes wide alert. 'Rose and rosemary were apothecary remedies for fertility.'

Cat inches closer to Hazel, nestling gingerly against her chest. The room holds a communal breath. Hazel quietly weeps.

'Five years trying,' a high-pitched squeak, a sob. 'No luck with IVF, either.'

Anna manages to say nothing in words, everything with her eyes.

Cat returns to her nest, satisfied that Hazel knows what to do, and elated that her wisdom has been witnessed. *What do you think of that, then, Freya?* Except Freya isn't here, but she'll hear all about it soon enough.

Cups of tea, huddled conversations, the sun crosses the afternoon sky, Clary draws the class to a close and Cat emerges from her reverie at the mention of Freya's name.

'From one end of the fertility spectrum to the other,' Hazel says, 'that was a fabulous piece you wrote for the BBC news website about Freya and her hot flushes.'

'Thank you, Hazel. I wasn't sure how much to say about the

cheating, but judging by the hundreds of comments people posted, women were generally understanding and empathetic, sharing their experiences of struggling through brain fog at work, trying to hide their sweats and covering for their blackouts.'

'Also, quite a few who've had readings in the past endorsing her accuracy,' adds Anna.

'No trolling, no negatives?' asks Pixie.

'Oh, yes,' Milly says, 'a dozen or so people asking why she markets a cat as her psychic assistant. If she's that good, why does she need to lean on an everyday, innocent, clueless cat, that sort of thing. Or she's obviously no good or she wouldn't have to make up stories about a domestic ginger being a magical cat.'

Cat shrieks and streaks from the room. Everyday, innocent, clueless, domestic, and worst of all, ginger? Two paws forward, ninety-two backwards.

Pearl glints in the moonlight, over by the row of topiary Reclining Women with Children.

'You'll be locked out,' Pearl says as Cat approaches, short of breath. 'Sun down, moon up, all good cats should be inside the building, contemplating their day's work.'

'I needed to find you, couldn't wait until morning,' Cat puffs.

They walk together, threading their way between the topiaries, as Cat tells her story and Pearl's attentive ear lightens her burdens.

'How did you know about the crushed woodlice?'

'I didn't. The words came to me.'

'Where did they come from?'

'Deep down inside,' Cat says, slowing her pace.

'Not a spirit message, then?'

'Not something I heard or sensed. Something I knew.'

'I wonder how much more you know.'

Cat looks around. The rows of topiary women have faded, all but the constant one. 'I don't know why these other women come and go, why I only see them sometimes.'

'That's interesting,' says Pearl, stock still against the full moon, shimmery, ethereal, mesmerising. 'What does @animal_instinct say?'

'My vision comes and goes.'

'That's so much wiser than you may think.'

The moon suspends time. An hour, a moment, a stirring of Cat's heart.

'Sometimes I see and know things, like knowing Hazel was struggling to conceive, like knowing crushed woodlice, rose and rosemary is the medicine she needs, then the knowing fades, like memories drifting in on the flow of the tide, retreating back into the ocean on the ebb.'

'It can happen in the ninth life.' Pearl of wisdom, Pearl of few words.

'Memories from my eight previous lives?'

'Run, Cat! Emmy's calling you. Lucky for you it looks like they've had a late night. Get back inside, into the building, into the depths of your magnificent being. Keep a lookout for the Silver Crescent Nest I told you about, and follow your nose, @ninth_life.'

🐾

Freya looks different today. Still essence of tangerine mist, but her long, wild, brassy locks have been chopped into a neat, chin-skimping, silvery style, a demure amethyst choker in place of her usual tumble of oversized baubles.

'Amantha, darling, what do you think? More professional?'

Less bowerbird. Less witch. Less abandon. Cat sniffs the air. More confidence: Freya has a plan. This will be interesting.

Tanya takes the green velour chair, smoothing down her

dress, a striking melody of watermelon slices and mint leaves against a caramel background, her fingernails a perfect melon match. She extracts a notepad and pen from her caramel clutch. 'Can I take notes?'

'If you wish, but better still, I can record the session for you for an extra ten pounds.'

'Or maybe I can record it on my phone?'

A touch of fluster brushes Freya's cool, but she remains calm. 'You're most welcome, Tanya. Now, what brings you here today?'

What? Cat sits up tall and semaphores a couple of loud meows in Freya's direction. *What about me? Where's the spiel about Amantha, your psychic assistant? Hello?*

'I read the article about your hot flushes,' Tanya says, chestnut fringe sweeping the frames of her fifties-style cat-eye glasses, 'and I could relate. Not for me, as you can see, I'm a long way off that time in my life, but my mother has been experiencing some difficulties staying focused at work and is thinking of resigning, and, well, I admired the way Milly put the case forward for women in your situation.'

'Are you here for a reading, or are you a journalist, Tanya?' Freya asks.

'Oh, no, sorry. I'm nervous, and when I'm nervous I talk too much. I'm here for a reading. What I was really trying to say was that I was impressed with the comments people left on the article, their affirmations for how accurate you are. It enticed me. Here I am. And I'm trying not to give you any clues about me and I've already blabbermouthed far too much.'

'That's okay.' Freya relaxes back into her chair. 'It's been a difficult time for me, and my heart goes out to your mother. I'm learning to live with it for however long it takes, letting it challenge me to grow. But this hour isn't about me, it's about you, so let's continue.'

'Oh, just one more thing before we start.' Tanya points at Cat. 'Is that Amantha?'

Thank you for the reminder. Cat does her best to look cool.

'Yes, she's a comforting presence. I like having her here, little darling.'

So, that's all I am now? We'll see about that.

'Tanya, we'll start by seeing if any spirits have come to offer you messages. They come and go, so there might be messages for you at any time during the session. Sometimes they offer precise information, and other times they bring you love but not the answers to the questions you seek. So, we'll also consult the tarot, and we'll conclude the reading with some time for you to ask me direct questions, for me to help guide and counsel you. As you may have seen in Milly's article, I am a qualified counsellor, and studied psychology as part of my social work degree.'

Cat slinks her way from the windowsill, pads across the floor and prances up onto the coffee table to view the tarot cards, stacked in a single pile, a pristine, untouched odour. The card on top features a cat stepping out, a dark path behind, a golden-bathed light path ahead. *Cats! She's going to consult cards about fictional cats instead of a genuine psychic cat, a wise cat in her ninth life, a cat capable of diagnosing fertility problems and prescribing a medicinal cure.* She lowers her belly onto the table, as close to the cards as she can wager. Close enough that a miniscule flick of her tail, seemingly unintentional, might scatter them across the table and onto the floor, if need be. She eyes Freya. Freya eyes her back. They both turn to look at the door. A spirit has arrived for Tanya.

'I have a spirit here for you, Tanya. He's presenting as a man in his forties, but just so you know, they can alter their appearance, and many of them are fond of presenting a younger version of themselves. He's showing me a rock ... no, he's lifting it to his eye, looking closely, mimicking looking at it through a magnifying lens. He's drawing a picture in the air. It looks like a spiral.'

Tanya stiffens. 'Can you ask for some more information, please?'

'He's shrugging his shoulders, rolling his eyes, like he's

making fun of you, like he's saying, *How much more proof does she want? Typical Tanya.* Let's give him a moment. Okay, he's showing me a pile of books, acting like he's reading them. I'm getting the sense he's telling you to get a move on and write a book, or more than one book, but I don't understand how the rock part works into that, do you?'

'His name is Conrad. At least, that's the name he gave me. Just Conrad. Don't know if it's his first or last name. I met him on a rocky beach in South Wales five years ago. We only spoke for a couple of minutes, but I've always remembered him. Percy, my terrier, ran over to sniff out his dog, a poodle cross, I think. Anyway, we had a little chat, as people do when their dogs are interested in each other, and he showed me a fossil he had just found. It was a nautilus, a spiral shape. He gave me a magnifying glass to look closer. And said the strangest thing, "I'm Conrad. Remember my name. Life is a mystical spiral. What seems like it's going round and round and going nowhere is actually progressing, offering you a step up to the next level, wider possibilities, more potential each time you cycle round. The trick is to look for the opening when things seem to be closing in on you. Look for the step up, the higher view, and know that small increments are okay, they all add up, in the end, to massive change."'

'That's a beautiful metaphor. I love that,' Freya says. 'It's true, too.'

'I was entranced, looking at the nautilus fossil the entire time he spoke. It was as if the fossil was speaking to me from ancient times, and I thought about all the small, incremental changes the world has been through between then and now. Overall massive change, for good or for bad, I don't know. When I looked up, Conrad and his dog were a long way down the beach. I slipped the fossil into my pocket. I keep it on my desk.'

Freya subtly reaches for her fan and gently waves it in front of her flushing face as the brain fog fills the air around her. Tanya, spellbound, doesn't notice, and continues to stare into space.

'I remember Conrad as being quite young, and I was surprised at his wisdom for his age. Handsome, too. If he's here in spirit, does that mean he's dead?'

'He's no longer in an earthly body, Tanya. I don't see the spirits of living people. Is he dead? That's another question. What do we mean by dead? He's very much alive to you in this moment, isn't he?'

Tanya cries, taking a tissue from the proffered pink box.

'There is one other possibility.' Freya leans forward. 'You were entranced by your meeting, and the message Conrad gave you on the beach was a metaphysical offering from a stranger, one who stayed only long enough to deliver. Might he have been a spirit? An angel? A comrade of sorts?'

A spirit mentor.

'That's pretty far out there,' Tanya whispers. 'It was certainly mystical at the time, and now, looking back on it.'

Silence hangs in the air, suspends conversation, extends contemplation.

Cat licks the pad of her right paw, massaging the spot where the end of her ninth life will be scored. *Might that be the nature of my future work? Manifesting as a stranger on a beach, delivering a message and fading away to my next mission?*

Freya's face comes back into focus as she replaces her fan on the table.

'I'm going to blabbermouth again, I know it,' Tanya says, 'but it's now or never and I need your guidance. First though, out of interest, your reading is accurate, but you could have got all that information from my mind, my memories, my dilemmas. That's amazing enough, but might you be imagining a spirit, seeing the shape of my thoughts and memories as a spirit?'

'All I can tell you is my perspective, Tanya. In my experience, today I saw a spirit. Spirits don't like to be tested. They don't respond well when you ask them for information that no-one else knows, like where gold is buried, or next week's lottery numbers.

They don't see their purpose as providing proof of their existence, unless it is to show love to family members, a subtle message of continuation of life, a gift of hope. They're not fortune tellers. They'll go as far as prodding someone to do something, to fulfil a mission, right a wrong, find forgiveness, that kind of thing. How do you relate to the book thing? It's odd. He's the second spirit recently that's talked about book writing.'

'I have an urge to write a book. I see myself writing a book. It's a vision I've had since I was a child, but I haven't known what to write about. Listening to Conrad, through you, I'm seeing a book – yes, perhaps a trilogy – about the spiral of life, a fictional ... no, I won't say any more. I have a definite sense that I know what to do now. Thank you, Freya.'

'We've still got some time.' Freya nudges Cat away from the tarot. 'Let's ask the cards for some extra advice. Shuffle these and think of a question, maybe about the book, or about something else. Don't tell me, just ask it quietly in your mind.'

Cat watches Tanya's face as she shuffles. A distinct knowing pulls at her belly, a sense of magnetism pulsing her third eye. She walks to the edge of the table, sniffs the cards in Tanya's hands and catches her gaze. One meow, two meows, three meows – transmit: *You are pregnant.*

Tanya drops a couple of cards, bends down to pick them up and places a hand on her belly.

'Are you okay?' Freya asks. 'Hand them back when you feel ready.'

Job done, Cat sits on her haunches at the end of the table and watches Freya turn over the top cards, examining them one by one, laying them face up in a fan shape. So many cats! A cat sunning itself, a cat jumping from a cliff, a cat hanging upside down from a tree, a cat amongst the pigeons, a particularly interesting card showing nine cats arranged in a circle.

'Keep your question in mind as I read the cards, Tanya. You've been taking some time out – see, the cat sunning herself?

NINTH LIFE

You're ready to take a leap of faith – that's obvious, the cat jumping from the cliff, but you're worried about how it will turn out. Will it leave you hanging – that's the cat hanging upside down from the tree – will it turn your life upside down? Will it provoke conflict, set the cat amongst the pigeons? Or will it end with a sense of completion, life coming full circle – that's the nine cats. From what you shared earlier, you might be wondering about evolving along the spiral rather than ending up where you began. It depends on what "full circle" means to you. Mythology tells us that cats come full circle when they have lived nine lives. They come back again for another round. Putting all that together, without knowing your question, I'd say have faith in taking a risk. You may feel like you're putting your life on the line, it may bring up conflict, but it will bring a sense of completion for you.'

Despite her confident voice, Freya looks unsure. She's trying, but this is all new to her.

'Do the cards mention a pregnancy?' Tanya's voice is a throaty wobble.

Freya bends her head to the cards, once more. Her anxiety spikes Cat's nostrils.

'I can't see it. Unless you'll have nine children!'

'You could say, looking at the cards,' Tanya offers, 'life is all sunshine and roses, I find out I'm pregnant, I wonder whether to jump off a cliff and end my life … No, I'm being facetious. I decide to take a risk and birth the child, even though I have no partner. My life, my career, goes into suspension, everything is turned upside down, conflict ensues, and I resolve the career side of things by opening a nursery and looking after eight other children in addition to mine. Sorry, Freya, I'm not sure I buy the tarot side of things. Your spirit reading was so accurate, and our discussion about metaphysical possibilities so engaging and helpful that the tarot reading seems trite in comparison. Sorry, blabbermouth, like I said.' She hangs her head, blushing.

'Let's move to the counselling part of your reading, see how

I can help you there. How do you feel about pregnancy? Do you want children?'

'I don't want children. Didn't want children. But I got a strong sense that I was pregnant when I was shuffling the cards. For a moment, I thought Amantha told me. She was looking at me over the cards, remember? I was still entrenched in spirit talk, and getting a message from a cat seemed, I don't know, normal, I suppose, until I looked at her, and well, she's just a gorgeous cat, isn't she? What would she know, truly? Perhaps it was the spiral image that implanted the idea, a sense of enlarging roundness, like a round belly, a foetus growing. On the other hand, writing a book would be like gestating a baby, starting with a nub of an idea at the centre that grows in spirals until it reaches a conclusion.'

Freya replaces her fan on the table, shaking her head. 'I think I follow what you're saying, Tanya. I do have to admit to a slight flush and brain fog there, but I'm still with you. Thank you for understanding. I do want to help you.'

'I went too deep, I think.' Tanya laughs. 'I'm sorry. To answer your question, I didn't want children, but today, it's as if the earth has moved and I'm ready to entertain both pregnancy and book writing. This has been a fabulous session, thank you.'

Freya shuffles the cards and replaces them in a pile, while Tanya gathers her things and prepares to leave.

'Bye, gorgeous kitty.' Tanya lifts Cat's chin to look her in the eyes. 'They say it's a dog's life, but I reckon a cat's life is the best. Come and go as you please, be fed and watered, no issues, worries or deep thinking required.'

Oops, did I twitch my tail a little too forcefully there? The tarot deck tumbles to the floor. *I'll just tiptoe through the spilt coffee here, and that's it, trample through the cards, nice soggy black paw-prints, back and forth, and oh dear, Freya has just noticed.*

Freya closes the door. 'Amantha, darling. Just as well they're plastic, washable. That went well, didn't it? Did some good channelling, managed my flushes and fogs, used the tarot to open conversation – although, I could do with a little more practice there. Finishing with a mini-counselling session grounded the whole session, I thought. Looks like I can keep doing my work without resorting to ... well, enough said.'

Cat catches Freya's gaze, at last. One meow, two meows, three meows – transmit: *Amantha told Tanya she is pregnant.*

'Telling Tanya she's pregnant. As if!' Freya cuddles Cat to her chest. 'Imagine that! I'd be out of business. Or I could hire you out as an added attraction. On which point, I must tell Serenity that I'm raising my fees now that I'm adding in the tarot and counselling.'

🐾

The smoky, nutty coffee aroma pervading the pow-wow room twinges Cat's conscience, the taste of last week's sweet revenge, her coffee paw-prints stamped across the tarot cards, bitter on her tongue. Her little tizzy didn't get her anywhere. She communicated zilch. There must be a better way. If only she could take human form, like Conrad, speak out loud in plain English, then disappear back into the ether, job done. Was Conrad a spirit-mentor cat? Or mouse! Or just a regular human being?

Cat stirs from her musing – *Or is that mewsing*, she thinks, congratulating herself on her growing language skills, teetering on the edge of zoning out to the conversation in the room again. Serenity's voice brings her back to the room. 'Coffee's done. Let's move to the purpose of today's meeting, the power part of the Power Hour.'

Cat tilts her head. *It's Power Hour, not pow-wow. How could I have got that so wrong?*

'First,' Serenity reaches up to loosen her bun and shake her raven braids free, 'big congratulations and profound gratitude to Abby for another stunning Amantha video. It's already topping the first one, currently at two-point-eight million views and only in its fifth day on the socials. The "rule three: support each other" theme for this one has clearly hit a nerve.'

When did all this happen? Cat eyes Abby. *Should I be careful about the way I move around, what I do, in case I'm being filmed? Just as well Abby didn't capture my tarot tizzy.* She pauses and drops her head, realisation heavily dawning. *The fictitious Amantha may be the goody-goody poster child for rule three: support each other, but I, Cat, in my fury, did little to support Freya's efforts to redeem herself. I, Bitch Cat, Snitch Cat. Witch Cat. Witch Cat? Cat wallowing in a ditch cat.*

'On that note,' Serenity continues, 'I'd like to dedicate this Power Hour to exploring how we can all best support Freya in what has been, I think we'd all agree, a tumultuous time.'

In a magnanimous gesture that takes her by surprise, Cat pads over and jumps onto Freya's lap, nudging her way beneath Freya's hands, unsure whether she is supporting Freya or asking Freya to caress and support her. Or asking for forgiveness.

'Small things,' Freya begins, 'can make a big difference. This lovely creature here brightens my days. She sits on the windowsill and whenever she purrs it grounds me. More than that, it's hard to explain, but it's like her purrs strum my heartstrings, like I'm a harp being played, in the nicest possible way. When I hear myself say that I realise she lifts my vibration, brings me harmony, lifts me heavenwards. I wonder even if she tunes me up, assists me to finely adjust my ability to communicate with spirits. It's like, we all know she's just an innocent cat – a poor stray cat that appeared on our doorstep, literally – but I sometimes wonder if she isn't a little more divine, like we say in our marketing.'

Freya looks around, three light-filled faces listening intently.

'She appeared when I needed her most. Mere weeks before the hot flushes and brain fogs began. When it happens, I try to focus on her energy, as if she's telling me to let it be, you know, the old "this too shall pass". It helps. She was there for me when things started to go pear-shaped, as if she understood, supported me in looking for ways to help my clients, even if those ways were misguided. I'm so sorry for the shame I brought on this place.'

'We're here for you, Freya.' Serenity gestures a palm to her heart. 'And you didn't bring shame. Milly's empathetic article put us in a good light, portrayed us as open, honest in admitting difficulties, contributing to the national conversation about the challenges perimenopausal women face in the workplace, and how we can evolve as a society to be more supportive. Yes, the article did attract some hurtful trolling comments about how we market Amantha, but we can explore that, maybe next week. Meanwhile, thankfully, Amantha is blissfully ignorant of all of that.'

'Thank you. I don't know what I'd do without you all supporting me. Amantha may be blissfully ignorant, but talking to her helps me. I chat to her before and after clients. It's like having a sounding board, hearing myself say things out loud that I wouldn't dare express to a person. Sometimes I imagine she answers back, gives me advice, but I'm guessing that's me projecting my inner thoughts and inner wisdom onto her, isn't it? Abby, you're a psychotherapist, you would know.'

'As far as Amantha's concerned, I do the same, chat away with her. She's like an old friend who loves me unconditionally.' Abby chuckles. 'From a psychology point of view, the way we all see things – living or non-living – reflects our personal perspectives, especially our unconscious views and judgements. I might imbue Amantha with the gifts and talents I keep hidden in my shadows. Assign her the wisdom I'm afraid to call my own. Another person might project their dark side onto things or people or their pets. They might say, "That cat, Amantha, she's full of self-righteous judgement" when they hide that aspect of themselves, working hard to be one hundred percent pure and non-judgemental.'

Cat wriggles. Something of what Abby says feels uncomfortably true. Does it work the other way? How cats see people?

'But you know what?' Abby says. 'We can also pick up on

what people think, can't we? We read their body language, hear inflections of their voice, read between the lines of the words they use. Not direct mind-reading, not telepathy, but reading a person's mind by reading how it manifests. Do you think we can do the same for animals, specifically Amantha?'

'That far, yes,' says Serenity, 'but as for telepathy, reading minds, not so sure about that. No offence, Freya, as far as I know you communicate with spirits, but you don't read people's minds, do you?'

Emmy emerges from quiet contemplation. 'That's so funny, Serenity, that you have a belief in spirits but not in telepathy.'

'Do you believe in telepathy, Emmy?'

'In my work as a hypnotherapist,' Emmy folds her hands in her lap, 'I help people to rewire their brains, change bad habits into good habits, introduce circuit-breakers for their anxiety or phobias, give them the confidence they need to pursue their goals. Sometimes I think of myself as a mind engineer, building, rebuilding and tinkering with the mind following precise rules and techniques I learned during my academic study. I'm curious about telepathy, but I'm more of a nuts-and-bolts kind of person. Sounds very dry, I know.'

Cat pokes her head out from under Freya's arm. *The importance of following rules. Well done, Emmy.*

'Do you believe in spirits, Emmy?' Freya touches the amethyst at her neck, momentarily exposing Cat's nestled form.

'I might be a lot better off financially if I did. People keep asking me to do past-life regressions, thinking I'm that kind of hypnotherapist. Have you seen how much Lou-Lou, the past-life hypnotherapist working out of her home along the coast, charges for her sessions?'

'I'm not sure that past-life therapy has anything to do with the existence of spirits, unless you're thinking about where we go between incarnations,' says Serenity. 'But we should probably save this conversation for another day and focus on giving our support to Freya.'

Cat eyerolls the three spirit cats hovering at Emmy's feet, and the human spirit dressed in sackcloth with medicinal herbs tied around her waist standing patiently at Emmy's side. One of the cat spirits sends her a telepathic greeting, 'Getting the hang of the eyerolls, Cat.'

A loud ping jangles Cat's left ear, wrenching her neck as she jumps to the floor for safety. The spirit cats and the medicine woman fade from sight.

'Sorry, forgot to turn off my phone.' Freya examines her screen. A soft gasp, her hand flies to her mouth. 'I, um ...' A frown gathers on her forehead and travels to her voice. 'Tanya is pregnant.'

'Tanya?' says Serenity. 'Who's Tanya?'

'A client I had last week,' Freya exhales, 'not sure how to take this.'

'Slowly,' says Abby, 'take a moment to breathe. We're all here for you.'

Cat sashays over to Abby, wraps herself around her soft shoulders and purrs in her ear.

'We had a powerful session. At one point she had a feeling she was pregnant, said she had one mad moment where she thought the message came from Amantha, but then she decided ... I can't remember what she decided. Look, this is confidential information. I shouldn't be discussing this with anyone.'

'No need to tell us about Tanya, Freya,' Serenity says, 'but it looks like you've just had a shock. How can we support you?'

'She asked me if the tarot cards mentioned a pregnancy, and they didn't. Not that I could see, I'm still attuning to the tarot, to be honest. Looks like I got it wrong.'

'That's okay, Freya,' says Abby. 'Like you said, you're still attuning to the tarot. Did you have any spirit backup?'

'We'd had a brilliant session with a spirit, but he disappeared with my first hot flush, and that's when I turned to the tarot. After that – look, I might as well bring you all in on it, now. I've developed a three-part approach to my readings, one part spirit communication, one part tarot reading, one part counselling. I studied psychology and counselling as part of my social work degree. So, if I have a hot flush, I can shift to the tarot or counselling. It's still challenging, working with brain fog for however long it takes, but I can fumble through, take my time. It's working for me, and for the clients who've experienced it so far.'

'So pleased for you, Freya,' Emmy says. 'Sounds like a good practical solution. If ever you want to try some hypnotherapy to help you cope with the hot flushes, I'm here for you. I've never treated anyone for hot flushes or brain fog before, but if we apply the tried-and-trusted formulae, I think we can make some headway.'

'That would be wonderful, Emmy. I'm ready to try anything. Sorry, that didn't come out in the way I intended. I'd love to do that, thank you.'

Cat meows loudly. *Focus, everyone, focus*, she purr-screams, but without eye contact her plea goes unheard.

'Anyway, back on track.' Freya shakes imminent brain fog from her inner eye. 'This is how brain fog goes, folks. Okay, focus. Yes, after the tarot reading, that's when Tanya said she thought Amantha told her about the pregnancy when she gazed into her eyes, but then she dismissed it. I invited her to explore her feelings about pregnancy in the counselling part of the session, and it went well.'

'And?' Abby says. 'It sounds like you handled the session very well, but I'm getting the feeling something's still not sitting comfortably with you.'

'It's the rest of the text message,' Freya wobbles. 'Tanya says, "Maybe I was right in the first place, maybe Amantha did deliver the message. Maybe she is psychic, after all. I can't explain it more than that. I'm blown away."'

Cat slides imperceptibly along Abby's right shoulder until their gazes meet. One meow, two meows, three meows – transmit: *Tell them about the crushed woodlice.*

'There's a story I can't tell in detail,' Abby begins, 'because I can't betray any confidences. But what I can tell you is that I personally witnessed a woman receive an astounding message about fertility medicine in an instant.' She tells them what happened without revealing the woman's identity. 'I don't imagine she's going to crush any woodlice, let alone eat them, but we were all gobsmacked. I've been thinking about it a lot, and the only thing that makes sense is that Amantha was somehow involved. Is she psychic? Did she give her the message? Why would she give her an ancient – probably ineffective – remedy? Or did the woman's close encounter with our gorgeous cat somehow awaken a feline, intuitive, psychic knowing within her? Obviously, she already knew she was struggling with fertility issues, but did she access the woodlice treatment from one of her past-life memories, or from her unconscious mind? Had she read about it years ago and forgotten about it? Or did she somehow pluck the fact from the collective unconscious?'

No need to read minds, Cat thinks. The silent tick-tock of cogitation, four pairs of eyes tracking from left to right and back again, perceptions shifting, *tick-tock*, what fits, what doesn't fit, *tick-tock, tock-tick*.

'They're both messages about fertility.' Emmy breaks the spell.

'And today's Power Hour was focused on supporting Freya through perimenopause,' adds Serenity.

Tick-tock, tock-tick.

Cat slides from Abby's shoulders and holds her head high as she trots from the room. *Fertility queen. Hadn't noticed the connection. Just don't ask me for tomorrow's lottery results.*

🐾

Eyes half-dozy closed, Cat purrs a lazy summer song, June sunshine warming her back, pearlescent butterflies dancing in her peripheral vision. Or flutterbys, as she prefers to call them. Though these ones aren't so much fluttering by as making her the focus of their attention. Trying to tell her something. She opens her eyes a little wider. Would a butterfly doze away her morning, one of only a handful of mornings a butterfly is gifted before she swaps her earthly wings for a more heavenly kind?

A 'handful' of mornings ... I've been around people far too long.

Butterflies, as every cat knows, rarely live more than four pawfuls of mornings, or clawfuls, to be precise. She counts her claws, five on her front left paw, five on the right, four on her back left, four on her ... *Oh, what's that?* A splodge of beetle dust between her toes. She shifts her body to better reach the beetle dust with her tongue, when a warm hand scoops below her belly, lifts her above the butterfly ballet and plops her into a soft weave basket.

'Keep us company, Amantha.' Clary's welcoming voice. 'Let's see if we can find some woodlice, crushed or otherwise.'

Us, it turns out, is Clary and Milly, all summer frocks and pealing laughter. The basket, it turns out, is lined with a soft butter-yellow cotton cloth with a couple of fish biscuits tucked into the corner begging to be eaten. It's a cat's life, indeed.

'Or rose and rosemary.' Milly laughs. 'I'm sure Briar's herb patch is more culinary than medicinal, and I'm well past needing a medieval fertility treatment, so any woodlice lurking in his garden can stay out of my sight, chomping away contentedly on their dank, rotting wood.'

'I did a quick google,' Clary gently swings the basket, 'and apparently, cooked woodlice – you have to boil them – are good, nutritious food if you're stuck out in the wilds.'

'Does Briar live that far out?'

The basket shakes with their laughter. Cat doesn't recall whether the crushed woodlice remedy is made from live or boiled lice. The mortar and pestle they used to do the crushing had a distinct earthy aroma and ... What mortar and pestle? Whose was it? When was it? The memory fades and then it's gone, a mousetail slipping down a mousehole, lost to her senses.

'Does he know I'm thinking of researching the history of the area?' Milly asks.

'I told him one of Freya's spirits suggested you did some digging. I didn't give any details. Just said the reading inspired you to follow your nose. He said he'd be happy to help.'

'Do you know much about him?'

'I've only met him a couple of times when I've been sketching in the garden. I think he knows Hazel more. She told him about the crushed woodlice thing, and he asked me, as "someone who knows Amantha well", given all my sketches of her, whether I thought she had given Hazel the message.'

'And you said?'

'I told him about my reading with Freya, how Amantha jumped onto my lap, and how I instantly got the feeling Freya had read my altar message. The more I think about it, the more I get to watch Amantha, the more I feel she might be a psychic messenger. Then, after Hazel's experience ... Anyway, that's what I told Briar and that's when he invited me over to see his herb garden.'

'You didn't think it was some kind of come-on?'

'No. Well, a little, yes, that's why I asked if I could bring you.'

'Oh, I see, to be your chaperone, huh?'

'No, I've got Amantha for that.' Clary lifts the basket to look Cat in the eyes, digging Milly in the ribs with her free elbow. 'And I'm happily single.'

🐾

Clary pushes open Briar's garden gate, a mouse squeak of rusty hinge heralding their arrival. Cat pokes her head above the edge of the basket, nose aloft, whiskers aquiver, lavender and mint on the air.

'Oh,' Clary gasps. 'It really is a secret garden.'

Essence of Briar approaches, quickly followed by Briar himself. 'Welcome to my world, come in, come in.'

Clary sets Cat's basket down on a chamomile lawn, beside a stone sundial. High stone walls stand sentry over a heavenly concoction of herbs and flowers, blue sky above, no sign of the topiary gardens or the Serene Lotus Centre for Health and Wellbeing from here. Cornflowers dance in blue and clary sage beguiles Cat's nostrils.

'It's my garden within a garden,' Briar says, 'although I don't know which came first, all of that out there beyond these walls or all of this in here. Folklore has it that the herbs and flowers in my garden have grown from the same stock for at least four hundred years. I've never had any die on me. Just followed the gardening rules my family has passed down through the generations, and the plants just keep on giving.'

Following the gardening rules, high five, Briar. The evidence is right before us. Rules are in place for a reason. No work for me to do here, except maybe bestow my approval, encourage Clary and Milly to learn from Briar's example. And from his family's example.

She catches Milly's gaze: one meow, two meows, three meows – transmit: *Write about the rules.*

'You're right about the rules,' Milly says. 'Your family gardening rules ... sorry, I don't know where I was going with that. But am I right in thinking this is a chamomile lawn, Briar?'

'Well spotted.' Briar stoops to brush his fingers through the softness of the flowering lawn. 'According to our family logbooks and our stories passed down through the generations, the garden started with this lawn. Chamomile is reputed to revive any plants in the vicinity, so it's like a base medicine for the entire plot.'

'Do you reap it?' Clary says. 'Is that even the right word? Do you clip it for teas?'

Briar turns on his heel. 'Would you like some? I'll put the kettle on.'

He saunters over to the corner of the garden, lights a match under a grill in the shelter of the stone wall and puts a cauldron – a cauldron! – of water on to boil.

'Full garden-picnic experience coming up,' he says, shaking a rug onto the lawn and opening a picnic hamper. 'I've got deli bread, cheeses, salads laced with my centuries-old herbs, and some nut cake if you've still got room. And some treats for Amantha.'

Clary and Milly beam, Briar exudes contentment, and Cat wonders if mouse is on her menu.

'I know chamomile is good for calming you down before sleep, relaxing you,' says Milly.

'Sedative. That's the official purpose as documented in our family logs. One day, I might show them to you for your research. They've always been a family secret. No-one else is supposed to know about them, let alone see them. I don't know why I blurted it out to you, Clary, when we first met, but ... let's talk about that another time.'

'If all the herbs in this garden go back, what did you say, nearly four hundred years, are they all medicinal herbs, planted for that purpose?' asks Milly.

'Many of them are listed as medicinal in the logbooks. See that one, over there? That's clary sage, it's an eyewash. Over there, plain sage for cleansing venom and pestilence. Thought about marketing that one during COVID. Joking aside, I do wonder if this very sage was used during the sixteen sixty-five to sixty-six plague, though I think bloodletting and purging were the focus. And quarantine.'

'Is that comfrey?' says Clary.

'Yes, sage Clary. Comfrey for healing wounds and infections.

See that over there? That's betony, a general cure-all, and that, behind it, is hyssop. It will flower next month. It's a purgative.'

'Any poisons, toxins?' Milly asks.

'I'm sure there are, if you administer too much. But no, nothing listed as such in our logs. Kettle's boiled. Let's eat.'

A bowl of cream and some nutbrown biscuits call Cat to Briar's side. She sinks into the chamomile softness and takes a botanical inventory of the garden's scents: clematis, larkspur, lavender, mint, phlox, roses, rosemary, campanula, scabious, hydrangea, sweet peas – ah she has always loved sweet peas – snapdragons, delphinium, nigella, sweet william, lady's mantle, yarrow, feverfew, cow parsley, corncockle, stinging nettle. Not all medicinal, but all good for the soul.

'Do your logbooks mention crushed woodlice?' Milly asks.

'Ah, your prescription for Hazel, eh?' Briar tickles Cat. 'See that woodpile near the apple tree? Endless source of woodlice.'

'You're avoiding the question, then.' Clary laughs, reaching out for a piece of blue cheese. 'Personally, I prefer mouldy cheese to decaying wood, or crushed woodlice, boiled, dead or alive. Though, would I go that far if I was desperate to conceive? Probably.'

'I have a dilemma with the woodlice.' Briar butters a slice of bread. 'I couldn't crush them alive, and I couldn't boil them alive, so either way, they wouldn't be for me. Also, I'm not trying to get pregnant.'

'Are you vegetarian?' Clary nibbles at her cheese.

'More of a do-no-harm approach, don't kill potential food inhumanely.'

Oh, Briar, Cat purrs, forgetting he is a person and can't understand cat language, *you don't need my guidance, oh Great Keeper of the Rules.*

'Still avoiding the question,' Milly says, very much in investigative-journalist mode.

'Suffice it to say for now, I'm supposed to make an offering of crushed woodlice to the Reclining Woman with Child topiary on every new moon.'

'But you haven't because you don't want to harm living beings?' Clary asks.

Cat pretends to focus her attention on cleaning her whiskers, which sadly only serves to remind her that she eats mice every day. The do-no-harm-to-whom conundrum. *Do no harm to mice, or do no harm to my health and longevity and ability to stay alive long enough to fulfil my mission? Do no harm to the structure of the centre, keep it free from mice damage? Do no harm to woodlice? Do they come under my guidance and protection, too?*

'I still make the offering every new moon, but I use garden compost and I choose my words carefully, talk about the blessings of the woodlice ... I think I'm saying too much. You must think I'm unhinged.'

'Would crushed woodlice have made good fertiliser back then?' Clary asks. 'Is the family tradition more about good horticultural practice with a nod to symbolism?'

'That's how I sell it to myself.' Briar reaches out for a slither of cheese. 'But I do feel a twinge of guilt every time I do it, like I'm letting down my ancestors or the Reclining Woman with Child.'

'Either way, the topiaries are healthy and thriving, as far as I can see.' Milly sips her tea.

'Cake all round?' Briar licks his fingers and picks up an antique-looking cake slice. 'I've got to get back to work soon. Lawnmowing, least favourite job. Noisy and smelly.'

'Have you lived here all your life, Briar?' Milly says. 'Not meaning to pry, it's just that I'm wondering if it's worth me researching and writing about this place. I'm getting the feeling there are secrets to uncover, but are they interesting gardening secrets, or is there something juicier to this village than meets the eye?'

'Apart from when I was away at university, this cottage has been my home, so that's some forty years now, and completely on my own since my father died three years ago. Give me some time, Milly. I need to reflect on a few things, but I think I'll be able to help you.'

'Thank you, Briar. You've got me thinking about what it really means to do no harm, too. It was the theme of Serenity's yoga class this morning, the centre's first rule, and number thirty-seven from the Rajpapa system. Seemed straightforward at the time, but it's not, is it? You don't want to do harm to the woodlice, and you don't want to do harm to the topiary, and you're in a quandary over changing a centuries-old ritual because – no, let's leave that for another day.'

'What do you think of Rajpapa Yoga?' Cake devoured, Briar walks them to the gate, eyeing Cat in the basket looped over his arm.

Me? thinks Cat. *Nice, tight system, tidy rules. Easy to follow. No work for me to do there. Serenity's got it all under control.*

'Not sure yet.' Clary takes the basket from Briar. 'I've enjoyed every single class, but I wonder if it will feel repetitive after a while. Too regulated, no room for individuality or creative freedom. Speaking as an ex-yoga teacher.'

'Like maintaining my beautiful herb garden.' Briar smiles. 'Sometimes I want to break free, change up the landscape a bit.'

'But for now, lawnmowing, hey?' Milly says.

For now, a little nap, Cat thinks, as her basket nest rocks on Clary's arm. *Clary questioning Rajpapa's rules? The very essence of the Serene Lotus Centre for Health and Wellbeing? Maybe a little work for me to do there later. But first, sleep.*

😺

A single chime, a final chant of *Om*, an echo of *namaste*s, a gathering of things, an airy blissfulness before the grounding caffeine, the women – and three men – emerge from the yoga floor all Rajpapaed up for the day. Cat watches them float down the staircase, chitter-chatter breaking the silence, laughter bubbling, a million miles away from the high tension of Abby's arms clutching Cat firmly to her chest, waiting for Serenity to complete her ritual, pick up her bag and walk towards them.

'Abby, are you okay? You're shaking. What's happened?'

Abby steers Serenity back to the yoga floor, sits her on a bolster, draws Cat closer, tries to speak, squeaks and hands Serenity her phone.

Serenity stares at the screen, mouth ajar. An eon passes. A passing housefly breaks the spell.

'When did this come out?'

'Breaking news half an hour ago, while you were still teaching. Café staff told me. They'll all know about it now.'

'The students?'

'Those you know, your online students, people who have nothing to do with yoga. It's gone national already, Serenity.'

Cat feels a stirring in Abby, a knowing. 'This isn't news to you, is it?'

'I thought we had it under control,' Serenity says. 'Came to an agreement for the highest good of all.'

'What are you saying?'

'Remember I told you all that he was stepping back from his public role?'

'You said he was getting tired. That he'd maybe make an appearance at the next annual convention in New York, and that Rajpapa Yoga would otherwise continue as usual.'

A patter of rain against the window. A strangled sob.

'Oh.' Abby reaches out for Serenity's hand. 'You got wind of the abuse and you asked him to step back.'

'It was one woman's word against his. She said he demanded sexual favours in return for giving her a teaching role at the ashram. He said they were lovers.'

'One woman?'

'I didn't know whom to believe, Abby. He was my saviour, my guru.'

Abby's phone pings and both women jump.

Abby scrolls. 'From Emmy, okay, there's more news breaking ...'

Cat's heart somersaults. Bones chill.

Abby's hand flies to her mouth. 'The woman, Penelope, says she was paid to keep quiet, but when another woman confided a similar situation, she decided to go public. There are now ... hang on, let me read some more ... *ten women claiming historical sexual abuse at the hands of Guru Rajpapa.*'

'Ten!' Serenity slides from the bolster and melts into a foetal position, eyes tightly shut, seemingly blind to Emmy's sudden presence beside them.

'Give us an hour, please, Emmy,' Abby whispers, releasing her tight hold on Cat. 'Can you block the stairwell, stand sentry, maybe even close the café, lock the entrance door? The media will want a piece of this.'

Cat slides over to Serenity, nuzzles her cheek, awaits her invitation to snuggle into her chest, then coils within her foetal embrace, purring a calming rhythm she didn't realise she knew. Rule two: help and heal, a rule but also an instinct. Rule three: support each other, a rule but a natural given. Serenity's heart begins to synchronise with Cat's, a resonant breath of approaching calm. Cat opens her eyes and meets the forget-me-not blue of Abby's.

'Serenity.' Abby crouches beside her, holding her hand again. 'We have one hour to prepare you for the onslaught. I don't think the media will be kind. I'm asking you to trust me as a psychotherapist, and more importantly, as someone accustomed to helping people present their best face to the media. And even more than that, as your friend. Squeeze my hand if you're ready.'

Serenity sits up, cradling Cat like a baby.

'The media were all over you at the London convention. You were the golden girl, the one who made good after her father's imprisonment for fraud and embezzlement. They're going to have their sniffer dogs out for any information on the hush money, specifically if it was you who paid Penelope. Can you see the angle they'll be going for?'

'It didn't feel like hush money. She asked for funds to buy a house and pay for the care of her elderly mother, who has dementia. She had given the ashram eleven years of voluntary service and done some admin work for Rajpapa Yoga in the early years of setting up the business. I believed Rajpapa's story. I felt she was slightly unhinged and desperate to provide for her mother. It seemed a small step to take to help a loyal follower and stop a rumour in its tracks.'

'But you asked Guru Rajpapa to step back, so you must have had an inkling that something wasn't right.'

'I need to tell you everything, don't I? The only way out is through.'

'You'll work through this within yourself in time, Serenity, but what we need to do now is come up with a plan, and to do that, yes, the truth helps.'

'After we made the payment – it went down as a business expense, a property investment – it began to niggle me. I remembered some things Guru Rajpapa had said to me in the early days, mild sexual innuendoes that I dismissed at the time but took on a different context looking back. I spun him a story, told him I could see he was getting tired, so I wanted to buy him out. I asked him to step back while we worked out the details.'

'He may have stepped back, but you're still in business as Rajpapa Yoga. You're the one carrying his name.'

'Surely, our students will respect the classes, the formula, the universal teachings ...'

'Number one, Serenity, you need to call your lawyer before leaving this room, get her advice on the payment you made to Penelope, where you stand legally, and how to best progress. Number two, you need to call your accountant. I imagine there'll be a backlash. People will be hesitant to do Rajpapa Yoga. You may need to shore up your finances, make plans. Get her started on that. Number three, you have to make a pitch for Rajpapa Yoga as a lifestyle option, something you've developed – give yourself the kudos – and stress that it's not a cult. And I think we need to write a statement encouraging women to speak out about sexual assault. I'll start drafting that while you call your lawyer and accountant. We'll dump the statement if your lawyer comes up with different advice.'

Cat yawns, every muscle crying for release. So much for leaving your troubles at home. If only Serenity could. But the cat is out of the bag now, as they say in the human realm. And this cat is out of here. *I have calls of my own to make to prepare for guiding them all through this. Beginning with Pearl.*

🐾

White vans parked higgledy-piggledy along the driveway, jacketed journalists jostling for the best position – the stately entrance doors, the majestic signage, the abandoned café patio – last-minute hair adjustments, lapel mics winking, cameras ready to roll, and rolling. Pieces to camera, raised eyebrows, nodding heads. A crush of yoga students caught leaving by the back door, the same exit Cat chooses.

Click, flash, click, click, flash.

'Is that the so-called psychic cat?'

'The witch's cat. Samantha, isn't it?'

Click, flash, click, click, flash.

'Amantha, might as well be Samantha, for all I've heard.'

'Here, kitty, kitty, puss-puss!' *Flash, click.*

'Poor innocent moggie, marketed to death. Just as well she doesn't know anything about it.'

'Yes, it's her. That honey marmalade, that way of walking, one inadvertent viral video star.'

Click, click, flash.

'The old cat-video trick to divert our attention from what's really been going on here: cheating psychics, pervert yoga guru. Is it a cult? Can we say it's a cult? An international cult?'

Cat sinks her teeth into a paparazzi ankle or two. *Nip, nip, flash.* Out of sight before they can recover their vigil.

'Leave your troubles at home, kitty kat. Haven't they taught you to walk your talk?' The final words reverberate as she top-speeds away.

🐾

Cat bowls Pearl over, knocks them both flying into the prickly base of Reclining Woman with Child.

'Cat out of hell, I see,' purrs Pearl.

'Sorry, saw you, but engine running on adrenaline,' Cat puff-purrs. 'Couldn't locate my brakes.'

'Yup, you need a break. Who's on your tail?'

'Were on my tail. Shaken them off now. Paparazzi. Paparazzi hunting out the Rajpapa story. Breaking news. Rajpaparazzi. Like that? I like that. Wish I could communicate that one to Milly. She'd love that.'

'Oh, so droll, Cat. Would you care to rethink your mission and purpose beyond your ninth life? Comedy writer, entertainer?'

'On that note, Pearl,' Cat licks the remaining sweat and leafy bits from her belly, 'I'd appreciate your ear. You predicted, some time ago, that there were storms coming. Let me run back through my memory ... Ah, here it is: "Storms approach, you think you've seen it all, but you've seen nothing yet." I thought I'd already weathered some storms, but is this the big one?'

'You want the good news or the bad news?'

'Okay, so I've weathered some, but a lot more to come?'

'Let me just check the barometer. Hmm, that just about sums it up. Storms can be the making of us if we're open to navigating them rather than seeking safe harbour. What have you learned so far?'

'I thought – no, I still know in my bones that I'm here to guide and protect this place and all who sail in her. Can't resist extending the nautical theme, sorry. Got to laugh off the stress, too. See the funny side of life, particularly the funny side of a challenging ninth life.'

Pearl wavers, luminescent, shimmering in the sunlight. One of their best tricks. Only a pearl cat can do that. Cat examines her tail. Honey marmalade is a more solid, absorbing, grounded kind of colour.

'Stay on track, Cat. Time to stop trying to be clever. Trying to avoid the issue. Focus.'

'The issue is,' Cat takes a deep, arching breath, 'keeping everyone following the rules is harder than I thought, and unless I succeed, I'll be doing another round of nine earthbound lives, and I don't want to do that.'

'Why not, Cat? Remind me.'

Cat shakes her head. 'It's not that I don't want to do another nine earthly lives. It's that I want to be a spirit mentor to an earthbound being. It's a calling. I feel it in my ...'

'Bones,' says Pearl. 'You feel a lot in your bones, don't you?'

'Bones I'll be leaving behind when I graduate.'

'What will you take with you?'

'My spirit, my soul, my learning, my wisdom, a lightness of being.'

'What is the heaviness of being you feel now?' Pearl edges closer, eyes looming large and intense.

Cat closes her eyes, drawing deeply. 'The responsibility for guiding and protecting people I can't communicate with, people who dismiss me as an innocent animal, a lovely kitty to exploit in their branding, their videos, or to divert attention from their shortcomings.'

'You want to be a spirit mentor to an earthbound being, a being clothed in a body: human, caterpillar, donkey, oak tree, or whoever you are assigned. You want to guide and help them through their challenges, their troubles, right?'

'Right, Pearl, yes.'

Pearl prowls to the right, to the left, spots a mouse, pounces, paw-presses it close to the ground as it squeals and wriggles, fighting for its life, then lets it go. 'To mentor an earthbound being, you need to know what they're going through, to know what it is to be clothed in a body with all its apparent limitations and illusions, to feel what they feel, see what they see, guide them from where they are at, not from where you think they should be. You've had eight lives to draw on, and if you want to know what I think ...'

'I do.'

'We sometimes leave the toughest learning until last. The things we haven't wanted to face in the last eight lives come back to taunt us in our ninth life. Go home, consult your bones. Listen and learn.'

'Ever thought about being a spirit mentor yourself, Pearl, when you graduate? Which life are you in now? I've never asked.'

Pearl jumps up into Reclining Woman with Child and nestles within the child's arms, an echo of Cat's curling inside Serenity's foetal embrace, a return of the calming rhythm synchronising Cat's breath. A rising crescent moon pauses beneath Pearl, peaking through the brush box before ascending into the late-afternoon sky.

Cat practises her regal walk, her wise walk, across the topiary garden, past the sleeping daffodils' bed and into the warmth of the hallway, inexplicably hoping for vegan bites instead of the usual meat that Emmy lays out. *Cream, yes, please. Mice and meat, not tonight, thank you.*

🐾

'The one thing to appreciate about the media,' Milly lifts a single buttercup from the jar of cornflowers and buttercups at the centre of the café table, 'is that they're always chasing the next story. Today's news is simply that. Three weeks ago, we were surrounded by paparazzi, and now look, nothing but July sunshine and blue skies.'

'Buttercups and cornflowers, sunshine and blue skies.' Clary extracts another buttercup and holds it under her chin. 'Do I like butter?'

'The answer to that is on your plate, oozing from your croissant, Clary.' Pixie licks the butter off her own muffin-crumbed fingers.

'And yet,' Milly replaces her buttercup in the vase, 'it may be all sunshine and blue skies out there in the world, but inside these walls, Serenity must be hurting. We turn up every morning for yoga, but she's losing Zoom numbers fast and furiously.'

Cat cocks her head, pausing her grooming routine from her vantage point on the shelf above the table to pay closer attention.

'How do you know that?' Anna drains her coffee. 'Serenity hasn't mentioned it. She's been, well, quite serene, I think, throughout the trouble.'

Milly examines her over the rim of her cup. 'Once an investigative journalist, always …'

'… an investigative journalist,' they chant in unison, laughing.

'I was curious. Went to the page on the website where you can book online classes, and there's a count beside each class, so you can see how many people are booked in. Must be a hangover from the days when they had to cap the numbers because of technicalities. I looked three weeks ago, and I've been checking every day since.'

'Snooping! Stalking!' Anna gives Milly a cheeky, admonishing look.

'Investigating. If I'm going to write a history of this place, I need to compare it to where we're at today. Or, okay, maybe I'm also just nosy.'

'I suppose we know Serenity as a person, trust her,' Pixie says, 'see her before and after class, see her around the village, in the supermarket, looking like butter wouldn't melt in her mouth.'

'What is it with you guys and your word plays?' Anna reaches for a buttercup, knocking the vase over.

'Butterfingers!' Pixie got in quick, before the others.

'You're right, though,' Clary says. 'I don't know what happened. I try not to read the media stories, well, try – curiosity gets me into the first couple of paragraphs before I realise it's all negativity and spin. I can't imagine Serenity would pay money to shut someone down from reporting abuse, can you?'

'We can't imagine it,' Anna says, 'but people who only know her as the big business guru, the immaculate teacher who guides them through their classes over Zoom, where they can't feel her true gaze … What do they think when they read the news?'

'Like she begins to fit the archetype of "super-rich guru steps too far and goes down for fraud",' Pixie says. 'If there is such an archetype, but you know what I mean.'

'Icarus flying too close to the sun?' offers Clary.

'Can she afford to lose Zoom numbers?' Anna asks.

'That's the burning question,' Milly says, 'no Icarus pun intended. How much of her business relies on her international yoga income – and let's not forget, her associated social media income, those Amantha videos, her paid endorsements – and how much relies on her property investments?'

'And if she has bought Rajpapa out,' Pixie steeples her fingers, 'is she cash-strapped?'

'I hope she can keep this place going, given that she leases it.' Clary eyes Cat. 'What do you think, Amantha?'

One meow, two meows, three meows – transmit: *Let's do what we can to guard and protect this place.*

'Let's do what we can to guard and protect this place,' Clary says, blinking. 'Actually, I think that message came from Amantha. After what she said about Freya reading my altar message, and what she said to Hazel about the woodlice, I'm beginning to think she's the guru we need to be paying attention to.'

All eyes turn to Cat as a buttercup-yellow butterfly glides

in on a sudden lavender-laden breeze and delicately perches on her right paw. Too stunned to do anything other than bask in its tender glory and wonder about its proximity to the point, on the underside of her paw, where graduation from her ninth life will soon be etched, Cat simply breathes. *Is being a guru the pathway to graduation*, she wonders? Will they all listen to her and appreciate her guidance if she becomes their guru?

'Not so sure the crushed-woodlice recipe is the best remedy for Hazel, unless she's one very adventurous and courageous woman.' Pixie pulls a mock-horrified face.

Milly looks at Clary, and they both nod. 'Clary and I have been chatting to Briar about the early history of this place. Scratching the surface at the moment, not much to report, but it turns out that crushed woodlice were used in a gardening ritual going back about four hundred years, and there's a spot in Briar's garden where the woodlice still thrive. So, if Hazel's interested ...'

Anna looks at Pixie, and Pixie bursts into laughter. 'Oh,' Anna says, 'thought you were being serious about Hazel for a moment there, Milly.'

Cat snaps into action. *Enough of this frivolity. Crushed woodlice mixed with rose and rosemary is exactly what Hazel needs, and the rosemary is not only a key fertility ingredient, but it also enhances the nuttiness of the woodlice, making it more fitting for the human tongue. Maybe Clary can whip some up. And while she's at it, maybe she can be my mouthpiece and whip this place into shape.*

Abby pokes her head into the café, marches over to the table and pulls Cat up and onto her shoulder. 'Sorry to break up the tea party, guys,' she winks, 'Amantha's presence is required at HQ.'

Cat whips her tail, confirming serendipity's message. *Whip, whip, whip*, she feels it in her bones. A clear mission.

'Is there something we don't know?' says Pixie, as Cat is whisked away beyond earshot, and bustled into the high tension of the Power Hour room.

'Here she is.' Serenity's voice is slightly muffled, bouncing from the walls, but nowhere to be seen. There's no trace of her jasmine-citrus essence, no clicking of her mala beads. Cat takes a moment and follows Freya's eyeline, watching as the tiny, coloured boxes on the wall shimmer and resolve into a moving picture of Serenity. *Ah*, the penny drops. Serenity is here on Zoom.

Abby joins Freya and Emmy at the oaken table – new to the room – pulling out a high-backed oaken chair, also new to the room. The beanbags huddle in a corner, displaced by the seriously formal furniture Cat now remembers seeing in the reception area. Her favourite purple velvet cushion awaits her on the table, in front of Abby. She plonks down, mystified, then rearranges herself in keeping with her envisioned guru status. Sitting tall, emanating a controlled aura of mystery and wisdom, readiness to *whip, whip, whip* once she's gathered the appropriate intel. HQ, she gathers, is the new name for the Power Hour room, a serious-business-table-and-chairs kind of room, not a lounge-about-beanbags pow-wow.

All eyes are on Serenity.

'Sorry I couldn't be with you in person today,' Zoom Serenity says, 'and sorry if the reception wavers. As you can probably see, I'm in the back seat of the car. The driver's got her headphones on, so we have privacy. I had to leave straight after teaching the yoga class this morning, heading to London to tidy business with my lawyer and accountant, business I can only do face to face.'

'How are you feeling, Serenity?' Freya asks, her trembling fingers touching her amethyst choker.

'I'm okay, thank you. How are you all feeling?'

Cat swishes her tail, the only sound in the room.

'You're not running away from us, a hot plane ticket to Peru, are you, Serenity?' Abby snaps everyone back to reality. There are guffaws, chuckles.

'As if.' Serenity laughs. 'I want to keep you all up to date with what's happening, in the broadest sense. I know all your main livelihoods depend on the continuation of the centre, and I want to protect you and the centre.'

Cat takes serious note, glancing sideways at Freya, Emmy and Abby. *Got that, guys? Serenity wants to protect you, and that is my mission, too. We've got this.*

'I have to be honest with you.' Serenity freezes on the wall for a moment, then returns with a squeaky fast-forward jumble of words before her voice settles back into its usual rhythm. 'I think we dropped out there, so I'll repeat that. I want to be clear. Before I bought Rajpapa out of the business, we bought a property, a house in Scotland, and gifted it to Penelope, the first woman – the only woman, as I thought at the time – who accused Rajpapa of sexual abuse. I'm deeply ashamed to admit that I didn't believe her back then. Rajpapa said they were consensual lovers, and as devoted as I was to him, I believed him. Penelope wasn't a popular woman around the ashram. Some saw her as manipulative, and I fell into the trap of judging her based on that. She asked for compensation, said she'd be happy to let the issue go if we bought her a house, so we did. The purchase went down as a business expense, an addition to our portfolio. That's how it felt at the time, investment in a property that we then gifted to a valuable employee.'

Emmy uncrosses and recrosses her legs. Freya pours herself a glass of water. Abby leans forward and caresses Cat's shoulders.

'The worst-case scenario, my lawyer tells me, is that it could be argued that we falsified our business accounts, listing the property as a business investment, not as a potential gift. Or, if so framed by an adversary, hush money. She doesn't think it will come to that, but I need to let you know. If I were to go down for mismanagement of funds, or fraud, you might not want to be associated with me. You might want to cut loose now.'

A June bug taps at the window.

'The second worst-case scenario is that the other nine women who have since come forward – and yes, I do believe them – may seek compensation from the business that we jointly owned, rather than suing Rajpapa, personally. I'm not sure how it works. I need to be in London to get clearer on this.'

Cat lifts onto all fours, stretches her back and sits down again, utter confusion disguised as all-knowing wisdom.

'I don't really expect either of those worst-case scenarios to occur, but better to let you know than have you suffer in conjecture. What I can tell you, and this is really the point of today's Power Hour, is that our Zoom numbers have absolutely plummeted. A significant number of students have cancelled their monthly online class memberships, and new memberships are just not happening. I'm trying to manage my feelings around my classes being measured by Rajpapa's behaviour, not by my dedication to my students, and not by the profound benefits the practice brings. I recognise that our formula of beginning and ending each class with Rajpapa's quotes and wisdom is perhaps damaging the offering. I'm prepared to rewrite the rules. I'm inundated with emails from Rajpapa teachers asking me for advice. But that's not for you to worry about ...'

Rewriting the rules, Cat ponders, no longer sure if this is a good or bad thing. Rules, as Clary says, are meant to be broken. But then Rajpapa seriously broke rules when he abused the women. *Focus, Cat, focus. Today is more about rule three: support each other, isn't it?*

'I've only got another five minutes and I'll have to take a call from my accountant, so apologies for talking at you rather than with you, but I have to get this out.'

Abby gives a thumbs up, while Freya places her hands on her heart, and Emmy sits stock still.

'As you know, I lease the centre. And you also know that I recently bought the businesses in New York. My accountants are trying to channel my finances into the New York investment to make good on the purchase and because those entities are not tainted, shall we say, with Rajpapa Yoga. They advise that I cut loose the businesses that are not making money. Our lovely village centre costs me more to lease than your rents and the current diminishing returns on the yoga classes. My accountants suggest I give up the centre, video the classes for our online students and channel all the remaining yoga income into the New York businesses. Unless, and it's a big ask, we can cover the lease of the centre through a combination of your rents, bringing in other practitioners and doing some clever marketing. All of which brings us back to Abby.'

Emmy clears her throat. 'Am I hearing this right? You may raise our rents?'

'Yes, or no, depends on what else we can do to raise income. Look, the bottom line is my heart is in this place. I love the personal contact, the friendships, living here in this village. Abby has some brilliant ideas. I've got to go. Oh yes, before I do, I've asked Mariana, one of our London Rajpapa Yoga teachers, to cover my classes for the next couple of weeks. I know you'll make her feel welcome. I have great faith in you all. Let's weather this storm and emerge stronger.'

One click, and she's gone.

'Before you panic,' Abby pulls her chair back, 'I really do have some fabulous ideas, and Serenity forgot to mention that she has booked the amazing Frankie Jay to give us a workshop on abundance on Saturday. Can I suggest we all take some time to chill, maybe grab some lunch and meet back here at, let's make it twelve-thirty?'

😺

Cat races up the staircase and crash-lands in the middle of the empty yoga floor in *savasana* pose, on her back, belly exposed, limbs spreadeagled, eyes heavenward, peace. *What was it Abby said? Take some time to chill. Chill. Chill. Chill. Breathe in for four, hold for four, breathe out for four, hold for four. In, out, in, out. What is it Serenity calls this in yoga, box breathing?* Body sinking down, muscles she didn't know were tense now relax, letting go. One big jaw-cracking yawn and her tight face relaxes. As her throat opens, the surprising release of a soft, humming purr floats in a starry purple sky.

Movement on the edge of the room, essence of bergamot and vanilla, signals Emmy. Cat opens one eye, sees Emmy kneeling at the yoga altar, then closes her eye once more, holding her space. *Mustn't move until I've got this clear. Listen to my bones. The best way to guard and protect this place is to be heard, to be respected, to communicate my wisdom, to help people keep to the rules, show them the way. Possible best way to gain their attention is to get Clary – who does hear me – to interpret for me, or to set me up as a wise being, a guru, if that's what it takes. Thank you, bones, that feels good. So, that's step one. Step two is to get some money flowing into this place so Serenity can keep it going, so all who sail in her can keep sailing – uphold rule two: help and heal.*

Cat stretches, rolls onto her side, sees Emmy no longer kneeling but prostrate at the altar, mumbles of prayer plucking Cat's heartstrings, drawing her altar-ward, purring softly so as not to startle Emmy, dropping to her belly and adjusting her purring to the rhythm of Emmy's prayer.

Emmy dries her eyes, sits back on her heels and pulls Cat into her lap. 'I can't go back to working from home, Amantha, having clients come into a space saturated with Ben's desperation.' She pauses, pressing her fingers into her temples. 'No, it's not the clients, it's me. I can't focus when Ben's in the next room gambling the last of our savings on the next sure-fire investment destined to go up in flames.'

Cat shivers, seeing an oil lamp falling, straw catching fire, a heavy wooden door closing, essence of skin scorching. She shakes her head and the vision fades. *Was it something Emmy said?*

'Working here,' Emmy lifts Cat's chin and peers momentarily into her eyes, 'I feel free. I can concentrate, I can help and heal, and I can put aside a little of my earnings in case I need to escape my marriage. My freedom fund. Just knowing it's there helps. I can't go back to working from home. And I can't afford to lose my place here, but paying more rent would mean less going into my freedom fund. Or worse, drawing on my freedom fund to pay the extra rent. It feels so good to give voice to my thoughts and fears. Thank you for being here, Amantha.'

Emmy gazes long enough for one meow, two meows, three meows – transmit. But Cat draws a blank. What to say? Her tail drops. *Some guru!*

'Some guru!' Emmy spits, looking up at the framed portrait of Rajpapa hanging beside the altar. She stifles a scream, springs to her feet, tears the portrait from the wall and smashes it over the cast-iron coat stand at the top of the stairwell. Glass splintering, Guru Rajpapa is nothing but tattered shreds of paper. 'That's what I think of you, Mr Guru King-daddy!'

She grabs Cat and marches back to HQ, softening a little with every step, before entering the room as if nothing has happened.

😽

A citrus aroma hangs in the air at HQ, a zingy tang on Cat's tongue, a refreshing pep to the senses. She knows, in her bones, that cats are repelled by citrus, but she also knows that, clearly, she's not a normal cat. Citrus tingles her curiosity, draws her in, magnetises her and compels her to pay attention. It's no coincidence, surely, that Freya's perfume is tangerine mist, Emmy walks in bergamot-spiced vanilla and Abby exudes amber citrus.

She traces the fragrance to three dainty gift boxes gracing the table, each topped with a sprig of lemon thyme and a stick of Palo Santo.

'From Serenity, one for each of us,' says Abby. 'Palo Santo

to clear the air of any negativity, and lemon thyme to offer a fresh start, to remind us to take time as we explore our options.'

'On the subject of time, I've only got an hour.' Freya softly rubs the lemon thyme and brings her fingers to her face to inhale the citrus. 'I hope the force will be with me to do my best for my afternoon clients after what we've been through this morning.'

'I've rearranged my afternoon bookings.' Emmy eyes the gift boxes as she takes her seat. 'Lucky they were both flexible.'

'Sorry, guys,' Abby says. 'I wanted us to be able to go home tonight with a feeling of opportunity and possibility, rather than doom and gloom.' She sits opposite Emmy and Freya, and lifts the lid on her gift box with an air of knowing. The others follow suit.

'A gift token for a Kahuna massage down at that new place on the coast, and a tiny jar of marmalade. I need to explain the marmalade. Serenity said it's to symbolise the gifts our own very lovely marmalade cat, Amantha, has bestowed upon us, the way she brightens up our mornings, brings zest to our days, something like that. It's a bit of a clumsy segue, but she intended it to open conversation on a change to our branding.'

'Sorry, not sure I follow.' Freya laughs, opening the lid on her jar and dipping her little finger in the jam. 'I guess we're in a bit of a jam now, aren't we, with the Rajpapa lotus so tightly woven into the branding of the centre?'

Abby twists her sprig of lemon thyme into a ring, threads it onto her right thumb and turns it absentmindedly. 'None of us know how the Rajpapa side of things is going to turn out for Serenity, or for her yoga brand. But she feels we need to focus less on yoga and more on the other services we offer here if we're going to make our centre viable in the wake of all this. Whatever happens for Serenity, she thinks we should drop the Rajpapa lotus symbol, plus any mention of him from our branding, and – until she decides what to do – drop his name from the yoga classes but otherwise keep them the same. As you know, we've already incorporated Amantha into our brand and marketing, and – as

I said at the time – I thought it was a clunky marriage, Amantha and Rajpapa, but we're now looking at enhancing Amantha's image in the brand.' She pauses to sip some water.

Cat examines her reflection in the window. *Not marmalade, I'm honey. Will they bring out my honeyed hues in their new branding? I can guide them from the sticky jam they're in, offer them the renowned healing powers of honey. Heal the harm that's been caused, bring them into line with the rules, attract the funds they need, be their honeypot in the shape of their wise guru, and when I'm done with all that, graduate my ninth life with full accolades.*

'The media have been disparaging about Amantha, remember,' Emmy says. 'Do we really want to throw everything behind the image of a psychic cat?' She cups her warm hands over Cat's ears a little too late. Cat bristles.

'Media, pfft.' Abby waves her hands as if batting away a fly. 'We're not marketing the centre to the media, we're marketing it to people within a fifty-mile radius from here, and a little further afield if we go ahead with some of Serenity's suggestions. Serenity says we've projected the centre as a yoga studio with side offerings, and she feels it's time now to reverse that.'

'So,' Emmy says, 'let's be clear about this. Abby, you and I bring in our fair share of clients, but it's Freya who's the honeypot. People love psychic readings.' She turns to face Freya. 'You've told us you still need to work at the post office every morning to make ends meet. I'm guessing you'd struggle to pay Serenity more rent, as we would. Shining a spotlight on our services isn't going to be enough to rescue this place, or us, is it?'

Cat zings from her nose to her paws to the tip of her electrified tail. Emmy hit the nail on the head: people love psychic readings. She meows to catch Abby's attention, pulling her forget-me-not eyes into her gaze. One meow, two meows, three meows – transmit: *People love psychic readings and people love cats. Let's put the two together.*

'People love psychic readings and people love cats. Let's put the two together,' says Abby, eyes wide in astonishment. 'I've got it. It's as if it just dropped out of the heavens. I don't know why we didn't think of it before.'

'Um ...' Freya looks at Emmy, subtly shrugging her shoulders. 'I've been marketing Amantha as a psychic assistant, a conduit to spirit, for the past few months, with varied success, wouldn't you say?'

'Go with me on this one,' Abby says, eyes flicking slowly from side to side as she completes her download from Cat, piecing together the practicalities, the implications. 'Freya, you're a winner whatever. Look at how amazingly you've come through the recent challenges, how you've widened your services, gained empathy for yourself and other women going through perimenopause. Look at all the people who came forward to endorse your accuracy following Milly's article. People love psychic readings, and they will always come to you, regardless of whether you include Amantha in your marketing. I'm thinking of something else.' She lifts Cat to her eye level to receive one more transmission. 'Freya communicates messages from spirits. Amantha gives guidance and wisdom.'

'How so?' Emmy glances sideways at Abby, her brow furrowed.

'I was there, at Clary's art class,' Abby says, 'when Hazel got a message from Cat about her infertility issues. She was new to the group, none of us knew she had been trying to conceive. Hazel said it was as if the message was downloaded directly from Amantha. You both know this story.'

'Weird guidance, though, to eat crushed woodlice,' Freya says.

'That's true.' Abby speaks slowly, measuring her thoughts. 'Maybe she needs a little practice, or maybe, looking back, it was perfect. The outcome was that Hazel shared her grief. It was the first time she'd talked about it openly. Told us it felt incredibly healing. As to the crushed woodlice, it got us all curious about how infertility has been managed over the centuries, and Hazel is thinking about embarking on some research with a wild plan to make a documentary on the subject. She told us, in Clary's class last week, there's evidence that some women fall pregnant once they stop focusing on trying to get pregnant – like people who adopt because they can't conceive and then do. She's going to stop IVF and switch her focus to something all-consuming – like making a documentary. Who knows what the result will be? But she felt that something within her shifted when Amantha spoke to her, and she has faith that, whatever the outcome, she's moving in a good direction. Is that wisdom? I don't know.'

Cat smells crushed woodlice. *It's a very simple message. Just eat the crushed woodlice mixed with a little rosemary and rose. Thinking too deeply, guys.*

'I'm ashamed to bring it up,' Freya says, 'but just between us, Milly, Clary, the media, the internet and the whole wide world out there, Clary felt it was Amantha who told her that I was using the information on her altar message. I don't know if it's true – she could just as well have put two and two together herself – but people believed Clary. I'm not sure how I feel, to be honest, about being upstaged by a cat.'

'If we promote Amantha as a psychic reader,' Abby doodles on the back of her massage gift certificate, 'and I'm unclear about how we would do that. Listen to us! Land of fantasy! But anyway, if we did, Freya, we'd be making a distinction: you give messages from spirits and provide people with evidence of the afterlife or hope in the face of grief and struggle. And with your levels of accuracy, you will always have customers. Amantha would be in a different field: guidance and wisdom.'

Freya's eyes brim with tears. 'All the effort I've put into my new service, surely, with all my academic training and experience, I've got more to offer than a domestic moggy?'

Cat supresses a hiss and focuses her mind on her mission.

And perhaps, if anyone was to give me the respect of using my real name, I would have more wisdom and guidance in my hard-earned ninth life than any domestic spirit-chatty middle-aged human moggy in her ninety-ninth life with another one hundred incarnations to go before she's ready to leave this earthly plane. The thunder cloud above her dissipates, leaving a tear in her eye, much to her feline surprise; a crashing to the ground in deep remorse. Rule three: support each other.

'Oh, Freya.' Emmy reaches out and touches Freya's hand. 'I don't think Abby meant it like that. She's coming from a marketing angle, and I'm not sure I understand it yet, but she's ultimately looking at ways to keep the centre open and to bring us more clients – hopefully without a rent increase.'

'Sorry, Freya,' Abby says, 'Emmy is right. Give me some time to get clear on the idea, but in the meantime, can we talk about Serenity's thoughts about why it might be advantageous to enhance Amantha's presence in our branding? Just to be sure, we're talking about using her in our imagery, on our website, on our building, on our marketing materials and replacing the Rajpapa lotus with something that evokes Amantha – or cats. Time is ticking and I know you both have clients to attend to.'

'Yes,' Emmy says, 'let's end on that feeling of possibility and opportunity that you mentioned at the start of this afternoon, please.'

'Rajpapa sounds masculine, all Yang,' Abby says. 'Raj for king, papa for, well, papa. And we know what else we and everyone else associates with him, now. A cat, as a symbol, is the opposite. We see cats as intuitive and – whichever gender – kind of more Yin. We see cats as curious, less Yang left-brain – reductionist, logic and rules – and more Yin right-brain – wholistic, creative, spiritual.'

Cat counts her virtues: *Yes to curious, intuitive, creative, spiritual, but in this cat's kingdom ... um, should that be queendom? In this cat's queendom, rules rule. Have me associated with your brand and you've got all the feelgood Yin elements, plus solid, rule-based guidance.*

'Isn't that what we want our brand to reflect, moving forward? Our intuitive, wholistic, creative and spiritual services, a mecca for the curious and open-minded?' Abby asks.

'Sounds good to me.' Emmy checks her watch. 'Definitely on board with distancing our brand from Rajpapa.'

Abby reaches out and swings the whiteboard into view, revealing her neatly handwritten list. 'Some of Serenity's ideas for bringing in more money, and hopefully keeping your rents at their current level. You might want to take a photo to study it at leisure this evening, but I'll read it out quickly before we wrap: bringing in more practitioners – no-one in your fields. This might mean hot-desking or sharing your rooms when you're not here to save you rent. Hiring out the bigger spaces for workshops or talks. Hiring out the café and gardens for weddings and festivals. Regular art-and-craft classes in the room Clary's been using. Putting on our own festivals, hiring out marquees and kiosks in the garden for vendors. Showcasing artists in the café and taking a percentage of works sold. Hiring out the yoga space to other practitioners when it's not being used for yoga, maybe dance, martial arts, Pilates. Garden tours – I think we can bring the landowner and Briar on board for this – as part of coach tours from London, lunch included in our café. This presents an opportunity for them to purchase the art on show in the café as well as discover our services. Possible coach tours from London for Freya's psychic readings – we're thinking of you working from a stage in the yoga space, Freya, doing readings for people in the audience. Offering weekend-package experiences or retreats, accommodating people at Airbnbs in the village, or at one of the boutique hotels with paid commission to us. This is just a starting list. Does it give you hope?'

'Yes,' Freya wobbles to her feet, 'give or take the terrifying thought of having a hot flush in front of a large audience, and the other terrifying and mind-boggling thought of Amantha offering her own psychic consultations, whatever that might look like, I can't imagine. But one step at a time. And yes, thank you, Abby, I do feel a renewed sense of hope.'

'Yes, thank you,' Emmy chimes, lifting Cat off her cushion, folding her into her elbow and gathering her things. 'I feel much better. Got to go and prepare for my client.'

'Oh, this Sunday, nine am start, all day, the abundance workshop. I'll email you details. Be there …' Abby's voice trails in their wake.

🐾

Emmy closes the HQ door behind her, lifts Cat to her cheek and waltz-sings her way to her office door: 'One, two, three, one, two, three, one, two, three,' and, crossing the threshold into her safe space, 'free.'

'So, now you know, Amantha,' Emmy says, settling Cat into a sunny spot on the window seat behind her desk and filling her bowl with fresh cream. 'It's one, two, three, free from working from home, one, two, three, free to build my freedom fund, one, two, three, free to be me. I've got to trust that Serenity's ideas will keep me on my path to freedom. I'm not going back, not now that I've come so far.'

Cat laps at the cream, eyelids heavy. So much to process, so many possible future scenarios requiring her guidance and protection, her attention to rule-keeping detail. Her responsibilities keep multiplying as her envisaged graduation day scurries further into the future, a mouse outpacing her and diving into a thicket, beyond trace.

But then a stirring, her heart misses a beat, leaps a dance of its own, electrifies her tail, heightens her senses as she recalls: Amantha, psychic reader. Amantha, as seen in viral videos worldwide. Amantha, renowned for her psychic guidance of Clary,

Hazel and Milly. Amantha, assisting those who consult her, those who queue for her guidance as she lounges on her plush consulting cushions, bowls of cream and nutbrown biscuits laid abundantly at her paws. Amantha, acknowledged for her wisdom. Amantha, lauded in the media. Amantha, saviour of the Serene Lotus Centre for Health and Wellbeing. Amantha – no, she will tell Clary her name is Cat. They will call her Cat. Afternoon tea with Cat. That has a ring to it. Could there even be a world where she abandons her increasingly complicated mission to graduate her ninth life and instead relaxes into a long, enjoyable ninth life as a psychic reader with no cares and responsibilities, even if she does have to go round another nine lives afterwards? Perhaps her next nine lives would be easy, gift lives in return for her services as a psychic reader in this life. Might it be more rewarding to see people like Clary, Hazel, Milly and thousands of others follow her guidance and evolve personally and spiritually, than to be an unseen, unacknowledged spirit mentor to one single earthbound being?

She sees a fork in her path. One way leads to her long-desired graduation through guiding everyone associated with the centre to keep to the rules. The other leads to a long and rewarding earthbound life focused in the present, guiding thousands of people to their best future, without the added responsibilities of being their moral guardian. Each way begins with being able to communicate, being heard, and if accepting a role as psychic reader means that people will listen, then that's the thing to focus on for now. She breathes out, long, slow, steady. No need to make any major decision yet.

🐾

Essence of tobacco enters the room, stinging Cat's nostrils.

'Hello, Martin. I'm Emmy. Pleased to meet you.'

'Hello, Emmy.' Martin looks around the room, shoulders

slightly hunched, aroma of anxiety surfacing through the veil of tobacco. 'My wife made the booking for me.'

Emmy guides Martin to sit in the oversized chestnut leather armchair, gives him a glass of water and delicately folds her body into the seat, facing him. 'I see she booked you in for a quit-smoking session, but it will only work if you want to give up your cigarettes. I'm happy to cancel the session and return your fee if you're not ready to do this.'

Martin sips the water and slips off his running shoes. 'Look, I'm willing to give this a try. I've tried everything else. Yes, I do want to stop smoking, but how do I feel about hypnosis? That's another question.'

'You're totally in control, Martin, even when I hypnotise you. Hypnosis is a way of making you so super relaxed that a deeper part of yourself feels more open to my suggestions. If you really want to quit smoking, that deeper part of yourself will stop resisting your efforts to quit and start assisting you. It's all about appealing to your unconscious mind to get on board with your conscious intentions and stop sabotaging you.'

'Suggestions?' Martin raises an eyebrow. 'What do you mean?'

'I don't tell you to make changes, I don't give you orders. We agree, before I hypnotise you, on the changes you'd like to make and the general nature of the suggestions you'd like me to offer to your relaxed unconscious mind. Most of the time – the method isn't a hundred percent effective – the way the suggestions are pitched softens your unconscious barriers. It's the difference between me telling you to sit back in your chair and me suggesting that you do if you want to feel more comfortable.'

Martin relaxes. 'Let's do it.'

Emmy suggests Martin reclines and closes his eyes, and Cat falls asleep, only to be woken, sometime later, by a change in Emmy's pitch.

'And you feel so very relaxed that you'll book weekly sessions throughout the summer to seal the good work we've done today. And, waking up now on the count of three: one, two, three.'

Martin blinks, looks around the room, notices Cat, then looks at Emmy. 'That felt like a nap. I expected to hear the suggestions. Did I conk out on you? Did I snore?'

'No, the session went perfectly, Martin. You heard all the suggestions under hypnosis, and you responded whenever I asked you to confirm, but on coming round, your conscious mind drops the memory. Rest assured, your unconscious mind was open to the suggestions, so now we wait.'

'How long? I have a meeting.'

'Oh no, you don't have to wait here. I meant now we wait and see what happens over the next few days, what happens when someone offers you a smoke, or what happens when you encounter the situations where you would normally reach out for a cigarette. It will feel odd. You'll probably not want one. The thought of a cigarette or the smell of it will most likely be a complete turn-off. I suggested to your unconscious mind that cigarettes taste like ... well, I won't tell you, but under hypnosis you agreed on the plan.'

'Thank you, Emmy.' Martin shuffles forward in his chair and slips his feet back into his shoes. 'Whatever happens, I do feel unusually relaxed. I'll stop by the reception on the way out and book another session for next week.'

The door closes and Emmy collapses her head into her hands. Cat doesn't need to wait for her to speak. The misdemeanour is glaringly evident. She has heard Emmy deliver her spiel to other quit-smoking clients. It's a once-off session. No need for further hypnosis. Emmy broke her code of ethics and Cat knows why. Should she reprimand Emmy? No, Emmy is already suffering remorse. Should she guide her to have more faith in the future, or guide her to ... Cat stretches her legs and calls on her innate wisdom. That's it, should she guide her to raise her fees?

'I suppose that's what you'd call suggestive selling,' Emmy

sniggers, reaching for a tissue to blow her nose. 'Don't worry, Amantha, I won't do that again. I don't know what got hold of my tongue. Or was that you? You know the saying, the cat's got my tongue. No, I'm jesting with you. At least I'm seeing the funny side of my wrongdoing, and I now understand the depth of my insecurities as far as money and my freedom are concerned. I'll take it as a lesson learned. As to what I'll do with Martin next week, we'll see.'

Cat extracts herself from her cushion nest and saunters towards Emmy, casually brushing by her legs, long enough to communicate her admiration of Emmy's conclusions, not long enough to signal approval of the misdemeanour itself, and heads to the door. Emmy springs forward and opens it for her. 'Thank you, Amantha. Somehow, I think more clearly when you're around.'

      🐾

The familiar hallway envelops Cat, wraps her in kindness and suggests she go outside to taste the late-afternoon air.

The time will come when she will help people to hear the suggestions and whispers of all things, aromas, buildings, nature. But for now, she is content that her mere presence in the room was sufficient to nudge Emmy into reflecting on her rule breaking, learning from her experience and vowing to stick to the rules in future. Though there was, Cat admits, a frisson of shared curiosity over what will happen when Martin turns up for his next session, one devoid of assigned purpose. What is it people say? Curiosity killed the cat?

And with that, she runs into the rose-scented garden and spies Clary and Milly, heading, it seems, to Briar's cottage. She covers the distance at speed, arranges herself in casual composure on the stone wall flanking Briar's squeaky garden gate, and feigns a flicker of surprise when the two women stroll into view.

Milly's dark curls bounce alongside Clary's blonde ponytail, Yang and Yin, Milly's sharp cut and thrust, Clary's soft nurturing, Milly's investigative reporting, exposing secrets, Clary's gentle teaching, drawing out people's natural, expressive gifts. Milly strides towards the gate, sensible black jeans and T-shirt, a long purple-and-red silk scarf trailing from her shoulders, while Clary glides, oversized sunshine-yellow shirt dress loosely gathered at the waist with a black sequined cummerbund, black sequined earrings catching the late-afternoon sun. Cat has nothing but attitude to ring the style changes, and today's attitude is cool psychic reader; no, make that psychic reader queen, or maybe cool cat; too cool for leaping into Clary's arms, which is what Cat really wants to do.

'Amantha. Are you psychic or what?' Milly lifts Cat down from her stone perch. 'We were looking everywhere for you. Where were you hiding? Briar says he's made you a sweet treat for our inaugural afternoon-tea-slash-history-interview, so he's expecting your royal presence.'

Afternoon tea with Cat. A royal, queenly Cat at that. Cat catches Milly's gaze, does the meow trick and transmits: *My name is Cat, not Amantha.*

'I know you're a cat, Amantha, but there's something mystical and special about you. Your psychic whisperings for a start, and your knowledge of medieval folk medicine, if your crushed woodlice advice is anything to go by,' Milly says.

'Or maybe your presence unlocks our own psychic insights, our wisdom, or access to ancient knowledge.' Clary unlatches Briar's garden gate. 'We're not sure yet and maybe we don't need to understand it, but you are some kind of conduit for us, and we need your energy to connect with the known and unknown history of this place. Let the magic begin.'

'And the afternoon tea,' Milly adds. 'I'm starving.'

NINTH LIFE

🐾

Essence of Briar intensifies inside his cottage, mingled with ... what is it? Beyond the coffee, fishy biscuits and the transient aromas of afternoon tea, there's beeswax, a touch of turpentine and the wonderful abandon of windows thrown open to the summer breeze.

'Oh, very witty.' Milly runs her fingertips over the vase of magenta roses spiked with sprigs of rosemary, the first thing she sees when Briar welcomes them across the threshold. She bends to sniff the combined aroma. 'Just missing the crushed woodlice, that's all.'

'Knew you'd pick up on the symbolism straightaway.' Briar steps aside to leave room for Clary and Cat to squeeze into the boot room – not that anyone needs to kick off muddy boots and hang up dripping coats today. It's such a tight space that Cat wonders why they didn't come in through the front door. Make a grand entrance. 'I picked them fresh for today, but it's a ritual I keep. Pick them weekly during the rose season and use dried roses and rose essence with the evergreen rosemary through the rest of the year.'

'For fertility?' Clary winces at her faux pas. 'For creativity, I mean?'

'Spot on, Clary. If you look closely, you'll see some bark chips scattered on the surface of the water in the vase. There are more, and they tend to sink. Any guesses?'

Cat bites her tongue. *Isn't that what humans say when they try not to let the ... oh no, here it comes*, she cringes ... *try not to let the cat out of the bag? See if Clary or Milly get it. A good challenge for them. Let them flex their curiosity, think outside the – um – vase. The best way to come up with the answer.*

Milly's in first, eyebrows dancing, giving a squeal of delight. 'Bark from your woodpile near the apple tree, the one where the woodlice live. No harm done to woodlice, but you're adding something of their essence that has seeped into the decaying wood. You have the fertility trifecta: crushed woodlice – in essence – rose and rosemary.'

'That's it. I have one at the front door, too. No-one ever enters that way, but it feels right to bless the flow of energy through the house. A Briar twist on feng shui. But come in, come in.' He stands aside. 'Step into my parlour.'

Cat leads the way, chooses the best vantage point, an ornately carved, broad-stepped oaken ladder propped against the far wall, springs to the middle rung, and settles back into psychic-queen attitude, sphinx-pose version.

'Parlour, you got me there,' Clary says, wide-eyed and grinning. 'Classic historic cottage that's been in the family for generations, medieval-medicine-inspired garden, solid traditional boot room and then this. A million miles from any parlour I've ever seen or envisaged.'

Cat takes a more considered look at her surroundings. *None the wiser*, she thinks. *Not a style guru, a psychic guru. Psychic reader, not guru. Queen not guru. Queen psychic reader. Hungry queen psychic reader.*

'This room is just a beginning.' Briar runs his hand over a pearl-studded oak cabinet tipped with wizardly curlicues. 'The other rooms are more traditional, as Dad left them. He would never have approved of this.'

'Didn't you say your dad died three years ago, Briar?' Milly extracts her reading glasses from her leather satchel and examines the pearl inlay, closely. 'You haven't made all this furniture in just three years, surely?'

'How do you know I'm the artist?'

Cat feels it in her bones and purr-congratulates Milly on her insight, forgetting that Milly doesn't speak cat language.

'Have more faith in me, Briar, I'm an investigative journalist. There's something about the shapes and lines in your garden that's reflected in here but given a modern twist. No, given a unique

Briar-shaped twist. The materials are traditional – timbers, pearl – but the designs speak to someone finding a new voice while encompassing the past. Am I right?'

'I'm impressed, Milly. I've been told since childhood that I'm responsible for our ongoing legacy, keeping the gardens intact, adhering to the rituals our family has been following for almost four hundred years, and I'm honoured to do so. It's been a hands-on legacy since the start, all recorded in the logbooks. I was trained in the practicalities of gardening, and Dad didn't really understand why I wanted to go to university to study landscape design. "You can't change these gardens," he used to tell me. "Your legacy is to maintain and protect these grounds and their secrets." I accept that, but I also want to develop my own ideas.'

'It's the secrets that excite me,' Milly says, 'but I understand the need to break free and cut your own path. After my twin sister, Jade, died four years ago, I struggled to see myself doing the same job for the rest of my life, constrained within the rules of investigative television journalism. But I didn't know what else to do. In the end, I resigned and moved here on a whim. It's only since my reading with Freya, when she conveyed the message from Jade to do some digging, that my mojo has returned, but with a new direction. It's like finding a way to use my old, more traditional skills to create a new voice, to contribute in a different way. Not sure if I'm making sense.'

'You're making complete sense, Milly.' Clary reaches out and touches her arm.

'I went along with Dad's vision while he was alive.' Briar walks over to the ladder to stroke Cat. 'I did a little landscape design for other people, but it was working with wood that called to me. Tim, the old bloke down the road, gave me the run of his old shed, and I started experimenting with crafting furniture there. Sold a couple of pieces. Stored the rest because I couldn't bear to part with it. Glad I did. It's what you see here.'

'What did you do with your dad's parlour furniture?'

Clary gives up waiting for an invitation to sit, dropping onto a cushioned chaise longue carved in a shape reminiscent of the topiary Reclining Woman with Child.

'Most of it is squeezed into the other rooms here,' Briar vaguely points upstairs, 'though he didn't have that much. Some church pews going back a few centuries, but woodworm got the best of most of the older furniture. Dad inherited his father's early Victorian pieces, not at all my style, but I've yet to let them go.'

'This pearl inlay,' Milly traces her fingers over the smooth, translucent shapes embedded in the oak cabinet, 'they're tiny crescent moons, aren't they? When we came for the picnic, you mentioned the traditional new-moon ritual, making an offering of crushed woodlice to the Reclining Woman with Child. Are these pearl crescents related?'

'You are standing before the altar, Milly.' Briar steps towards the cabinet. 'Did you notice all the drawers? No, of course you didn't, because they're disguised. Stand back and watch.' He bends down, presses his thumb on some unseen point underneath the cabinet, simultaneously touches several of the pearl moons, then flicks one of the wizardly curlicues embellishing the top. The cabinet springs open, like a toolbox popping out a multitude of trays. 'Glad you stood back?' He grins. 'Takes up twice the space when open, but it's easier to look through the files this way. And yes, these are the secret family logbooks, and yes, yours are the first eyes outside our family to see these in almost four hundred years.'

Cat jumps down to get closer. Clary bounds up from the chaise longue to catch Cat before she can dig her claws into the enticing, parchment-scented papers inside. 'Let's look from here, Amantha,' Clary whispers.

Briar lifts a file from the cabinet, his hands shaking, his body trembling as if caught in an earthquake. 'Such is the power of my father and my long line of forefathers,' he says, a high-pitched squeak of a voice, his tight throat strangling his words. 'I had no idea this was going to be so emotional.'

Clary gently touches his shoulder. 'You don't have to do this today if you need more time, or never if it doesn't feel right, Briar. Family secrets are family secrets.'

Briar carefully places the file across the open cabinet, smiles a thankyou at Clary, swallows hard, and pulls a pair of soft white gloves from another secret compartment. 'I need to break the ice, show you one page today, sleep on it, then reconvene to show you more later in the week. One quick look, then I'll find my feet and get our afternoon tea underway.

'No photos today, Milly,' he says. 'I'm not sure about the effect of light on the parchment. That's something we'll need to research, but let me show you a page from one hundred years ago. I prefer not to handle the older pages just yet.'

Milly and Clary lean forward, Clary's hands firmly clutching Cat.

'The format of each page is identical right from the start on the fifteenth of April sixteen twenty-three, except that an extra item was added on the third of September sixteen ninety-eight, the date Henry Gable completed his Reclining Woman with Child topiary. From that date on, all the pages include that extra item to log the maintenance and care of the topiary. So this one, from one hundred years ago, has been unchanged in format since that autumn day in sixteen ninety-eight.'

Cat sees only columns, lines, squiggles and inky handwriting in various styles. She swishes her tail and wishes one of them would read aloud or make some helpful comment.

'Lots of symbols, I see,' says Milly. 'What do they stand for?'

'Some of them are family symbols, meaningful only to us, my ancestors' way of hiding our gardening formulae and medicinal remedies from prying eyes.'

'Let me guess.' Milly pushes her reading glasses further up her nose. 'I can't see the point of hiding gardening formulae or commonly known medicinal remedies unless these relate to witches or healers your family was protecting from persecution.

But my journalist's nose tells me there's something else. Am I right?'

'About the witches and healers,' Briar says, 'I believe so. About there being something else, I don't know. I feel it, too, and I'm as curious as you, which is why I'm ready to consider looking into this with your help. But the time is also right because ...'

Cat shudders, the sense of a hand gently lifting her overwhelming, despite Clary's firm grasp. Heart pounding, aroma of red raspberry leaves, essence of fear, sweat of hurry, a nearby jet-black horse glistening in the rain, stomping a hoof, a whispered thankyou, a hand resetting her onto her cushion, no, into a basket with a soft cloth, posies of daisies, raindrops as the horse departs, the air quietening, a rainbow.

Clary stoops. 'Are you okay, Amantha? You're shaking.'

Cat looks at Briar and understands, her vision fading. He has no children, no heirs, no-one to keep the logbooks, no-one to tend the land, no-one to keep the family secrets. No-one to follow the rules.

'She's probably hungry.' Briar regains his humour. 'Tea time!'

A short time later, stomach replete with exceptionally tasty fishy biscuits and cream, Cat nods off, sprawled across Clary's lap, waking later, much refreshed, to the chink of wineglasses and Milly's voice saying, 'We'll drink to that, Briar.'

'To the book, then the National Trust.' Briar raises his glass and takes a sip. 'This is such a relief. Even if I did have children – and who knows what the future may bring on that score – I wouldn't want to saddle them with the obligation to be the hands-on gardeners, to stay here, to protect secrets that they – like me – don't really understand. I'd want them to be free to follow their passions, create their own legacies, or just enjoy living day to day without the burden of ancestral expectation.'

Cat yawns. *To just enjoy living day to day without the burden of an increasingly heavy mission. To picnic with Clary and Milly, to play with Pearl, to create my own legacy in the shape of my psychic readings, to follow my nose and do what I want to do, to write my own rules instead of checking, checking, checking that other people are following rules laid down long ago by someone else. Wouldn't that be nice? But where would that get me? And why do my bones urge me to guard and protect this place and its rules like my life depends on it?*

'Come round again on Wednesday,' Briar opens the back gate for Milly and Clary, 'and we'll begin the detective work.'

A silver moon guides them home just in time for Cat to slink inside before Emmy locks up for the night.

🐾

'Come on, video queen, puss-puss.' Abby crouches down to Cat's level, holding out her fingers as if she has food, which Cat clearly sees she does not.

'Watch out, she'll scratch you,' Hazel says, passing by in a beeline for the café. 'She hates being called puss-puss. I know, I tried it the first time I met her, before she changed her mind about me and gave me the crushed woodlice message. I still have a scar on the back of my hand – look.'

'I know. I do it to tease her.' Abby pulls out her phone and holds it close to Cat's nose. 'Come on, puss-puss, show me your snarly face.'

Cat can tease too. She pulls her hoity-toity face, holds her head high and walks into the classroom like she's got all the time in the world, like she's the keeper of psychic secrets, the one who will decide what to tell whom and when. Then she lowers her head, looks straight into the camera and gives her best transmit look: star-spangled, hypnotising eyes.

Abby stops videoing her. 'Lovely work, Amantha. Subject for this week's video is "Amantha: Psychic Queen". What do you think?'

'Teasing, or for real?' Clary pulls open the blinds in the room.

Morning light strikes Cat's nest of cushions, her stage, occupying pride of place in front of the art tables. Last week's portraits still perch on the easels, no longer reeking of wet paint. Cat takes the long route to her throne, as she now sees it, a slow prowl past the paintings before the students arrive. One looks exactly like her reflection in the café mirror, all honeyed limbs and self-satisfied repose. One or two are more fluid, feline shapes, snatches of colour close to her own. One is a bunch of leaves, no, rosemary sprigs, and is that really a woodlouse in the corner? And the tip of her nose, or some cat's nose, whiskers a touch too thick, some clumsy brushwork, but quite intriguing, a sense of her entering the picture, exploring nature. One painting is a whorl of orange golds, nothing more, but astonishingly mesmerising.

'For real,' says Abby. 'As a teaser, so both, really.'

Clary starts unloading an assortment of picture frames and craft supplies from her backpack. 'A teaser for Freya's psychic readings?'

'Not really, or maybe, not decided yet. We're about to launch our new branding, dropping Rajpapa's lotus from the imagery, and making Amantha our focus symbol. She's to be the Yin face of the centre, a much-needed energy shift after the Rajpapa debacle.'

'Is Serenity going to change the yoga style, then? More towards Yin yoga, you mean?'

'It's more than that.' Abby picks up her painting, the mesmerising orange whorls. 'She's undecided about the yoga at this point. She asked Mariana to teach the usual formula but without reference to Rajpapa until she returns. Have you been going to her classes?'

'I've done a couple. She's a good teacher. I miss Serenity, but Mariana is guiding us to focus on the yoga rather than on the guru behind the system, and it feels right. I feel like I'm getting more in touch with my intuition rather than being restrained by one of Rajpapa's themes. And none of us, given what's happened, want to hear his name bandied about.'

'Look, we'll be rolling out the new branding and marketing starting from next week, so you might as well know, and I'm interested to hear your thoughts. With Serenity in London, it's mostly been left to me to come up with the ideas and then run them past her. I'm loving the creativity, wondering even if this isn't more in line with my passions than my psychotherapy work.'

'If your portrait of Amantha is anything to go by,' Clary draws up a stool beside Abby and gazes at the painting, 'creative work suits you. This is off the wall, way beyond left field, yet spot on. You've captured Amantha's essence perfectly, the way she mesmerises us, the messages she transmits. I could sit in front of your work and let it speak to me, just as Amantha does. Discover what I need to know. A psychic reading with Amantha but without her in the room. You may be onto something with your new video idea.'

Cat's stomach flips. This whole psychic-guru gig is about having a platform to communicate directly with people, to give them her wisdom and guidance, to help them follow the rules, to protect and save the centre, and, let's face it, if she is to be the icon for the centre, people will want to sit in her presence and meet the real video queen. On the other paw, thousands of people could purchase her portrait to hang in their homes or above their altars, helping to fund the continuation of the centre. And when she finally graduates her ninth life, people would have something to remember her by before she adopts the mantle of invisibility as a behind-the-physical-scenes spirit mentor to an earthbound being.

'Thank you, Clary, I appreciate your encouragement. You're superbly skilled, and we'd love to see your art classes continue and expand in some way. We're looking at flipping the concept of this place on its head so that rather than being a yoga centre offering some services on the side, it becomes a health, wellbeing and creativity centre, with a range of services, classes and retail spaces, including yoga.'

'And how does your proposed video of "Amantha: Psychic Queen" fit in?'

'You've just commended me for my off-the-wall creativity, well, here it is in action. She's already a top cat in viral-cat-video land, so we can leverage that in any direction we choose. There's chitchat around the village already about her reputed psychic skills – Hazel's story is spreading like wildfire. I don't fancy the chances of the local woodlice if there are any around here. I'm half running on humour – use the videos to get people interested in our offerings, old and new – and I'm half serious. You've experienced her messages. What if we set up an open day, or a fundraiser, and get you to sit with Amantha and interpret her messages for people? It could be a fantastic promotion for the centre. An opportunity for us to see what she's capable of while passing it off as a bit of fun to draw people in. Anyway, here come your students. Think about it and let me know.'

🐾

It's strange having people in the centre on a Sunday, an intrusion into Cat's weekend solitude, but she knows in her bones that her quiet days are numbered. If the centre is to flourish, it needs to operate seven days a week, and perhaps evenings, as well. She bounds up the stairs to check out the preparations in the yoga room, where today's abundance workshop kicks off in an hour. When people start to arrive, she'll take up her welcoming position on the altar. Yes, on the altar, not beside it. Take command, get their full attention, keep everyone in line, because today they're expecting eighty-eight people to crowd into the space: practitioners, regular clients, people from the village and a group coming down from London in a minibus.

'Are you ready for eighty-eight adoring fans to pat you or call you puss-puss?' Abby greets Cat at the top of the stairs. 'Better be on your best behaviour – no scratching. They're only human, after all. People love cats.'

It takes Cat a moment to realise the eighty-eight people are Frankie Jay's adoring fans, and most won't know Cat from any other sweet-looking, honey-coloured feline pet. Though, some might recognise her if they've been watching the videos. *No scratching. Be humble. Stick to her job.*

'We could have sold this event ten times over if we had more space.' Abby drops to her knees to push a heavy cardboard box from the landing into the yoga room. 'Come with me, Amantha. Help me unpack.'

Cat slinks onto her belly to sniff the box, essence of printing ink, no further clues.

'Or twenty times over. It's going to be a tight squeeze as it is. That's how famous Frankie Jay is. That's how much Serenity is willing to invest in Freya, Emmy and me to give us the confidence to raise our fees. Can you imagine! The tickets were sold out within an hour of release, and at five hundred and fifty pounds a pop, that won't even touch the amount Frankie Jay has invoiced. People want to know how they can charge the kind of fees she commands, and they'll throw their savings and next week's rent into discovering the secret formula. They'll get more than their investment back, they think, so what's there to lose? That's how the model works, I suspect. It's a scam, if you ask me, but shh, don't tell. And I'm willing to suspend my disbelief given that the workshop is free for Freya, Emmy and me. So glad I can confide in you, Amantha. It helps to hear my thoughts spoken out loud. All you need to do is sit there, and I feel so much better.'

Cat's ears prick at the word *scam*. *What's Serenity doing inviting a scam artist into the centre? What message is that giving about us? Us?* She sits bolt upright. It's the first time she's referred to herself as being one of them – their resident psychic cat? She prowls around Abby's box, flicking her tail from left to right, discomfort unsettling her bones. Which is it? Their guardian and protector, or a practitioner, helping and guiding those who seek her wisdom? Which is it, Cat on her way to graduation via all the responsibilities that entails, or letting go of that dream in favour of a less-pressured life as a psychic reader and another round of earthbound lives?

A rip of packing tape and the creak of cardboard announces the grand opening of the box.

'Oh, look.' Abby pulls out a neatly bound journal. 'Oh, hasn't that turned out well. Look, Amantha.'

Big, bold and orange, Abby's mesmerising whorl painting of Cat adorns the cover. 'I'm being cheeky, testing the waters, you'll see.' She pulls another few journals from the box, all with the same cover, and soon there's a mountain of them piled on the table just inside the entrance to the yoga room. 'Okay, let's take our places and let the fun begin.'

Cat trots back out to the altar and leaps into position, sending a couple of crystals and an incense stick flying. Clumsy for a sure-footed cat, one, as it turns out, slightly put off balance by the sudden realisation that Abby's original painting now occupies the space where Rajpapa's portrait once hung. Her head spins. Is she the new guru, or is this all part of Abby's test-the-water plan? And what on earth does that mean, anyway, 'test the water'?

Cat sits tight through the onslaught of arrivals, focusing her gaze on every pair of eyes that looks her way, transmitting, as best she can, do no harm, help and heal, her anti-scam, rule-abiding mantra.

Last up the stairs is Emmy, her cream pantsuit, soft rose-coloured silk shirt and triple-pearl necklace a stunning contrast to the voluptuous, magpie of a woman she accompanies. The magpie, long floating tapestry coat, a rainbow of expensive-looking baubles draped across her chest, their cousins sparkling from every single finger, false eyelashes blinking at Cat, must be Frankie Jay. 'What a gorgeous puss-puss,' the magpie drawls, American accent, digging her red-painted claws into Cat's skin, her long black hair with its single streak of white flicking Cat's paws.

'I'll let Abby know you're here, Frankie.' Emmy pops her head into the room and signals a thumbs up. 'She's going to introduce you, then I'll walk you down to the podium and it's all over to you. Everything else you need is already set up at the front. Give me a sign when you're ready for your first break, and we'll bring everyone down to the café for morning tea. I'm so looking forward to your workshop.'

Cat jumps down from the altar, gives the magpie a wide berth and slips into the back of the room and onto a windowsill. Eighty-eight excited bodies, mostly women, the scent of just about every perfume Cat knows underscored by essence of anticipation, sitting tall in rows of hard-backed chairs, bright-orange journals on laps.

'Welcome to the Serene Lotus Centre for Health and Wellbeing.' Abby waits a heartbeat while the room stills. 'I know you're as excited as I am to meet Frankie Jay and learn how you can pump up your abundance and enjoy a wealthier future. I'm Abby, the resident psychotherapist, and it's my job to warm you up. I'm the support act, if you like, to the big ticket. But don't worry, the support act is all of forty-five seconds long and is in the shape of our latest cat video. I know some of you have enjoyed our videos of Amantha, our resident psychic cat, on social media. She has a huge following. Not as many as Frankie Jay, but who knows what she may learn after today's workshop to enhance her profile. There she is, in person, or should I say in cat, gracing the windowsill behind you.'

The shuffle of bodies, craning of necks, waves, blowing of kisses, Cat's blood pumping in her ears. She manages to sweep her eyes across the crowd, trying to exude wisdom.

'Sit back and enjoy the premiere of "Amantha: Psychic Cat". Just for fun, we'll keep tabs on the number of views as the day unfolds. If it's anything like her previous videos it will go massively viral before afternoon tea. Think of it as a metaphor for the rapid soar in abundance you will experience when you take Frankie Jay's teachings home with you at the end of the day.' Abby turns to face the screen behind her, clicks the remote and there is Cat, as seen by Abby down the camera lens, in tiny, pixelated boxes too difficult for Cat to appreciate, but the audience bursts into a rapture of claps and adoring laughs as the video comes to an end. The final shot is Abby's painting, a glorious, mesmerising orange finish that lingers on the screen as the audience quietens.

'The same picture as you see on the journal you found on your chair. A touch of magic from Amantha. Take a minute to stare at the picture. I'll let you know when the minute is up. Ask a question, expect an answer from Amantha as you enter the mesmerising whorls. First, a moment to think of your question.' Abby drops her head and waits. 'The minute begins now.'

Cat asks a question in her head, not sure if she can consult herself through the picture, but eager to try. *Which way should I go, guardian and protector, or psychic reader?*

A crystal tone rings and Abby steps back from the vibrating singing bowl. 'The minute is up.'

Cat's bones have spoken. *Find the Silver Crescent Nest that Pearl mentioned.* Not the answer she was expecting, but it feels right. Although, she has no idea what it means or where to start.

'You can write Amantha's message on the first page of your journal, if you wish.' Abby holds her palm against the singing bowl to still the sound. A flurry of scribbling and pages turning. Time for Cat to remember something Milly said at Briar's, something about the pearl crescent moons on the cabinet he built to store his family secrets.

'And now, let me hand you over to the woman who needs no introduction, the woman who will take you on a fabulous, life-changing journey on this beautiful day. Please welcome the magnificent Frankie Jay!'

'Are you ready to feather your nest? To build your nest egg? To see your fledgling ideas take flight, spread far and wide, and bring you all the financial returns you desire?' The magpie spreads her arms like wings, baubles a-jingling. 'Let me hear you. Speak up. How are you going to make more money if you can't make yourself heard? Are you ready?'

A muffling mumble rumbles around the audience, as the magpie points a finger at Freya. 'Are you ready, Freya?'

'Yes,' Freya warbles, 'yes, yes, yes,' resonance cautiously mounting.

'Are you ready,' the magpie leans in to read a nametag, 'Anna?'

'I'm always ready for a bit of extra money.' Anna's neck burns red. If she had feathers, they'd be severely ruffled.

'Let me hear it, Anna – yes, yes, yes!'

'Yes, I'm ready.'

The magpie cups her hands to her ears. 'Everybody, can I hear you? Are you ready?'

'Yes!' the chorus gains shaky strength.

The magpie signals for more noise, a conductor gaining control of her orchestra, and here they go, an echoing reverberation of yeses and head nods. The moment has come: the magpie has them eating from her jewel-encrusted hands.

Cat makes her way over to Abby and climbs onto her lap. The magpie is talking about feathering nests, with money presumably, with gold and silver. Is this a sign, something to do with Pearl's Silver Crescent Nest? She engages her antennae ears, not wanting to miss a word.

'Let's start with your nest.' The magpie clicks the remote and points at the screen. Nothing much for Cat to see other than squiggles and what the magpie is calling flow charts. Or pie charts, or ...

'Actually, let's not look at charts.' The magpie double-clicks and a single white feather appears on the screen. 'Abundance and attracting money into your life have nothing to do with science and everything to do with feelings, visions and a few simple tips I'm going to share with you today. One feather doesn't go far in lining your nest, but get the vibration right and ...' she clicks the remote once more, 'everything you need comes to you.' Feathers float into vision and magically line the nest on the screen.

'A bird cannot fly with one feather alone.' The magpie mimics a hapless bird trying to get airborne. 'But with an abundance of flight feathers, the world is her oyster.' She rises to her toes, as if to take flight. Cat readies for her take-off, but there are no hidden wires and the magpie remains grounded.

Oysters, Cat thinks. *Pearls, Pearl, pearly silver nests.*

'Open your journals and write down how much you charge for an hour's work if you offer a service. If you sell products, write down how much you receive for an hour's work. If you don't have a business yet, write down what you would probably charge per hour if you were a coach of some kind, maybe a life coach.'

Cat purrs into the silence. Her nest is already feathered; she doesn't need money. She has a home here at the centre, she is fed and loved, and her market reach is measured in millions. She is an attraction, and if people paid to consult her as a psychic reader, she could save the centre and help Abby, Emmy and Freya keep their jobs. What would her hourly rate for that be?

'Now add a zero to your figure,' the magpie says. 'So, if you wrote eighty pounds an hour, write down eight hundred pounds an hour. Go on, don't think about it, just do it. Look at that number, how does it make you feel? Close your eyes, picture a client paying you that amount in cash – make it cash, it's more tangible. How does it make you feel? Write down how you feel.'

Cat zones in and out. Maths makes no sense. A distant lawnmower starts up, Briar probably. Sunlight strikes the window and plays at highlighting everyone's hair. Cat extends a leg into the light, more hues of honey and marmalade than she's ever noticed before. Even ginger, gold, pink, yellow and flecks of silver where her whiskers flicker into her peripheral view. She floats for eons. Or maybe she flies, a bird leaving her nest, feeling the uplift of her powerful wings, or the sense of weightlessness she will enjoy when she leaves the earthly plane and becomes a spirit mentor one day.

'So now, you're all comfortable with charging at least ten times your current fee,' the magpie screeches. 'And feeling sexy about finally letting your divine energy shine. Let's up the ante. Think beyond selling your services for an hour, or your single product. Think packaging. What add-ons can you, um, add on? I'm not thinking, "Do you want chips with that?" I'm thinking your client gets you for an hour plus access to your online course for a year, plus membership of an elite private social media support group, where you post podcasts and tips, plus an invitation to share their story for your next book (and save you from looking for more material), plus VIP invitations to your book or product launches. Maybe you add another zero to your fee, maybe your package is eight thousand, or add another zero and maybe it's eighty thousand, for very little extra work on your behalf and a guarantee that you'll have plenty of people turn up for your launches and they'll talk you up in the support groups and do the work for you by chatting to and supporting each other. You might add gift certificates for other businesses and services that are keen to offer a free session as a promotion. I'm talking about passive income: there's only one of you, and you're not going to be able to enjoy your feathered nest if you're working hard all the time. Break up into groups of four, please, and help each other out. Give each other suggestions, make them silly, over the top, wild, outrageous. That's where the magic is. Go do it now.'

Suddenly Cat is flying, tucked under Abby's arm as she rushes from the room, whispering, 'Just checking on the morning-tea situation,' to Emmy on the way out.

But they go nowhere near the café. They fly into the garden, out of earshot from anyone save the cloud of silvery-blue butterflies hovering above Abby's head. Abby pulls out her phone and jabs the screen.

'Hi, Serenity. Yes, it's going very well. I'll fill you in tonight, but I want to run something past you now if you've got a minute or two.'

Cat wishes Abby would lighten her hold, give her a little more room to breathe, but she also wants to stay close to hear Serenity.

'I do, you sound excited, breathless even.'

'I have an idea to save the centre. I want to run it past you so you can chat with your legal team and advisors, then perhaps we can talk about it in more detail tonight.'

'I'm all ears, Abby.'

'I'm not going to dress it up. You're happy with bringing Amantha into our brand, the new Yin energy we've talked about ...'

'Yes.'

'I want to take that further. You've been happy with the Amantha videos I've created, and I know from the number of views that they're generating income from the ads, a small amount in your terms, a very significant, rent-paying amount in my terms, so for starters I'd like to formalise our arrangement, receive a fee for creating the videos and eighty percent of the advertising revenue and ...'

Cat's ears strain, but she still hears Serenity's voice. 'Keep going, I'm listening.'

'I want to copyright or trademark – not sure which applies – Amantha as a brand, so that only we, no-one else, can use her in business. I'm going to make her famous. She's going to be our psychic reader and we can charge people to consult her. I know it sounds silly, but stay with me. People will pay to consult her and they'll pay big. She's a cat, she doesn't need money, but the centre does and so do I. I'd also like to write a book about her or bring her into a book I write about psychotherapy, and I'd like to think we could stop anyone else from doing the same, because with the fame she's going to get, other people will think of it. On a smaller scale – or maybe larger, I don't know – we could sell licensing rights to a jeweller to make iconic Amantha jewellery, or cups with her image, or, I don't know, this is probably your territory not mine. On that score, I'm thinking whatever money we make from her psychic readings, and products, licensing fees and so on, you get twenty percent, the centre gets twenty percent and I get sixty percent.' She gulps, strong essence of endorphin tickling Cat's nostrils.

Cat leans in, eager to hear Serenity's response. 'It's a lot for me to think about, Abby, but in principle, yes. I'll talk with my people and get back to you this evening. We need something wildly outrageous, and I trust you. I have no idea how a cat can give psychic readings, but I like a good marketing idea. Why don't you give it a test whirl at the Open Day this week? Got to go. Enjoy the rest of Frankie Jay's workshop.'

Abby cradles Cat as they walk back towards the café just in time to welcome everyone in for morning tea. 'I still think Frankie Jay's a scam artist,' Abby whispers in Cat's ear, 'but she triggered that idea and I feel like I'm bouncing off the walls, as if I've had ten cups of coffee. I'm so excited for us, for you and me.'

Bouncing off the walls? Cat feels responsibility overload, a severe need for time out with Pearl. She meows, gives Abby what she judges to be a warm, conspiratorial look, and speeds into the topiary garden, far, far away from the deafening café noise and its tsunami of contradictory essences.

🐾

'Up here, in the Reclining Woman,' Pearl calls, a beautiful pearly snowball puffed up in the reclining woman's lap, the pale full moon glimmering in the clear summer sky, framing her face, a halo, an ethereal crown.

'Dare I? Isn't she kind of sacred?' Cat stalls, looking up through a dancing cloud of pearly butterflies. 'Is it allowed?'

'I don't think there's a rule, Cat. I know rules are sacred to you, but consult your bones.'

'This isn't one for my bones, Pearl. This is one for the written rules, the rules I need to ensure everyone follows if I am to graduate.'

'Run through them, then.' Pearl yawns her snowball shape into a fluffy cloud, and settles it into a pearly thinker's pose, chin resting on raised paw, eyes slightly upturned.

'Rule one: will I harm the topiary if I jump into it? I think not. The reclining woman has withstood well over three hundred years of weather extremes, Briar's topiary shears, nesting blackbirds and heavy pearly cats. I'm light of paw and also in awe, so much awe, perhaps, that my appreciation and gratitude will seep into her branches and uplift her heart. So, joining you up there would do no harm and can only do good. To her and to me. To me, because I need your comfort and support, which brings me to the second rule.'

'Rule two,' Pearl purrs benevolently. 'I'm here to help and heal you, and since all transactions are equally balanced, you will help and heal me, too. Rule number three?'

'Rule three: support each other. Well, you've just covered that one, Pearl, which brings us to rule four. That's a tricky one.'

'How so?'

'If I leave my troubles at home, I bring you what I consider to be the best of myself, my focus on the present, my mindfulness, my love, light and joy, but it's my troubles I want to talk about. How can you support, help and heal me if you don't know of my troubles? And how can I heal a troubled heart if I bury those troubles so deep that I cannot hear them or resolve them? And – so many ands, I didn't realise there was so much to consider – what use is home as a refuge if all I face when I go back there is a bunch of troubles?'

'Which is more important to you, Cat, to abide by the rules or resolve your troubles?'

'I'm torn.'

'And so you will remain unless you jump up here and bathe in this sweet, sacred daytime moonlight with me. Listen to your bones, Cat. Bones trump rules.'

Tonight, Cat knows, she will sleep beneath the stars, nestled in Reclining Woman's lap, as Pearl traces the constellations with their right paw, shares their sacred stories and soothes her troubles. The magpie fled hours ago, ego replete – no doubt, with a dozen converts to her ten-thousand-pound 'Live the dream: become an abundance coach' course – the London minibus in her wake, eighty-eight pairs of dollar-dazzled eyes heading home to put an end to their financial troubles. So easy to see from this higher topiary perspective.

'You told me to meet people where they're at.' Cat shifts her balance on a particularly prickly brush-box twig. 'Serenity has been honest about her situation, she cares for the practitioners and she's trying to address her wrongdoings or miscalculations. It's easy to judge her, but I'm meeting her where she's at, ready to remind her of the rules if she falters again. Emmy's fear of not being able to pay extra rent led to her making a hypnotic suggestion to her client to book extra sessions, which broke several rules including her professional ethics, but she noticed straightaway and admitted her error. I didn't need to reprimand her. I'm meeting her where she's at, rulebook in paws to refer to if necessary.'

Pearl eases their body back, reclining cat aligning with Reclining Woman. Cat follows suit.

'I'm trying to cool-cat it around Freya. She still sees me as just a cat, but she's making a good job of rule keeping after her cheating episodes. My bones are troubled around her and I'm listening to them, moment by moment.'

'From what you say,' Pearl tilts their chin further skywards, 'you're keeping pace with your mission to guide and protect.'

'But where do my responsibilities end, Pearl? Guarding and protecting the centre and all who sail in her feels impossible. Do you know how many hundreds of thousands of people this involves, including people who enter the hallowed halls, and those who step inside from the dark side like the magpie scam queen?'

'A tsunami of troubles, I see.'

'And then you ask me to look out for a Silver Crescent Nest because it holds the key, and I'm overwhelmed, confused, lost. A few clues that seem to contradict each other. On top of all this, I'm experiencing those weirded-out visions, the ones you said might be flashbacks from one of my earlier eight lives. I'm a hallucinating detective as well as rule keeper, guardian and protector. How's that for troubles?'

Pearl rolls onto their side, nudging Cat off balance.

'Whoa, what are you trying to do?' Cat regains her position.

'Tell me about Abby.'

'I'll come to Abby. Briar's caught between following his ancestors' rules and breaking them, but breaking them for the betterment of all, as far as I can tell. Milly is on an ethical crusade, and Clary is creating courses where she teaches some classic art rules and advocates breaking others. All their work looks good, but it does my head in trying to navigate where they need my guidance and protection, and whether their pioneering – and my apparent condoning of their rule breaking – will hinder my graduation.'

'So, it's about hindering your graduation, not about people doing good work?'

'I didn't mean it to sound like that.'

'But that's what it is.'

'Which brings me to Abby.' Cat shakes her head, resisting sleep, as the first glimmer of light breaks in the eastern sky. 'She's got this wild plan to set me up as a psychic reader ...'

'Stop right there, Cat.' Pearl raises their paw. 'You've talked to me before about wanting to be acknowledged for your psychic wisdom, so don't fob this off as Abby's wild plan. At some level, you manifested this opportunity. If you want my help and support, you need to be honest with me. Replay that thought for me.'

Cat hunches her shoulders, cowers her head and takes a deep breath. 'Anyone would think you follow me around, or live inside my head. Do I even need to tell you the truth? Don't you know it, already?'

'It's always good to express yourself in words in an empty room, or to someone who will keep your secrets. Isn't that what Abby, Emmy and Freya have each told you, and others, I imagine? Hearing things spoken can give you new perspective. A cat, or a therapist – and I happen to be both – afford you that safe space.'

'You're a therapist, Pearl?'

'For the sake of this argument. Don't nitpick. Except for that little nit right there in your groin.'

Cat sits up and lifts her back leg to take a closer look.

'Got you,' Pearl sniggers. 'You're far too clean a cat for nits.'

Cat rearranges herself, demurely. 'Okay, I'll come clean. At the last HQ meeting, Emmy said Freya is the honeypot for the centre because people love psychic readings. It hit me there and then, the potential for attracting more people and bringing in much-needed cash to guard and protect the centre from closing. I experienced that moment when two things collide and make sense. What do you call that, serendipity or something? I did my "one meow, two meows, three meows, transmit" on Abby. She's as good as Clary at receiving my messages.'

'What did you transmit?'

'"People love psychic readings and people love cats. Let's put the two together." She got it straightaway, and the same words tumbled from her lips. Her plan evolved from there.'

'Excited though you are, you're calling the plan wild.'

'Nitpick!'

'The observation stands.'

'I'm all wobbly in the guts, Pearl. It's one thing to see something like Hazel's need for crushed woodlice, or Freya cheating on Clary, or giving a wise nudge here or there. But if people are paying money for my psychic advice, what if I draw a blank?'

'You'll find out soon enough. When's your first gig?'

'At the Open Day this week.'

'Keep an open mind, see what happens.' Pearl yawns and hefts themself onto their paws, a long, slow back arch, the prelude to a parting shot. 'Look out for the Silver Crescent Nest, Cat.'

'About that nest ...' Cat's words evaporate as Pearl shimmers inside a dewy morning mist rising from Reclining Woman's lap, and the grind of gravel announces the arrival of Emmy's car. If she runs fast, Cat can slip in through the door with Emmy and eat last night's dinner if it's still there, maybe breakfast, too. She's ravenous, exhausted and ready for a nap.

🐾

It's all Cat can do, after a quick kip, to haul herself up to HQ, a Monday-morning meeting she can't fail to miss. She doesn't need her bones to tell her the obvious agenda. Open Day, with some possibly contentious discussion about her psychic-reader debut. And some juicy gossip in the aftermath of the magpie's visit.

What she doesn't expect is an extra attendee. Mariana, wafting in wearing loose muslin yoga pants lightly embellished with silver daisies, a cream cashmere post-yoga shawl, and an exquisite jay feather – turquoise stripes like luminescent piano keys – slipped into her raven topknot. Essence of violet, matching eyes, aquiline nose, unlined skin. Cat hesitates, giving her a wide berth, unsure about the jay feather. Windowsill seat for today.

'I loved your class this morning, Mariana.' Abby appears, skin glowing red, essence of shower soap, flyers in hand. 'You have a magic touch. I feel refreshed and energised yet slowed down, a smell-the-roses kind of feel, I guess.'

'Close.' Mariana takes the seat Abby offers at the table. 'I used violet leaf in the infuser today, a modern witch's love spell, a pick-me-up after a relationship breakdown. That's what's been so good about standing in for Serenity for a while, leaving London, the scene of a spectacular relationship breakdown if ever there was one. Girlfriend was cheating on me.'

Cat focuses on Mariana. Leaving her troubles at home? Abiding by rule number four but not addressing her troubles, according to Pearl's pearl of wisdom.

'Oh, Mariana, we didn't know.' Abby beams compassion.

'Thank you. Violet leaf is also a spell for abundance and confidence. Appropriate, I thought, in the wake of Frankie Jay's workshop yesterday.'

'Ah,' Emmy says, 'hence the jay feather in your hair.'

'Well spotted.' Mariana removes the feather and shakes out her hair. 'I'm experimenting with combining symbolism and yoga.'

Cat sits tall, pointing her ears in Mariana's direction. A rule breaker. Experimenting with the ancient rules of yoga.

Essence of tangerine mist enters the room. Freya, always last to arrive. 'Sorry, guys, it's so tight finishing at the post office at nine am and our meeting starting at, oh my goodness, five minutes ago.'

Abby places the pile of flyers on the desk, face down, amethyst crystal on top to weight them, a secret yet to be revealed. 'Serenity's going to join us by Zoom any moment now. She invited Mariana, and I think we can all say we're delighted to have you with us, Mariana. You've been a lifesaver for our yoga classes, and from the feedback I've heard, all the students are enjoying your classes and your careful curating to exclude references to Rajpapa.'

Serenity pops up in all her pixelated glory on the big HQ screen. Cat squints to see if it makes the picture clearer. She seems to be in a blue room today.

'It's so lovely to see you all and imagine being back with you in the centre of village life. I miss you and thank you for your continued support and efforts. It's been full on here. I'm at my solicitor's today, this is her boardroom, all quiet, just me, so we're free to talk. I've got another meeting with my accountant coming up, so our time is limited. First up, I want to know how Frankie Jay's workshop inspired each of you.'

Emmy, red-rimmed puffy eyes, clears her throat. 'It was entertaining, Serenity. It nudged me into thinking about possibly raising my fees, but I'm bound, to some extent, by the fee structures recommended by my professional hypnotherapy association for clinical therapists. I know there are people out there who charge a lot more than I do, but they're generally more out-there practitioners, like past-life hypnotherapists.'

'Can you expand your services,' Abby says, 'offer past-life hypnotherapy at a premium price? I know Lou-Lou down on the coast charges three times your fee.'

'I'm not trained in it, and I'm not sure that I agree with it.' Emmy wrings her hands. 'Not sure that I believe in it, I should say. I use tried-and-trusted, evidence-based, clinical techniques to help people with their challenges.'

'On that note,' Serenity's voice cuts in, 'I've been advertising for expressions of interest from other practitioners wishing to hire space, and Lou-Lou put her hand up for a couple of days a week. I didn't think she would compete with your services, Emmy, but let me know if you feel she does. I want our services to complement each other, and ideally, our practitioners to recommend each other, to work in synergy.'

'Thank you for letting me know.' Emmy sits back. 'I'm still thinking about Frankie Jay's workshop. I might raise my fees a touch, or develop some self-help programs, or the occasional workshop.'

'What about you, Freya,' Serenity says, 'did Frankie Jay inspire you?'

Freya touches her amethyst choker. She seems to wear it all the time now. 'Yes, she did. I'm raising my fees, for starters. Quite a lot, especially if you're going ahead with that idea of bringing coachloads of daytrippers from London. If they're coming all this way, they're expecting something exceptional, and I believe I offer that. I'm also thinking about setting up a social media group where people can share their experiences of the spirit world, then developing some products I can sell to them. Not sure what products yet, but ideas will come.'

'Nice work, Freya.' Serenity takes a sip of water. 'And yes, we have daytrippers trying us out from next month. I'll keep you all in touch with practicalities as we get closer, but basically the trip will include each person pre-booking one or two sessions, so you'll all benefit.'

Cat's heart backflips, her stomach wobbling. Will the daytrippers be making bookings to see Amantha, the psychic reader? And how will Freya react to that?

'Mariana, I don't know what I would have done without you.' Serenity brings her hands in *namaste* to her third eye, her lips, her heart. 'How did Frankie Jay's workshop inspire you?'

Mariana lifts her jay feather to her cheek. 'It was a powerful day. Before she even came into the room, I did Abby's exercise, posing a question to Amantha and focusing on the picture on the front of the journal. I got a message within seconds. It was to move here, to the village, and offer my services as an Ayurvedic medicine practitioner by day and build an online business to sell spells by night.'

'Spells?' Freya, Abby and Emmy ask in unison.

'I've just finished a PhD on witch lore, based on my research into the history of medieval witches from this part of England and their medicines and remedies, including their spells. What we might call affirmations or manifestation intentions today. I'm halfway through writing a book for the popular market – no academic jargon – and the online business would help keep my finances flowing. I'll only sell ethical spells, and do podcasts and tell stories ... I'm talking too much.'

'I like it,' Serenity says. 'I'll have a chat with you later about maybe working from the centre, and I hope you'll still have time to teach some yoga classes.'

'You might enjoy chatting with Milly,' Abby says. 'I'll formally introduce you if you wish, but you'll know her from your yoga classes. She's researching local history. She keeps giving us teasers about uncovering local secrets.'

'Before Abby shares her ideas,' everyone turns to look at Serenity, 'a quick update on where I'm at. It's still early days, but it looks like I'm personally in the clear as far as any legal proceedings or criminal charges are concerned. The women are suing Rajpapa as an individual, and my advisors tell me that gifting Penelope the house is above board. Financially though, I've taken an enormous hit because of the loss of the Zoom memberships and the purchase of the New York entities. It looks like I'll be able to keep the New York businesses, but at the expense of other properties and investments that I've had to put on the market. I've decided to stop offering teacher-training courses. I'd have to develop a different style of class and that's all too much for me right now. So, courses gone. Anything Rajpapa, gone. In my heart of hearts, I just want to return to the village and curl up beside the fire in my cottage, like a cat with no worries. And I still want to keep the centre going if we can make it financial. I don't know if you feel this is good news or not such good news. The pressure's on for us all, and I thank you for the efforts you're putting in and for your support in the coming weeks with our Open Day, our London daytrippers, and making new practitioners and workshop facilitators welcome. They're helping to keep your jobs. And on that score, I'll leave you with Abby. Till next week, *namaste.*' The screen blinks and she's gone.

'Did Frankie Jay inspire you, Abby?' Freya slides the bowl of chocolates on the boardroom table towards Abby and unwraps one for herself. 'Ah, tangerine crème, my favourite.'

Abby takes time selecting a chocolate and places it, still wrapped, on her notepad. Cat cowers down on her windowsill. Is Abby losing her nerve, or – no, there it is, essence of confidence ramps up as Abby lifts her chin.

'I'm jumping all in with some wild, fun ideas. Not sure where they will lead, but I've enjoyed making the Amantha videos and splashing the paints around in Clary's classes, and yesterday's workshop fired me up to do more of that. I'm looking at ways to bring more money into the centre.' She removes the amethyst paperweight from the pile of flyers and holds one up. 'Starting with this for our Open Day.'

Cat's face, all regal and a little snooty looking, stares out from the flyer against a background of orange whorls from Abby's painting. Large letters Cat can read from the windowsill: 'Amantha: psychic reader. Free readings.'

'You're not serious!' Freya splutters through her second tangerine crème.

'Look,' Abby says, a pink flush splotching her face, 'it's a bit tongue in cheek, a tease for Open Day, playing on the popularity of her videos. It will get people talking, and who knows, she may even transmit one of her messages. It's a way to test the idea.'

Mariana reaches out for a flyer. 'As I told you, I got a powerful message just from staring at the orange picture on the cover of the journal yesterday, whether or not the actual cat was involved.'

The actual cat? Cat's upper lip curls, exposing her fangs; her claws protrude, and with supreme effort on her part, retract. *Am I just another cat to Mariana?*

'Although,' Mariana continues, 'who knows whether staring at the picture got me in touch with my inner wisdom, or whether the cat's – sorry, I know you all love her, Amantha's – spirit heard my question and somehow transmitted the message. It's a fascinating thought. Maybe there's a PhD in there one day. I can imagine setting up some experiments.'

'So can I.' Freya rolls her eyes in Cat's direction, then pops another tangerine crème.

'How will it work on the day?' Emmy plays with the bowl of chocolates, spinning it this way and that.

'We'll have a section curtained off inside the marquee, with Amantha on Clary's lap – Clary has agreed to be part of the fun, and she has a way with keeping Amantha in tow. We don't want her slinking off mid-reading. We'll make the readings ten minutes each. Clary will tell the person to spend time with Amantha, look into her eyes, or just watch her for five minutes while, Clary will explain, Amantha tunes in. After five minutes, Clary will pick up Amantha and stare into her eyes, expecting a message. Clary will relay the message to the person. We'll give everyone one of the journals – I had an extra few hundred printed – and suggest they write the message in the journal. Then we dip Amantha's paw in a paint tray and imprint her paw-mark under the message. What do you think?'

Cat inspects her front paws. She might offer her right paw for her signature, so the marks denoting the ends of her sixth, seventh, and eighth lives show in the paw-print, sealing her wisdom as a cat in her ninth life.

'It will certainly attract interest.' Emmy chews her lip. 'And that's what we need. Personally, I appreciate the hypnotic quality of your artwork, and I can see the potential of that to draw people into their inner world, where they may find the answers they seek. I wonder if the same applies to sitting in silence watching Amantha? You've piqued my curiosity. On a practical note, is there any chance you can fold some of our brochures into the journals so people can learn about our services? Given that she'll most likely be the big attraction, it would be great to leverage that.'

'Good idea, yes.' Abby scribbles on her notepad.

'I'll mention it to the students after my yoga class tomorrow,' Mariana says, 'get them to spread the word.'

'Freya?' Abby raises her eyebrows.

'My hands are tied, as I see it. Before I changed my format, I advertised Amantha as my psychic assistant, my conduit to spirit, so what can I say? I endorsed her back then, even if it was only for marketing purposes. I didn't really believe she had those qualities. Goodness, we do all know she's just a cat, right?' Freya shrugs her shoulders, lifting her upturned palms heavenwards. 'But look, you're playing the same game, Abby, creating a persona for Amantha as a marketing tool, and I get that. So yes, you have my support.'

Marketing persona, marketing tool, my paw! Hackles raised, blood curdling, lips snarling, Cat flashes from the windowsill, speeds under the table delivering a ferocious whip of her tail to Freya's plump ankle and exits the door, detouring to the basement to snag a mouse. *Just a cat, hey?* She tosses the frightened mouse in the air. 'Just a cat' about to eat 'just a mouse'. Time suspends, a vision of Pearl in her mind's eye. Time enough for the mouse to land under Cat's nose and scuttle away, for Cat's hackles to settle, and to haul herself from the basement and out into a summer breeze ripe with essence of rose. She drops into sphinx pose at the top of the steps, coaxes her spine into alignment, looks out towards the Reclining Woman with Child and purrs a rolling roar of *Oms*.

😺

This will be fun. Cat weaves her body sinuously between Martin's legs as he tries to follow Emmy into her office for his return hypnotherapy session. No essence of tobacco today. In its place essence of, what is it, daisies, oranges, both?

'You trying to trip me up, Amantha?' Martin stoops to pat her, and receives a playful paw-punch with a deep, honeyed meow.

'Sorry, Martin.' Emmy grabs Cat and carries her over to the

corner, where a bowl of cream awaits. 'She's been cooped up at a staff meeting for the last hour, and I think she's ready to let off steam. She'll calm down when her tummy's full.' She wags her finger at Cat. 'Hear that, Amantha? Calm down or I'll put you out in the hall.'

Cat belly-crawls to the far side of her bowl so she can lap up her cream while keeping an eye on Martin. *Yes, this will be fun. The hypnotherapy session with no agenda.* She settles in for the ride, all ears.

A petite iridescent-orange butterfly circles Martin's head and lands on the tip of his right thumb as he takes his seat. 'Am I out to it, already?' He carefully tilts his head towards his hand to draw Emmy's attention to the visitor. 'Is this a dream? Quite magical.'

'How beautiful,' Emmy's voice is hushed, reverent. 'Not a dream, Martin, but perhaps a synchronicity.'

'What's that?' Martin whispers, eager not to disturb the delicate creature fluttering and folding its tiny wings.

'It's when a symbol appears that matches what's going on in your inner world. I don't know how on earth she got into the room, and I'm not sure that I've ever seen one like this little beauty before, but butterflies are symbols of change. You know, the caterpillar becomes a chrysalis and after a while something completely different – the butterfly – emerges. Hypnotherapy gives you the opportunity to change, to transform from one way of being into a different, perhaps lighter, more beautiful way of being.'

'It's a tiny butterfly, so a tiny change?'

'What tiny changes have you experienced since last week's session?'

'Strangely, I haven't wanted a cigarette. Well, that's not entirely true, let me refine that. I'll make myself a cup of coffee, and because that's when I would reach out for a ciggie – one of my rituals I suppose – I reach out, but as soon as it's in my hand, I don't want it.'

'How does it feel when that happens?'

'Weird but exciting, because that's what I want, to lose the addiction, not smoke.'

'Any other tiny changes, Martin?'

'I've been on edge, and I guess my body is craving the nicotine or something, I don't know. I'm experimenting with going running, lifting weights and singing, trying to ride the withdrawal with things that make me feel good, raise my endorphins or whatever. So, yes, tiny changes in my fitness coming up.'

'We can explore ways to relax you more under hypnosis, if you like, or suggest changes to your routines to avoid the triggers.'

'My wife says I smoke – smoked, I should say – for a reason other than addiction. No, that's not quite right, let me think about it: she says if I could discover what made me start smoking in the first place, before the addiction kicked in ... no, I'm not sure what she was getting at.'

'She's right. I don't know why you started smoking, Martin, and we might focus on that in your session if you like. Some people start smoking to fit in, or to look cool, so when they quit the habit they can find themselves grappling with issues of fitting in, or looking cool. The prop, the cigarette, has gone, and they're left with the old problem.'

'Well, looking back ...'

'Wait, Martin, we could do this more effectively under hypnosis. Would you like to try? That way, you and I can check in with your forgotten or buried memories, which might be more useful than the tidy story you carry in your conscious mind today.'

'Will I still be able to hear everything I say while I'm hypnotised? I don't want to say anything I'll feel uncomfortable about. Will I remember the session?'

'It will be the same as last week. You'll feel deeply relaxed and you'll be aware of everything you say.'

'Okay, I'm nervous, but in an excited kind of way, and I'm very curious. Let's find out what's behind all this, and what might trip me up now that I've let go of my prop.'

Cat begins cleaning her creamy whiskers. *There you go, guys. It's all about what might trip you up. Didn't you get that message when I danced between your feet coming in? You're welcome. What would you do without me?*

'Martin, close your eyes now, and notice the lightness of your eyelids, or is that the heaviness of your eyelids, or perhaps the lightness ...'

Despite her best intentions to stay present, Cat falls into a deep, restful place until a tickly sensation at the tip of her nose brings her back to the room and the beautiful miniature orange butterfly now dancing beneath her nostrils.

'That's it, Martin,' Emmy's voice is deeply resonant, 'going back through the years now, that's right, that's it, and here it is, your first cigarette. Can you see it?'

'There it is,' a groggy Martin says with a slight teenage twang. 'I made it myself.'

'How old are you, Martin?'

'Twelve.'

'How did you make the cigarette?'

'Rolled it. The smell is like my dad.'

'Loose tobacco?'

'Fresh, loose. I'm pinching some to my nose.'

'How does the smell make you feel?'

'Closer to Dad.'

'Where's your dad, Martin?'

'He died. I'm the man of the house now.'

Cat smells rivers of tears, the room becoming humid with unleashed grief.

'You're smoking that first cigarette now, Martin. How are you feeling?'

'Burning, my throat is burning, my eyes are stinging, I mustn't cry, I'm the man of the house now.'

'Martin, I'd like you to go back to when you were younger, when your dad was still alive. Can you go back a year, two years, however many years, find a time where you remember playing with your dad. Go there now. Raise your hand when you see him.'

Cat sits bolt upright, breath suspended, the room shimmering. Martin raises his hand.

'How old are you, Martin?'

'Twenty-four.'

'Okay,' Emmy says, wobbly, 'where are you?'

'Galloping across a meadow. It's raining. Playing chase, my father in front on a black horse, me behind on a dapple.'

'You're playing?'

'Yes, but he's telling me to go home now, he has business to attend to.'

'What are you doing now?'

'I'm following him, keeping my distance, curious.'

'Can you still see him?'

Martin's eyes flicker from side to side, flutter, flicker, butterfly eyes. 'He can't see me, I'm a good rider, good at staying out of sight. He's at a cottage now, he dismounts. He's bending down, lifting a ginger cat from a big basket.'

'A ginger cat?'

'He's holding the cat to his face, like a kiss, and he's bending down to the basket.'

'Can you see what's in the basket?'

A long pause. Cat holds her breath, her heart all flicker, flutter.

'No. But he's standing up now, a little pouch in his hand. He got it from the basket. What is it?'

'I don't know, Martin. Can you get a little closer to see?'

'He's taking his coin pouch from his tunic, putting silver coins into the basket.'

'Silver coins?'

'Yes, I can see them glinting, the sun's coming out. Now, he's putting the cat back into the basket and mounting his horse. I've got to hide, quick!'

'Okay, Martin, can you move forward a little in time, maybe an hour, maybe a day, maybe a few days. Find the day where you can see into the pouch your dad got from the basket. Raise your hand when you're there.'

Martin sneezes then raises his hand.

'What are you seeing now, Martin?'

'I'm in my lady's antechamber. My father has placed the pouch on a table. I shouldn't be here, but I'm curious.'

'Look inside the pouch, Martin, what do you see?'

Martin's nose twitches. 'I smell wine, fruity wine, and amber, and wood. I'm opening the pouch. Oh, it's leaves, crushed leaves. I know what this is.'

'What is it, Martin?'

'It's red raspberry leaf.'

'How do you know this? Have you seen it before?'

'My grandmother was a wise woman.'

'Your grandmother knew about herbs and teas?'

'I'm not allowed to talk about my grandmother, shh.'

'Okay, Martin, we won't talk about your grandmother. Who is going to drink the leaf tea? Is it a tea? Or is it for smoking?'

'It's medicine for my lady. I need to go now. She's coming.'

Emmy's voice fades. Essence of rain-damp horse mingles with daisies and oranges as Cat feels herself lifted by the unseen hand, the jingle of coin, the glint of silver, the whispered thankyou. The rainbow. She spies the second horse, the dapple, turn and flee. The creak of the cottage door opening, the swing of her basket as she is carried inside, the golden glow of the orange trees in the tubs. The warm citrus smell of home.

Emmy clicks her fingers. 'And you're wide awake now. That was good, wasn't it?'

Cat looks for the orange butterfly – was it imaginary? No, because Martin and Emmy saw it, didn't they? But Cat feels it in her bones, a connection between the spirited flutterby and the flashback. It was a flashback, wasn't it? A repeat of the one she had when Briar opened his cabinet to show Milly and Clary his family logbooks, but with more detail this time. If it wasn't for that experience, she would have passed off today's vision as a daydream triggered by Martin's description, but no, she's seen this, or been there, before.

'That was so utterly real, like I was there.' Martin sits up and shakes his head, pulling a tissue from the proffered box to dry his eyes.

'Hypnosis can take you to some daydreamy places.' Emmy scribbles on her notepad. 'When we get in touch with deep or uncomfortable emotions, we may see them more symbolically, perhaps when we're not ready to bring back full recall, or when the emotional content is hard to put into words.'

'No, I was there. It wasn't like a daydream. It was real. Also, it was me, but my body was different. You asked me when it was, what year did I say?'

Emmy consults her notes. 'Sixteen fifty-five. But if we lay that aside for the moment, I see a connection between the loose tobacco leaf you associate with your dad and the loose red raspberry leaf you associated with another father figure under hypnosis. Might the red raspberry leaf be a more symbolic connection to smoking? You had to be furtive, hide from your father, not let him see you following him. You had to disappear before your lady came in to collect the red raspberry leaf. Could the lady have been your mother, or your wife, and might your vision have been about trying to hide your smoking habit?'

'That makes some kind of logical sense, but it felt too real. Can it work the other way round, going back to a past life to understand more about my leaf-smoking habit in this life?'

'To be honest, Martin, as you know I'm a clinical hypnotherapist, not a past-life hypnotherapist. I'm not trained in that area, I've never had a client visit a past life, and I'm not even sure that I believe in past lives. But I'm curious about why you had this experience.'

Cat rolls her eyes, a feat she has finally managed to perfect. No-one is watching, but it feels good to do, therapeutic. *People can be so dumb*, she thinks. *Past lives are a given. I'm in my ninth life, the marks are clear and easy for anyone to see, on my paws and in other places for anyone awake enough to notice. Same with spirits. Why do so few people see them? They're here, the recently departed and those who have chosen to hang around for a while. Not to mention all the spirit cats lounging about between lives. And the spirit mentors, but they're harder to notice because they change form, parade as flesh and blood, or leaves and roots, or breezes and rainbows. As for you, Martin, it seems you and I have history, and you may have had a different body, but I seem to have been much the same. Only don't call me ginger, please. Or marmalade. I'm honey.*

'You mentioned your grandmother, Martin. Is she still alive?'

'My grandmother in this life? I don't think the one back in sixteen fifty-five is still with us.' Martin grins. 'My family has lived in this area forever, as far as I know. A whole line of grandmothers. But no, both my grandmothers died before I was born, sadly.'

Cat sidles over to Emmy, meows for attention, locks eyes and transmits: *Red raspberry leaf is a medicine for pregnancy.*

'I think I've read somewhere that red raspberry leaf is a herbal remedy for pregnancy. Have you heard of it before?'

Martin pulls out his phone. 'I'll look it up. Sorry, is it okay if I look it up?'

'Fire away. Today's session's almost done, and I'm as curious as you are.'

Martin's fingers are speedy; *click, scroll*. 'Red raspberry leaf recommended for ... lots of things and ... may support pregnancy in third trimester, and historically used for easing childbirth.'

Cat meows for Emmy's attention again: *Keeps babies inside, keeps them alive.*

'I wonder,' Emmy says, 'just supposing you did visit a past life in sixteen fifty-five, maybe your lady had suffered miscarriages and wanted to make sure her latest pregnancy survived. She would pay good silver coin for such a remedy.'

Cat's stomach unclenches and her jaw relaxes. *Got it, Emmy.* Her inner Cat somersaults.

'Also, on the symbolism front,' Emmy's on a roll, 'we've now related death and leaves: you first smoked tobacco leaves when your dad died, and in your vision, the leaves were perhaps to stop your lady losing another pregnancy. And when someone dies, they "leave" you.'

'My imagination may be running away with me,' Martin sits on the edge of this chair, 'but my father seemed to be involved in a stealthy operation. He was very secretive. Did he get the medicine from a healer, a village witch? Was it specially grown, or did it come with a magic spell?'

'You have a fabulous imagination, Martin. Book another session for next week on the way out and we'll explore some more. I want to help you uncover the reasons why you started smoking and resolve some of those issues before they trip you up now that you're heading out into the world as a non-smoker.'

😺

Emmy fumbles for her phone, *click, click.* 'Freya? Just a quick question. What are the chances of someone under hypnosis tuning into one of your spirits?'

Cat strains her antennae ears, catching Freya's faint response. 'If they're intuitive or psychic, quite possible, in my opinion. Why?'

Emmy explains what happened with Martin. 'I wondered if a spirit was relaying the information to him.'

'Hmm, that's interesting. When I channel spirits, I don't become them. I see them as separate from me. I communicate with them. When I'm not in a brain-fogged hot flush, anyway. I'd say if your client bodily felt the experience, it was one of his past lives. Don't you believe in past lives, Emmy?'

'Not sure. What do your spirits say about it?'

'I've never had a spirit mention past lives. The spirits I talk with have usually recently left their bodies, or they're staying around because they want to pass messages to their loved ones rather than pass on to another life. Some of them look like they're from centuries ago, but unless they want to talk with me, I can't verify that. They might be stuck, unable to find their way to their next life. But you know, spirits love to play dress-up, so I can't judge from their appearances. I believe in past lives, though. I did a couple of sessions with Lou-Lou once, and they made sense to me. Felt real.'

'Thanks, Freya. Maybe I should try it.'

'Better still, why not try it and then do a course so you can offer past-life regression here? It would bring you a lot more money. I can meet you for a coffee tomorrow, chat some more. I have a client coming in five minutes, but a quick word: remember Serenity said Lou-Lou was interested in renting a room here, so if you've got any thoughts about doing this yourself, best have a chat with Serenity. You don't want competition on your doorstep.'

Emmy clicks her phone, kicks off her shoes and lies down on the floor. 'What do I do, Amantha? The extra income would be good, though I'd have to pay for training first. I tried to stay rational with Martin, but I'm curious. Maybe it's time to open to more adventure in my life. Be less rigid about the way I do things, at home and at work. My goodness, did I just admit to being rigid?'

*

Bang, bang, bang, tap, tap, bang. There's no way Cat's going to be able to sleep tonight, the eve of Open Day. There are people all over the lawn erecting marquees, building a stage, putting up tables, clanging stacks of chairs into neat rows, testing microphones, *one, two, tap, tap.*

Nerves zinging, muscles primed, brain chatter on overdrive, nowhere to relax because the front door is open for people to come in and out, collecting bits and pieces from the storeroom and from their offices, so that everything's in place and ready for the nine am start. Where's a cat to go for peace and quiet, her last night before Amantha: psychic reader's launch?

Before she knows it, her body takes control and she speeds over the lawn, past the topiary, leaps up onto Briar's mossy wall, drops into his heavenly scented garden and pauses, stock still. Has anyone seen her? All is quiet. No lights on in Briar's cottage. The raspberry bed beckons, so she crawls in, sinks down into the lusciously leafy shrub, rolls onto her back and rests her eyes on the late-evening summer sky, which is exquisitely framed and embellished by an intricate pattern of raspberry leaves.

Here, inhaling the labour-easing raspberry-leaf scent, she meditates upon her imminent rebirth as a psychic reader. Dispenser of wisdom and guidance. A side-step from her role as guardian and protector, keeper of the rules.

A rising silvery moon peeps over Briar's wall, backlighting the top of Reclining Woman with Child. Viewed from here, the topiary woman appears to be gazing directly at her, crowned by the moon, emanating a magnificent peace that tingles deep into Cat's bones. Why the hurry to graduate her ninth life and miss soul-enriching moments such as this?

🐾

'You're a star attraction, Amantha.' Clary arrives just in time to pluck Cat from her chosen sphinx-pose position on the ticket desk as the gates open for the big day. 'We can't have you mingling with your fans, giving away your secrets before your advertised start. If we don't protect you, they'll ask for tips, want to have a selfie taken with you and wear you out before you begin your formal readings.'

'Oh, good, you've found her.' Abby arrives, somewhat breathlessly, and holds out a straw basket lined with bright-orange silk, a daisy chain threaded through the handle and trailing down the sides. 'A touch of pageantry, a basket fit for a queen. Your throne awaits, Amantha.'

Clary gently guides Cat into the basket and primps the silk.

'One more thing.' Abby drapes a daisy chain around Cat's head. 'A crown for the psychic queen.'

The daisies tickle Cat's ears, their scent adding a frisson of excitement as Abby lifts her basket high above the throngs now pouring into the garden. 'You've heard all about her, you've seen her videos, here she is, in the flesh, Amantha, psychic reader. Come in the spirit of fun, prepare to be amazed. Free readings, from nine-thirty am in the main marquee.'

Phones shoot up all around her, *click, click*, faces loom above the basket. 'Hold the selfies.' Abby stop-signs her hand, and it's only now that Cat notices Abby and Clary are both wearing oversized dark sunglasses and hefty black earpieces, fancy-dressed as her personal security contingent. 'Amantha will pose for selfies after your reading. Please take your place in the queue at the marquee. Free coffee while you wait.'

Freya's husky voice wafts by. 'All the fun of the fair, I see. Can I leave some of my flyers with you? I've got a talk on spirit readings at two pm. For people who want serious readings.'

'Serious readings?' Clary asks, still smarting from Freya's cheating but putting on a jesting, funfair voice. 'What are you suggesting, Freya? Can't get much more serious than divining fertility issues and offering an ancient remedy or two. If you can stomach crushed woodlice, that is.'

'My point exactly.' Freya laughs. 'Our Amantha is a little witchy for modern-day mortals. Talking of which, have you seen Mariana's stall? Remedies and spells. She got that up and happening fast. And she's got Pixie onside, womaning the stall over lunchtime while she teaches her free yoga class on the terrace. Witches and pixies.'

'All hail, Amantha.' Milly's operatic tone slices the air. 'If you discover any historic titbits in anyone's past, send them over to me and Briar. Our stall is near the topiary. We're collecting folk stories and inviting chats about local history.'

🐾

Cat's heart flips as they near the marquee, a dozen or so people already lined up, coffees in hand, waiting for her.

Abby passes Cat's basket to Clary as they walk along the queue. 'Here's the one you've been waiting for, folks. Amantha, and, let me introduce you to Clary, Amantha's interpreter.'

Clary takes a cheeky bow, swishes the indigo curtain aside to whisk Cat into the reading space and settles her, still in her basket, on the low coffee table. Essence of pine, beeswax, paint, dappled light and a pile of Abby's orange whorl journals on the table beside her. Clary removes her sunglasses and earpiece, and ties an orange silk turban around her head, a surprisingly elegant accessory to her dark-chocolate sleeveless tunic dress offset by a delicate amber amulet. Quite the part.

Cat reads Clary. Serious intent, curious, but keeping everything light and quirky to cover for nerves. And criticism. Ready to blow it off as a fun piece of marketing if Cat fails to impress. What words of wisdom would Amantha, psychic reader, offer Clary? Test case. She twitches her tail. Clary shuffles the journals and fluffs up the cushions stacked in the client's chair. There's no eye contact available to transmit a message, but what would she say? 'As with your paintings, Clary, it's all in the way you frame it.' She's not entirely sure that she understands the message, but her bones settle contentedly.

A silky rustle cuts the air as Abby pulls the indigo curtain aside a chink, admitting a short, freckle-faced, slightly flushed woman aged in her early twenties. Agitated, excited, eyes darting everywhere, as she struts towards the chair Clary indicates. Speckled Hen.

Clary offers Speckled Hen a journal and a pen. 'Welcome. Amantha works in silence. She'll tune into you during the next five minutes. If you have a question, bear it in mind. Watch her and look into her eyes as much as she will allow. You can write any messages you receive in your journal, and it's yours to keep. You don't need to share what you write with me. After five minutes, Amantha will deliver an extra message through me, and you'll have time to write that down, too.' Clary folds her hands in her lap, bows her head and stares at the floor.

Cat looks into Speckled Hen's eyes, which are russet-coloured, yearning. Fingers adorned with too many rings; the beauty of any single item overwhelmed by a forest of jewelled distractions. Peck, peck, pecking at possibilities, settling on none. An egg-laying Speckled Hen, and, ah yes, essence of early pregnancy, the tiniest heartbeat, a presence yet to be felt. Except by Cat. Male energy, lover of nature.

Speckled Hen bends to write a word or two. Odd, because Cat is still assessing, hasn't transmitted yet.

Clary gets up from her chair and kneels before Cat, then gazes into her eyes. 'What's your message, Amantha?'

Cat knows she needs to keep the message short. One day, Clary and the others will be able to absorb more, or she will learn how to transmit more, but for today: *You're pregnant, a boy who will love nature. You have too many distractions, you need to focus on one beautiful thing.*

Clary nods, then turns to Speckled Hen and repeats the message.

Speckled Hen gasps, her hand floating to her abdomen, her first motherly touch. 'Pregnant!' Her eyelids flutter, a tear spangling her cheek. She holds her journal out to Clary. 'It fits with the message I got during the five silent minutes. Look – I wrote it down: "Time to be still, save your energy for what's important."'

'That's beautiful,' Clary says. 'Would you like to write down the extra message, word for word? I'll repeat it for you. Then we'll dip Amantha's paw into the paint so she can add her paw-print signature.'

Speckled Hen chooses forest green for the paw-print. Clary guides Cat's right paw across the paint sponge and gently presses it onto the page. The space where the mark denoting completion of her ninth life will go stares back at Cat, a tiny white splodge amidst the forest green. How many readings will it take, once they start charging fees, for her to raise the money required to guard and protect the centre, to save everyone's jobs, to free her to graduate and become a wise spirit mentor to an earthbound being?

Essence of lemon with a touch of tangerine. 'Just a dab to remove the paint and nourish your paw.' Clary gently swabs Cat's foot. 'Well done, let's see who's next.'

Leopard Snake glides through the indigo curtain, taller than most, high heels adding even more stature, a cobra ensconced in a leopard-skin jacket, about to strike. But no, the forked tongue retreats, no need for defence. Leopard Snake finds ease in the tent, coils herself into the client chair, legs tucked under her hips, shoes abandoned on the floor for now. The five minutes of silence begins.

Leopard Snake watches Cat, a gaze, a glare, a narrowing of the eyes, a slow blink, then opens her journal and writes a few words.

Clary kneels before Cat. 'What's your message Amantha?' Cat gazes into Clary's eyes: *You have betrayed someone, but mostly you have betrayed yourself. You don't trust other people because you don't trust yourself.*

Clary smiles and takes a deep breath. 'You are at a crossroads: let honesty and trust be your guide.'

Leopard Snake nods and leans forward to show her journal

to Clary. 'Interesting,' the forked tongue lisps. 'The message I got was, "shed your skin, be more honest about who you are and what you want".'

A purple paw-print seals the deal, as Leopard slides through the indigo curtain, leaving her discarded snakeskin crumpled and curling on the floor.

Cat leaps at Clary and hisses: *Wrong message!*

'Amantha, darling, you can't be too blunt. Your message was spot on, as far as I could tell by reading her body language, but if I repeated your exact words, she would have tongue-lashed me to pieces. I needed to soften the language, reframe it in a way that would help her. Help and heal. Do no harm.'

Cat pokes at the discarded ethereal snakeskin with her left paw.

'Like my paintings, Amantha, it's all in the way you frame it. Ready for number three?'

Scattered Owl, essence of bookish wisdom and scent of worldly experience, takes the chair. Hair a little dishevelled, tawny cotton cardigan draped over her shoulders, telltale paper fan poking from the top of her soft leather satchel. 'It's a touch hot in here, do you mind if we leave a gap in the curtain to let some air through?' She pulls out her fan and flicks it into motion with obvious practised skill.

Any moment now. Cat keeps her eyes focused on Scattered Owl's head. Yes, here it comes. First the light mist then, ah yes, then the thickening, and then, wait three seconds, total brain fog sets in.

Cat pulls herself from her basket. Perhaps she shouldn't be doing this. Isn't the psychic reader supposed to stay on her throne? Essence of slight alarm from Clary, but Cat cautiously climbs onto Scattered Owl's lap, and remaining standing so as not to add her heated weight to Scattered Owl's already burning furnace of a body, gently places a paw on her belly. Carefully, she lightens her paw pressure, *one, two, three*, then gently presses, *one, two, three*, repeating again and again until the brain fog dissipates, and she returns to her basket.

Scattered Owl's journal, lightly speckled with droplets of sweat, remains closed, as Clary kneels for her message. Cat chooses her words, looking for good framing: *When the heat is on, breathe deep and slow, three breaths in, three breaths out, until the heat subsides. Brain fog is temporary. Just breathe and wait.*

When Clary relays the message, the Owl folds her fan. 'Amantha gave me that message with her paw pressure when she jumped on my lap, did you see? It helped too. Can I ask for a little more? The brain fog she so accurately saw meant I couldn't focus on asking a question during the silent five minutes. I wanted to ask if I'm going to lose my job.'

Clary checks in with Cat. 'Tell them what you're going through. Remind them of your wisdom and skills. Get their support. Take charge. Work from home.'

'They used to call me Night Owl,' Owl hoots. 'Maybe that's the answer, work from home in the evenings, go at my pace, not theirs. Thank you, Cool Cat. Anytime you want to exchange some of your cool for some of my heat, give me a call.' She chooses silvery moon for the paw-print signature and leaves her own footprints in the burned embers of her dilemma as she exits through the indigo curtain.

'Two more before we stop for a short break,' Clary says. 'A sip of cream for you, coffee for me. Are you okay to continue?'

Am I okay to continue? I am having the time of my life! This is fun. And that lemon tangerine paint remover is icing on the cake. It feels so ... Cat rolls onto her back, dances her legs in the air and paws at the sudden appearance of a bumble bee. She watches as it buzzes its way inside the orange blossom that now surrounds her, a grove of orange trees in tubs, a citrus sweetness buzzing through her body, now fading.

Clary reaches down, tickling her belly. 'I take it you're ready. Back on your feet now, please.'

Docile Mouse sits obediently in the client's chair, pushes her sunglasses on top of her head and blinks her big blue eyes, expectantly. Cat could toss her in the air, eat her for breakfast, and Docile Mouse would oblige. The five minutes pass slowly; Cat and Mouse eye each other; no-one moves.

'What's your message, Amantha?' Clary does her kneeling thing, eyeballing Cat.

A sixth minute rolls by, and Cat knows she must speak. Blank, blankety blank. *Quick, think, make up something. No, that would be wrong. Breathe deeply, just transmit whatever comes: Don't just sit there. Do something. Do something for you.*

Clary's pause is long enough for Cat to realise she's reframing.

'See life as a blank canvas ready for you to choose what to paint and how to paint it. You have that choice every day. You don't have to wait for permission. You don't have to do what other people expect you to do. If you don't know what you want, paint, draw or write in that journal you have on your lap. Do it every day, just write or draw whatever comes up. Your only goal is to turn the blank pages into a riot of colour, shapes and words. Nothing needs to make sense, but if you do this you will wake up one morning and know exactly what you want to do in this beautiful life.'

Cat hangs her head and droops her shoulders. There's no way she could have created or transmitted all those words, or found that magical way of inspiring Mouse, but Clary is right.

Mouse's docile shadow slips a fraction, exposing a posy of roses tattooed on her shoulder: an unseen hand sketching a flowery vine down her arm, reaching the fresh canvas of the back of her hand. Cat blinks and the vision recedes, but the future possibilities remain, ethereally marked for Mouse to discover.

Mouse opens her journal to the first blank page and courageously asks for a posy of paw-prints, not just one, and in as many colours as possible. One pink, blue, green, lavender, purple, silver and orange minute later, Mouse leaves, rosebud cheeks glowing.

'To help us out,' Clary settles Cat back into her basket after the last paw cleanse, 'I'll ask them to write a question down in their journal as the five minutes of silence begins. I'll tell them it's to help them focus. If they're focused, you can read them more clearly, I'm guessing. We handled the blank page well, and it was good advice for anyone, but it did seem right for her, too, didn't it?'

Abby pokes her head around the indigo curtain. 'The queue outside is bonkers. No way you can see everyone today. Looks like you're doing about six people an hour, so allowing for lunch, and if you agree, I'm going to count off thirty people and give them each a ticket with an appointment time, taking us to the end of Open Day. Do you think you can do that?'

'I'll need to slip Amantha out the back for a pee, and maybe you can look after her a couple of times so I can go to the bathroom, but yes, although it's a huge task, we did promise a day of readings in our flyers, so that's what we'll do.'

Cat lifts into a yawning cat-arch stretch. *Yes, rules are rules, good for Abby and Clary for sticking to them.*

Abby lingers, pen in hand. 'But there are maybe a hundred people out there, and they've all done the maths. They're asking me if they can make a future booking. Would you be up for that, Clary? It could be you sometimes, me other times, interpreting for Amantha. And we would charge a reasonable fee. We'll need to discuss details later, but if you're up for it I'll collect their email addresses and we can contact them once we've got a plan.'

Cat looks from Abby to Clary. *Anyone going to ask me if I'm up for it? Because yes, I'm up for the fun, and I'm up for it if it's making money for the centre, and no, I'm not up for it if I'm confined to a basket indoors every day of the week for the rest of my ninth life.* As if on cue, her left front leg numbs, a fog descends and a searing pain momentarily rips through her thigh muscle, essence of singed fur, burning flesh.

'In principle, yes.' Clary looks at Cat. 'We can't keep her in a basket tied up indoors, though, can we? Maybe we do three days a week or spread over a month.'

Cat eyes the curtain, a familiar male voice approaching. Emmy's client, Martin. No matter which way she looks at him, she can't unsee the dappled horse, can't block the aroma of red raspberry leaf, can't ignore the rainbow arching above his head. She breathes deeply, shakes off the image of Martin in seventeenth-century dress and focuses on his denims and navy button-down shirt with the rolled-up sleeves. Rolled up, rolled up, like the first cigarette he rolled after his father died. She paws at her eyes, smooths her whiskers and focuses again. If she hadn't been present for Martin's hypnosis, she wouldn't have known about the roll-your-owns; would she have seen them today, or is she only making the connection because of what she knows? What are the guidelines and rules for psychic reading? What are the ethics?

Clary settles Martin into the chair, then begins to explain the procedure.

'I'm curious,' Martin whispers to Clary behind his hand. Doesn't he know cats have exquisite hearing? 'Amantha was present for my hypnotherapy sessions with Emmy. I didn't know she was purportedly psychic. Didn't know she might have been listening in. I imagine today is a bit of fun, a marketing exercise, but I've prepared a question to which, if she truly is psychic, only she would know the answer. Unless Emmy shares details of her clients with you?'

'Emmy's a professional, one hundred percent, Martin. There's no way she would divulge anything that clients say during her sessions. What an intriguing experiment. Let's see. Write your question in your journal and focus on it during the next five silent minutes, then I'll ask her for a message.'

Cat's nerves spike sky high at the whiff of a test, her tail lifts to its full height and it takes all her focus to retract her hypervigilant claws. A minute ticks past, and she sees nothing beyond the roll-your-owns, feels nothing other than her stomach in her throat, her blood pulsing in her ears. *Focus on the question. What question?* A vision of the yoga altar flickers before her, the memory of reading Clary's message from the sound her pen made as she scribbled it down before class on the first day they met. Okay, she can do this. One more deep breath and she replays the last minute, listening for the sound of Martin's pen scratching the starchy page of the journal. *Not cheating, right? Using her psychic skills, right? Right.* The silence in the tent plays to her advantage as she pieces the written question together: 'What type of leaf, and what was the year? And tell me something I don't know.' Nick of time.

'What's your message, Amantha?' Clary seems on edge. She transmits: *Red raspberry leaf, sixteen fifty-five. And I was the ginger cat. But honey, not ginger.*

Clary, essence of confusion, lifts her eyes to meet Martin's and repeats the message. 'That's it. Sounds totally weird to me.'

Martin's hands shake so violently his entire body tremors, a rippling, seismic jelly, and his journal slips to the floor. Cat meets his eyes.

Clary steps forward, retrieves Martin's journal and hands him a glass of water. 'Are you okay? You're shivering. Should I call for the first-aid team? You look very pale.'

'I'm okay, thank you, Clary. Shaken, but not too stirred. Or maybe I am, stirred up. Not making sense, I know.'

'Anything you want to share?'

'Is it Amantha who's the psychic, or you? Can you read my mind, both the question I wrote down and the information? Everything you said I already knew, so you could access it if you're psychic. Except the bit about a ginger cat being Amantha, and about her seeing herself as honey, not ginger. If you read my mind, you could have seen the ginger cat and added a cheeky twist about honey. Are you an unwitting psychic, imagining that the messages come from this domestic kitty?'

'If I'm psychic, it's news to me. The only psychic thing

about me is being able to hear Amantha speak. But since Abby, Hazel and even Emmy, your hypnotherapist, can hear her, I'm far from alone.'

'If Emmy can hear her, they must have had a very interesting conversation after my last session.' Martin's voice anchors down, his body steadies, and he unrolls his sleeves and buttons the cuffs. 'I leave this tent with a sense of continuity with the past, as if nothing or no-one dies, just changes form. I can't explain it more than that. And on a mundane note,' he pauses, 'this is the first time I can honestly say that I'm not craving a cigarette.'

🐾

Cat can barely crawl from the marquee for a pee by the end of the afternoon. She's exhausted but determined to find her feet after being cramped in the basket for so much longer than she'd expected.

'Clary, wine?' Milly approaches, bulging satchel over her shoulder. 'Got some interesting local history snippets today, so the stall was worth it. Dying to hear about your day. Fancy dropping in on Briar, quick glass of wine before you go home?'

Clary checks her phone. 'My cousin's taken Benji to the coast for the day, staying overnight at her place. No texts from them, so they must have everything they need. I'm wiped but wired. Some weird stuff I wouldn't mind running past you. Look at that, "wiped, wired and weird". I think I'm still in lyrical-psychic-message mode. Yes, please, glass of wine. Coming, Amantha?'

Clary lowers the basket towards her, the silk lining and daisy chains discarded. Cat jumps aside and runs ahead of them, beelining for Briar's. Oh, the delightfully sweet, honeyed pollen of a late-summer night, the magnificent freedom of galloping across the lawn. Do cats gallop? This one does. She must talk to Abby about the basket thing. Can they do the readings on the run? Trot around the room with her clients? Meet them outside?

On the café terrace? Dance around them? Pass the movement off as part of the ritual? With a final grand jeté, she lands in a catlike arabesque on top of Briar's wall and turns to watch Clary and Milly saunter the last few yards. She curtseys, expecting a final applause for her work today, but the women are too deeply in conversation to notice. 'Sixteen fifty-five?' Milly opens the gate. 'Rings a bell. Not that we need one to alert Briar to our arrival.'

'Oh, so amusing.' Clary raises an imaginary wineglass to Milly, then turns to Cat. 'Get that, Amantha? Sixteen fifty-five rings a bell, but Briar's door is open wide ... never mind.'

Cat trots behind them. No bells to ring when Martin's father visited in sixteen fifty-five. It was all stealth, no noise. Hush-hush. No glass of wine, no cup of tea, no *hello, come inside*. No welcome at all. Why?

😺

'Look at her, she's flat out, like a tiger-skin rug in front of the hearth, a hunter's trophy.' Briar's gravelly voice awakens Cat from a deep slumber. 'Could almost warm my feet on her if she was a little bigger.'

She tries to lift her belly from the floor and feels her five limbs – four legs and a tail – splayed around her like the points of a star. Star indeed. Flat-out star. The only way up from here is to roll onto her back, but her legs are still asleep. A far cry from her earlier nimble grand jeté and arabesque.

'Don't listen to Briar.' Clary strokes Cat's belly, picks her up and holds her to her chest. 'Unless you can tune into his innermost secrets and give us the gossip.'

'She's joking, Amantha.' Briar pretend-swipes at Cat. 'Don't you dare. My secrets are innermost because that's where they belong.'

'But back to sixteen fifty-five, Briar,' Milly is razor sharp, despite the heavy wine aroma carrying her words, 'if the number is a year, and if – as Amantha's message suggests – it relates to red raspberry leaf, I wonder if there's any reference in the gardening logbooks. Do you have any records for when your herbs were planted?'

'The herb garden was well established by then.' Briar tents his fingers. 'But I did begin work on extracting a timeline last year when I went through some of the early logs. It's in my office, I'll fetch it. Wouldn't be wise for us to plunder the original documents while we're a bit tipsy, but the timeline might help. I've been tidying it up a bit, making it more legible for your research, Milly.'

'Does he mean a gardening timeline, or village history?' Clary whispers, as Briar's footsteps echo from his office next door.

'Gardening, I think. His focus in on the gardens, mine's on the question of what family secrets might be buried in the logbooks. But I think we should tread carefully, start with the gardening details, where Briar feels comfortable.'

Briar emerges from his office, cheeks flushed, carrying a pile of emerald-green notebooks. 'Ledgers, from Waterstones, nicely ruled lines and columns. And I prefer handwriting at this stage. It feels more connected to my ancestors than using Excel docs.'

Milly opens the first ledger. 'Sixteen twenty-three. The first year recorded in the logbooks.'

'That's what motivated me to start a timeline.' Briar looks over Milly's shoulder. 'The four hundredth anniversary, last year, of the first ancestor to put pen to paper for future generations. A man of vision, Will, son of John. I wonder if he's looking down on us now.'

'Johnson! Your surname!' Clary booms.

'That's it. Will's first entry in the logbooks is signed Will, son of John, but some ten years later he changes it to Will Johnson, and it must have stuck. All the following entries through the years are by various Johnsons. There's no record of who the original John was, or his occupation. It all starts with Will.'

'Where there's a Will, there's a way.' Clary giggles. 'Better not give me any more wine.'

'So, sixteen fifty-five?' Milly thumbs a few pages ahead. 'There's nothing for that year?'

'Nothing recorded, but the previous year is mentioned.' Briar finds the entry. '*November sixteen fifty-four: three orange trees in pots, lacemaker's cottage, keep fire burning, or try oil lamps.*'

'Orange trees?' Clary repeats, eyes wide.

'They need to be kept warm in winter.' Briar flicks ahead a few pages. 'But this is just a record of the timeline. The gardening and care details will be in the original logbooks. We can look at those tomorrow when our hands and minds are steadier.'

'No.' Clary's voice is an octave higher in excitement. 'I mean, orange trees? In England? On a seventeenth-century farm in winter? When were citrus trees introduced to this country? Would they have even survived?'

'From memory, from my days at university,' Briar runs his fingers through his gingery beard, 'England's first orange tree was grown in the early fifteen sixties. But they were expensive to import and maintain and needed to be kept inside in winter. That's how orangeries began, and why we think of them, historically, as being more of an aristocratic invention. They were an architectural fancy and indication of wealth, though they did eat their oranges, and make marmalade from them, too, I believe.'

'Nothing aristocratic or fancy architectural about this village back then, though, hey?' Clary, chasing her wine with a glass of water, is trying her best to sound intelligent.

'A gift, perhaps?' Milly says. 'To the lacemaker in return for exquisite lace for a wedding dress? Hope they paid her money, too.'

'Something like that, no doubt.' Briar empties the remains of the last bottle of wine into Milly's glass. 'But don't believe everything you read in our family logbooks. There's more than one secret encoded in everyday language to protect the information from prying eyes.'

'Ah, the healers, the witches, the makers of herbal medicines.' Milly pushes her wineglass aside. 'I'm done for tonight, thank you, Briar. We've kept Amantha up late. I think she might be locked out of the centre. Do you mind keeping her here overnight in case she gets chilled outside?'

'Delicate little marmalade cat, aren't you, Amantha?' Briar lifts her up and lovingly deposits her on a cushion near the hearth. 'You can sleep in my old Jess's spot.'

'You had a cat?' Milly looks surprised.

'Jess, died in November. I still miss her. And I had an orange tree in a tub, but I gave it away last year. Too tricky to keep healthy inside a low-light cottage like this one in winter, even for a green thumb like me.'

Cat catches essence of Jess on the cushion, glimpsing her pearly spirit watching from the hearth. 'Lace,' Jess purrs, 'remember lace? Red raspberry leaf in lace pouches. She who makes lace, makes herbal medicine. Do you remember?'

At least she's not confined to a basket wearing a daisy-chain crown, and the room they've chosen for her readings is more spacious than the tight corner in the marquee. Room to breathe, to stretch, to prance, to add a touch of drama to the proceedings, to communicate through body language, or to nestle up close to those clients who emanate a need for a little love. And room, Cat reminds herself, is what she needs to give herself if she is to fulfil her role as guardian and protector of the centre by doing as many psychic readings as she can to bring in the money.

'Thanks to you,' Clary, essence of earthy clay, touches her fingertips to Cat's chin, 'my shaky weekly income's going up a notch now that I'm your official chaperone and interpreter.'

Cat transmits: *Clay under your fingernails?*

Clary inspects her hands. 'Ah, telltale sign. I'm experimenting with making iconic Amantha ceramics. Statues, cups, mobiles, and my favourite so far, wall tiles. Our clients might like to buy them after a reading, and the café might take some on consignment if we supply them with a showcase.'

Cat strikes a possible pottery pose: sitting Buddha, Cat-style.

Click, click, Clary's phone flashes in her face. 'Got it, thank you. Another study for the series. Quite the guru. Okay, are you ready for our first paying client? Fifteen-minute sessions from now on, so take your time to get to know her.'

Stork wades into the room, graceful long legs struggling against the current of exhaustion, proud, capable beak of a nose held steady. An audible sigh of relief as she lowers herself into the chair, dropping her heavy sling bag to the floor; a moment to stop and rest. More than a moment, fifteen long, refreshing minutes.

Clary hands her an orange whorl journal, and gestures towards the jar of pens, pencils and crayons on the high stool at Stork's elbow. 'You might like to start by writing a question in your journal. It helps to focus on what you want to get from your reading. Then keep your eyes on Amantha and breathe nice, long, slow, relaxing breaths. Nothing else for you to do. After fifteen minutes, Amantha will transmit a message for you through me.'

Cat waits while Stork selects a purple pen from the jar, keen to enlist the first of the psychic-reading rules she drew up for herself during her post-breakfast whisker-cleaning meditation. As a proud, rule-abiding cat, what could be more efficient than establishing a system that conserves energy – so she can do more sessions and earn more money – while guaranteeing happy clients?

Stork opens her journal and puts pen to paper as Cat instigates psychic-reading rule one: listen to the question and discover what's important to the client.

The scritchy, scratchy pen is easy to read. '*What is the meaning of life? What's my purpose?*'

Pose a big question, why don't you? Pose a – Cat chooses Buddha pose, closes her eyes and psychically invites Stork to join her, ticking the box for psychic-reading rule two: strike a pose that echoes the question, and invite the client to find connection.

Cat counts twenty silent meows before moving, long enough for Stork to slow down, breathe deeply, become entranced, and spill the shape and smell of her secrets into the space between them: psychic-reading rule three.

Stork starts drawing in her journal. *Not supposed to happen at this stage! Focus on the rules.*

Engage psychic-reading rule four: Watch body language, interpret the clothes the client has chosen to wear, sniff the aromas and essences. Easy part, job done. The stork who delivers babies, her sling bag always at the ready to carry the next newborn, all heavy load, no replenishment. Holding steady with grace, can't go on for much longer.

Commence psychic-reading rule five: showmanship – or should that be catmanship, or catwomanship? Use the remaining time to relax, play and re-energise while looking like she's still working. Stork looks surprised, follows her prancy-dancy moves, then hurriedly returns to drawing in her journal. *Also, not supposed to happen!*

Cat takes a deep breath. *Note to self: Can I learn how to read drawings as well as writing? Possible next project. For now, no. Also, have I checked all the boxes for the centre's four rules? I have, except, rule four is a tricky one, but did I keep my head and heart in the present moment? I think so, mostly anyway, check.*

'What message do you have?' Clary kneels before Cat after fifteen minutes, as per protocol.

Cat experiments with more words: *You are exhausted, a midwife of babies and projects. You've lost your sense of meaning and purpose. Your purpose is to give life to others – you know this – but also to give life to yourself. The meaning of life is life.*

Clary gulps, cocks her head at Cat and nods. 'You are exhausted from delivering new projects, or babies. You're like a midwife. Your purpose is to give life to others, but to do this you must first give life to yourself.'

Cat nudges Clary.

'There's more, and I'm not sure if I'm hearing this right from Amantha, but I'll tell you what I'm getting, "The meaning of life is life."'

Stork opens her journal and lifts her page of drawings to show Clary. 'This picture is me, the midwife, and me, the baby. I'm birthing myself. And these,' she turns the page, 'these are the colours of life, all the colours of the rainbow emerging from a washed-out grey haze. It's the vision that came to me while watching Amantha. Every slow breath I took released another colour. Amantha's message reached me while I was drawing.' She falls silent.

Clary sits quietly. Cat purrs, absorbing the enormity of Stork's experience. Her messages are getting through without engaging her 'one meow, two meows, three meows, transmit' method. Without needing an interpreter. Is Clary thinking the same? Won't she always need Clary to set up the room, welcome the clients, give them instructions? Absolutely she will.

The colours return to Stork's face, the grey lines under her eyes flushing pink. 'I'm a midwife. I help women to breathe through their labours, yet I haven't breathed through my hard labours, until now. Breath brings life. It's time to let my life breathe itself into greater being.'

Stork chooses a fresh spring green for her paw-print signature. The waters in the room recede as she lightly glides to the door, her sling bag spouting rainbows in her wake.

'You made me work hard there, Amantha.' Clary clips Cat's ear. 'If it's a long message in future, let's maybe take it in stages, hey?'

Cat purrs in acquiescence.

'Although,' Clary's eyes swing heavenwards in deep thought, 'according to your message, I need to remember to breathe slowly and deeply to lighten what feels like hard work. I'll take that message on board for me, too. Looks like we hit home, though, wouldn't you say?'

😺

Ten paying clients later that day, Cat appraises the success of her psychic-reading rules. Eleven happy clients, each leaving the room transformed in some way, and with only one client to go before they finish for the afternoon, she has just enough energy to spare, thanks to the playful time-out built into each session. The centre is wealthier, Clary is financially enriched, and they can repeat this formula three days a week, which is what they agreed with Serenity. A squirmy worm flips in her stomach, a fledgling anxiety about her biggest secret to success: reading the clients' questions. She has undeniable psychic ability, but this reading of the question is what she needs to save her energy so she can give life to others and guard and protect the centre from financial harm. The worm settles, reassured for now.

😺

Lovelorn Nightingale slips into the room, plainly clothed, dainty of stature, mighty of singsong voice, as she chats with Clary about the beautiful topiary in the garden. Essence of loneliness, white band of skin on the ring finger of her left hand.

Cat listens for her question as the charcoal pencil sweeps across the page in extravagant flourishes at odds with her humdrum appearance. A song wishing to be set free. Or perhaps a phoenix preparing to rise from the charcoaled ashes of her broken relationship. The serifs and stylised letters are tricky to read, but Cat cracks the code: *'Does Sebastian love me? Should I sell Casa del Mare?'*

Cat chooses a plain sitting pose, matching Lovelorn Nightingale's posture, before shuffling a little closer to bridge the yawning loneliness. The questions are precise. If she addresses them specifically, chatty Lovelorn Nightingale will sing her praises far and wide, probably on social media, given her loneliness. People will pour into the centre to book readings. She twitches her tail then quickly stills it, remembering she is embodying psychic-reading rule two, inviting the client's engagement. Lovelorn Nightingale empties the jar of pens, selects three crayons and starts furiously drawing in her journal, turning page after page, humming gently.

'Your message, Amantha?' Cat thuds back into the present moment: *It's a long message, I'll break it into three, Clary.*

Clary nods.

Show the world your colours, sing to the heavens.

'It's a three-part message,' Clary says, and relays it.

Lovelorn Nightingale drops her jaw.

Cat transmits part two: *Be like the phoenix rising from the ashes of your relationship breakup.*

Clary does well with this one, too.

Lovelorn Nightingale puffs out her chest, visibly growing taller.

Cat struggles with part three, then: *It's more important to love yourself than to seek love from Sebastian or anyone else. You'll never be lonely again if you love yourself.*

Clary repeats, almost word for word.

Cat purrs loudly to gain her attention one more time: *And tell her to keep Case del Mare if it suits a phoenix rising from the ashes. Sell it if it belongs to the past.*

Clary, essence of complete astonishment, relays Cat's final message.

Nightingale flips the pages of her journal, opens it up to a double-page spread where – as Cat can see – a resplendent phoenix rises from a broken heart.

'I don't know if a phoenix sings,' Nightingale traces her finger along her throat, 'but my one does. Look, see the quavers and treble clefs I've drawn around her? I suppose she's a mythical bird, so she can sing as beautifully as I believe she can.'

'Do you sing?' Clary asks.

'I used to sing in school musicals as a child, but I lost my confidence, and then, you know, one thing and another. But I've been thinking about joining a church choir, not that I go to church, but to meet people and to ... yes, I need to sing!'

'Did the message about Sebastian make sense, or did I misunderstand Amantha there?'

'Perfect sense, or should I say purrfect sense, thank you. Casa del Mare is a rather exotic-sounding name for my rundown beach hut on the coast. Amantha has given me food for thought. If a phoenix rises from the ashes, what can rise from my rundown beach hut, or my rundown life? You know what? I'm going to drop by the art shop on the way home, get some colours and go home to fill more pages in this beautiful journal. I have a feeling the phoenix will sing to me through more drawings.'

Nightingale chooses blue – 'the colour of the throat chakra' – for her paw-print signature, and leaves the room accompanied by an angelic choir.

🐾

'Sorry, Ms Vernon, but we need that cat on a leash, or in a box with a lid, someone should have briefed you.' Toothy Doberman adjusts his headset and calls for support. 'Front desk here, Sally, I've got Ms Vernon and her cat here for you, but protocol demands some restraint for the cat, at least until we get her into the studio, and perhaps even more so then. Remember when they interviewed that zookeeper and his meerkat, and the creature pooped all over the couch? Live TV, too, went straight to air. Can you send someone down with a leash or a box? Thank you.'

Cat enlists her now well-practised eyeroll, directed at Clary, but deliciously soothing when she needs to be on her best behaviour and can't bare her fangs at Toothy Doberman to put him in place. Mere cat indeed. Her feline canines trump his stunted eye-teeth any day.

Being snatched from her deep sleep in the dead of night and packed into a moving beast of a car was not a good start to the day. But as Clary explained, appearing on breakfast TV, live from London, is good for bookings, good for them all.

Abby catches up with them at the front desk. 'Found a parking spot, finally. Just as well I dropped you off at the entrance. Glad you're still here. Wouldn't have wanted to miss this.'

'Not sure I can let you both in.' Toothy Doberman hands Clary a lanyard with her studio pass.

''Course you can, just print another pass, Toby.' Sally (must be Sally, though Cat recognises her as Intrepid Mountain Goat from her reading last week) breezes past Toothy Doberman and offers Clary a diamante-collared leash. 'Polly's, but she's tucked up in her doggie basket in the storeroom with a tasty bone. Polly's my labradoodle, so the collar might be a bit big, but we can tighten it. Or loop it over her tummy, that would do it. Least it's sparkly, fit for a star, hey, Amantha?'

'Thanks, Sally. This is Abby, our marketing guru and the creative genius behind the Amantha videos. Abby, this is Sally, the *Breakfast Show* producer.'

'I hear you had a reading with Amantha.' Abby tucks Cat under her arm and rolls the excess leash around her hand as they march down the hall and enter a musty rabbit warren of tunnels, twists and turns.

'I did. She picked up on my sense of adventure and gave me some tips on how to reach the top of my profession without burning out along the way. Inspired me to take a few more risks rather than follow the expected safe path, suggesting this interview being the first of these. Thankfully, the crew were all on board with it. Quick stop for hair and makeup for you, Clary. Shall I bring you both coffees?'

Cat watches in the mirror while Panda Eyes disguises Clary as a rosy-cheeked clown and blows her sleek ponytail into a candyfloss cloud. 'Can I add a touch of glitter to the cat? It will sparkle in the studio lights. Fit for a star – what do you think? Will she bite me?' Without waiting for a reply, Panda Eyes sprinkles a handful of golden glitter across Cat's back, some getting up her nose and making her sneeze.

'Truly a star.' Intrepid Mountain Goat bends to take a photo of Cat. 'And one of both of you, Clary and Amantha.' *Click, click.* 'Okay, time to go.'

They walk the rabbit warren in reverse, round one more corner, and as Intrepid Mountain Goat lifts her finger to her lips, they enter the suspended hush. The too-bright lights and aroma of nervous anticipation hit Cat in the bladder. *Easy not to poop, but mustn't pee, mustn't pee, mustn't pee.* Abby's touch reassures her, though Clary emanates enough anxiety to … ah, Clary breathes deeply, *three, two, one*, as Abby passes Cat to Clary and Intrepid Mountain Goat shows them to the couch.

'Hello, Clary, I'm Rick.' Tight Trousers leans forward and shakes Clary's hand. 'And this is Trace.' Trace wiggles her toes before thrusting her feet into show-pony heels and reaching out to welcome Clary and tickle Cat. Tight Trousers and Reluctant Show Pony.

A hand flicks in front of Cat, its fingers silently counting down, *three, two, one*. The hand rolls and Rick begins.

'And finally this morning, the interview we've all been waiting for. We have Amantha, England's one and only psychic-reader cat on the couch with us, and we're hoping for some interesting predictions, if our producer, Sally's, experience is anything to go by.'

The camera turns away from Cat as Intrepid Mountain Goat blinks in the bright light, a rabbit caught unexpectedly in the headlamps. 'You booked a reading with Amantha last week, Sally. What did this gorgeous marmalade guru tell you?' Tight Trousers flashes perfectly aligned bright-white teeth.

'She read my personality spot on.' Intrepid Mountain Goat speaks into the boom mic that suddenly appears before her. 'Gave me some tips on my career, but I'd rather keep them to myself, if you don't mind. Quite magical, is all I can say. I just knew we had to have her on the show.'

'Got any tips for me, Amantha?' Tight Trousers says. 'I understand you interpret for her, Clary.'

The allotted three minutes races past in a hazy daze.

'And cut ...'

'That was amazing.' Reluctant Show Pony descends from her mountainous heels and pads over to Clary. 'I was sceptical, but I'm going to book a full reading, bring some of my friends. It's well past time for a country jaunt.'

'You were great, Clary.' Tight Trousers releases his tie and cracks his neck. 'I don't know what's going on, whether the cat is psychic or whether it's you, a kind of ventriloquist psychic or something, but what you said to me was, to be honest, amazingly close to home. Glad this was the last segment for the day. I'm in a completely different headspace now. We'd love to have you both back sometime, maybe a regular fun feature? I'll chat with Sally. We'll get back to you.'

🐾

'Oh my God, Abby, you have no idea!'

London speeds by as Cat sits in the travel crate beside Clary in the back of the car. Much better this way than this morning, when Cat was all alone in the back and had to screech and mewl to signal her discomfort. Clary's real face emerges as she deposits the last of a whole box of makeup-remover wipes into a paper bag.

Abby's face is visible in the car mirror, keeping her eye on the road ahead. 'No idea about what, Clary?'

'The messages Amantha was giving me. So rude. I had to soften them all, and that's hard when you've got a camera in your face and the thought of however many thousands of people watching you.'

'Eight hundred thousand, maybe closer to a million.' Abby switches on the tick-tock thingy and the car sweeps to the left, along with the contents of Cat's stomach. 'Why, what did she say?'

'Her message for Rick was that he needed to loosen his belt and give Trace more respect. I told him she said there was value in presenting stories that show a variety of viewpoints, being more of a ringmaster than a ... and I had to work hard at that point because I wanted to say *circus clown*, but luckily, he nodded his head and said it made sense.'

'And her message for Trace?'

'She had a circus theme going in her messages. I guess that's why the word *ringmaster* came to me. Anyway, her message for Trace was to stop being a show pony, to get off her high horse and get real. Bit of a mixed metaphor, and I think the studio environment was hindering her psychic abilities. I told Trace Amantha said her superpower is relating to everyday people, and to see how she can find a way to do more of this in the show.'

'That's brilliant, Clary. You came across as cool and calm, like you were simply translating for Amantha while looking beautiful. Well, actually, I think you look more beautiful without the makeup and Marie Antoinette hair, but hey, now that I know what was going on, you were totally awesome.'

'Thank you. I'm not sure about a regular feature, though. I think once is enough. Let's see what happens to our bookings.'

Cat drops to her belly and folds her front paws to make a pillow for her buzzing head. People are a strange breed, she decides. They don't like to hear the truth. They need it wrapped up in stories, softened in lyrics, projected into positives, presented as a finger beckoning from a better future. *Come this way, little caterpillar, spread your butterfly wings*. Something she needs to practise.

Pearl is easy to spot rolling in the reds and oranges of the fallen leaves last night's winds tumbled across the gardens. Cat's honeyed body is more camouflaged, enabling her to creep up and pounce, but Pearl turns at the last moment and eyeballs her. 'Think I don't have eyes in the back of my head, Cat?'

'And what exactly do you see?' Cat twirls and does her best to curtsey, awaiting applause. It's been weeks since she's seen Pearl, weeks of indoor work doing psychic readings, no time to slip outside now that the evenings are colder before Emmy locks up after Cat's last client leaves. No time to seek Pearl's wisdom, only time to dispense it, over and over and over again, client after client, day after day.

'What do I see?' Pearl shimmies closer. 'I see your guru crown slipping over your eyes, blinding you to your purpose.'

'Guru?'

'Don't pretend surprise, Cat. Haven't people been calling you a guru ever since your appearance on breakfast TV? Haven't you felt that flicker of pride at the end of each day when you replay the insights your clients share when they show Clary their journals?'

'I do feel proud. I'm helping these people and bringing money into the centre, fulfilling my role as guardian and protector. What's wrong with that?'

'Do you have any idea how much Serenity is charging for your services?'

Cat holds her chin high. 'Abby told me Serenity took the magpie's – Frankie Jay's – advice, so yes, a lot, and people are paying it, so they must be happy. And I must be worth it.'

'How much exactly?'

'Four hundred pounds for the tier-one readings, three hundred for tier two.'

'Tier one and two?'

'It turns out that my superpower is just being in the room,

being a channel. The clients watch me, receive messages and write or draw them in their journals. Clary – or Abby or anyone who's free – welcomes the clients and collects them after the reading. That's tier two.'

'And tier one?'

'Like tier two, but Clary comes in at the end and I transmit an extra message for her to tell the client – like we did when we first started out back in the summer.'

'And the sessions are how long?'

'Fifteen minutes. Abby says we've got a waiting list, solidly booked up until after Christmas.'

'So,' Pearl jumps onto the lowest branch of Reclining Woman with Child to peer down at Cat, 'do you know how much Freya charges for her psychic readings? No? One hundred pounds, for an hour. Your tier one calculates out at sixteen hundred pounds for an hour. Are your readings sixteen times more valuable than Freya's?'

Cat jumps up to the same branch to meet Pearl eye to eye. 'They are if people judge them to be so. And remember, Freya struggles. I wouldn't be surprised if she still cheats occasionally, buffing up on a bit of client background before they turn up for their readings. My superpower allows me to channel constantly, and that's what people pay for.'

Pearl ascends a further branch and looks back down, dawn butterflies circling their head, a pearly queen's crown. 'Remind me of your psychic-reading rule one, Cat.'

'Listen to the question, discover what's important to the client.'

'And how, pray, do you do that listening?'

'I use my psychic powers to listen to the scratches their pens or pencils make when they write their question in their journal.'

'Their secret question? Personal information known only to them? Isn't that what Freya used to do? Read the altar messages, read their social media posts?'

Pearl's butterfly crown flutters down to Cat's head, drops over her eyes, and whisks into a dizzied frenzy that knocks her off her perch and sends her crashing to the ground.

'There you are, Amantha.' Clary races across the lawn and gathers her up. 'You're a bundle of fallen leaves, and your first client of the day awaits. Let's get you cleaned up and ready to face your morning.'

😺

Eleven clients done and dusted, Cat has time for a lunchtime dash up and down the staircase to burn off some energy and stretch her legs before returning to the reading room for a bowl of cream and an afternoon of practising reading her clients' drawings. It's quite an art, and good to be able to focus on learning something new. Helps get her through the otherwise boring tier-two sessions. It's the tier ones with Clary that she really enjoys, the challenge of summarising her assessments in positive, lyrical language, and hearing Clary repeat them aloud.

'Because I'm not a cat!' Freya's voice thunders down the hall, and lightning strikes Cat's heart, electrifying every single honeyed hair to frozen attention.

'No, that's not it at all. I was doing fine until that ginger moggie dragged herself into our lives.'

Cat drops to her belly and presses her ears to the floorboards relaying the angry vibrations from HQ. Serenity's Zoom voice filters through. 'What can I do to support you, Freya?'

'Shine a light on my work, get me on the *Breakfast Show*, treat me with the same respect you all have for Amantha?'

'Amantha represents our brand, Freya. And we're marketing the hell out of her. The shift from Rajpapa to the softer feline focus has helped our image, and Abby's videos have captured the online market to the extent that I can see not only rebuilding the online yoga numbers again, but perhaps bringing our practitioners – you top of the list – to the wider world through Zoom appointments. We need to step slowly, work out the details before I invest more marketing money. If you think being on the *Breakfast Show* will help, I'll ask Abby to sit down with you and work out a plan now that we've got Sally, their producer, on side. And we have Amantha to thank for that, after all. And the income she's bringing into the centre means I haven't needed to raise your rent.'

'I'm grateful for all that, Serenity, but – and I hate hearing myself say "but" – but my bookings have gone down since she's been the main attraction, and I'm struggling to pay the rent at all.'

'Have you thought about raising your fees?'

'Like to four hundred pounds for fifteen minutes? How is that even working? I don't get it.'

'You heard Frankie Jay. It's all about claiming your worth and walking your talk.'

'And robbing poor people of their hard-earned income, promising them psychic insight and wisdom from a mere cat? Sorry, that was harsh. I'm so sorry, Serenity. I retract that.'

'I do understand what you're saying and what you're feeling, Freya. But – I'll use one of your buts – you're charging a very reasonable fee, a fee the less wealthy have been happy to pay up until now. Do you think it's those same people who are choosing to pay four hundred pounds for fifteen minutes?'

'It seems so, doesn't it?'

'Then put your fee up. What if Frankie Jay is right, and people choose the services they perceive as more valuable because of their price?'

'It feels wrong.'

'Frankie Jay would say that if it feels wrong it's because you don't value yourself.'

'Did you follow these principles when you set up the Rajpapa Yoga business? Sorry if it sounds like I'm prying. I'm curious.'

'I did. It works. Worked – I acknowledge recent hiccoughs.'

'Communicating messages from spirits used to be considered

mystical, but a cat giving readings tops that in the woo-woo stakes. Do people want more woo-woo? Is she getting bookings because she's an animal, because she's super mystical, because she's a fad, or because people believe she has all the answers?'

'You may be right on any of those counts, Freya. But – there we go again – she's saving our centre from financial ruin, keeping the place open, saving your job.'

'Except she's not, is she? I have a flicker of a hope from your idea of doing readings by Zoom in the future. Maybe I can even do that from home, get my two lazy sons into action to build me a website or whatever, but then I'm back down to how do I market that?'

'And that's why we put our combined energies into Amantha. She's a marketing tool. A very lovely cat and gorgeous to have around the place, but primarily a marketing tool. And we've put her to work marketing this place, and ultimately, you and your services.'

'Do you believe she's psychic? Or is it Clary, Abby, even Emmy, who channel their own psychic abilities, or their intuition, when they slow down and focus on her?'

Cat's heart stops beating, splutters, stops, splutters, eases back into rhythm. She can't press her ear any closer to the floorboards.

'I don't know, Freya. People are reporting astounding insights when they sit with her and watch her. As a yoga student – every yoga teacher is an eternal student – I'd say it's possible that watching her puts people in a trance, or at least, a deeply meditative state, where it's easier to access their inner world, or the divine nature of the universe, however you like to put it. Access their own innate wisdom that is otherwise buried beneath the distractions and anxieties of modern life.'

'I think you're right, Serenity. If I stay objective, I can see an argument for charging for her services to help people meditate in a way they can't do alone or think they can't do alone. Charging people to slow down and focus, I guess, in a defined space, with no distractions and with a dash of hope. No, not a dash of hope, a dollop of complete and utter faith. That's what does it. Faith in the process. Faith that they will receive insight, so they do.'

'Four hundred pounds' worth?'

'I see your point, Serenity. The more they pay, the greater their faith that they'll be rewarded, so they are.'

'But I see your point, too. I value you, and I want to support you. Try putting up your fees for now, and I'll work on a timeline for getting you doing Zoom readings from here. We can try breakfast TV if you like, but they prefer off-the-wall subjects, and I think what you offer is more mainstream these days.'

'Thank you, Serenity. You've given me an idea. Off-the-wall subjects, hey?'

Cat scrapes herself off the floor and wobbly-paw-totters her way back to her reading room with moments to spare, before she hears Freya exit HQ, humming deviously.

🐾

Cat watches the dawn light play with the first frost on the patio, a magical moment to breathe and prepare before her working day begins. But someone else is up early, footsteps tip-tapping behind her, essence of tangerine mist announcing Freya.

'Come along, Amantha. Clary and Milly are staying in London until the end of the week, making progress with their research into our local history, so you've got me chaperoning your tier-two readings for another day. Sure you'll be delighted, whether or not you understand a single word I'm saying to you, and my guess is that you don't, sweety demon pie.'

Cat ignores Freya's threat. She plays along, purring demurely. She needs to stay focused for her clients, not let Freya ruffle her.

'We've had a few cancellations this morning, an accident blocking the motorway from London, so I'm taking you for a well-earned treat.' Freya swings the travel crate into view. She must have been hiding it behind her back. 'In you hop. Off to the beautician for you, a warm bath, chop out some of that matted hair that's been bothering you under your chin, nails clipped, fur brushed. You'll love it. It's a dedicated cat parlour, so no doggie smells to upset you. You'll be at your best for your appearance on breakfast TV next week. Don't know why Clary hasn't thought of it before. She gets all dolled up to be on camera, so why not you? You've been missing out.'

Cat's tail switches left to right, right to left, but her heart is not listening to her distrusting body. Why hasn't anyone thought of primping and priming her, their psychic-guru queen? Has it really been about Clary all along? Doesn't she, Cat, deserve to look her best for her TV performances? Doesn't she deserve time out from her long, hard and – let's be honest – sometimes boring days doing readings? Maybe Freya is feeling remorse for her outburst with Serenity. Maybe she's reaching out to rebalance the karma. Maybe ... Freya moves the travel crate closer and Cat jumps in.

🐾

Cat emerges from The Purring Diva Beauty Parlour the most relaxed she's been in weeks. Nothing but admiration, pampering and long, dozy chats with the other cats, who, it turns out, visit weekly to have their nails done, their long hair cut and curled, and in the case of a couple of the more adventurous breeds, their feline tresses sculptured into ocean waves, ornamented fairy wings or shell-encrusted dinosaur tails.

'I bet you'd like more days like that, Amantha.' Freya straps Cat's travel crate into the passenger seat of her car. 'Well, you could if you retired from giving your psychic readings. They must wear you out. People loved having you around as my psychic conduit when they came for spirit readings. What if you spent a couple of days a week relaxing in my office? You can sleep if you like – no pressure other than to be there. And in return, I take you for a full day's pampering at The Purring Diva every Wednesday. What do you say?'

Freya keeps her eyes on the road, not seeing the need to look at Cat, because, Cat knows for sure now, Freya has no belief in Cat's abilities to understand what she's saying. Freya is speaking to herself.

Cat stretches her front legs through the travel-crate bars, admiring the glow of the passing streetlights dancing across her glossy, honeyed fur, and the way her claws sit neatly within her paws, with no raggedy, rough bits spoiling her silhouette. Essence of The Purring Diva Beauty Parlour lingers in her fur, drifting through her silken whiskers, an incredible lightness of carefree being. Retire from her psychic readings? Possibly. She's made plenty of money for the centre and they're on track to financial stability. She has guarded and protected them well, but what have they done for her? Worn her out? Used her as a – what was it Serenity said – a marketing tool. *A marketing tool!*

'Emmy will have locked up by now.' Freya clicks the clickety thing near her steering wheel and they lunge to the right. 'You can stay at mine tonight, nice and warm by the fire, tasty tuna dinner, homemade nutbrown treat. We'll drive in tomorrow morning in time for the breakfast HQ meeting.'

😺

Freya bundles Cat under her arm as she shuffles along the hall, stops outside HQ, fluffs up Cat's fur and kisses her cheek, before pushing open the door. 'Ah, coffee.'

Serenity on the screen smiles and lifts her cup. 'Having a caffeine cleanse today: mint-and-ginger tea. Talking about ginger – sorry, Abby, I know you don't like us to refer to Amantha as ginger, but she's looking quite golden and glowing from what I can see.'

'Exhibit A.' Freya places Cat on the table, close to the screen, and settles her with a nutbrown biscuit. 'Oh, I should warn you, I'm hijacking the meeting this morning. Apologies in advance, but I have something important to say, something you all need to know.

'Exhibit A, one beautiful ginger cat, extra beautiful this morning because I dropped her off at The Purring Diva yesterday for a long-overdue beauty treatment. Her first ever, I believe. Not just beauty, standard feline care, including vitamin injections, worming tablets and so on. Extra beautiful today, too, because she had a day to relax, to have a rest from readings, a rest from being indoors around the clock, a rest from hard labour, a rest from our expectations and pressure. She had a chance to lounge with other cats, and let's face it, simply be a cat, as nature intended. Look at her: she's refreshed. What have we been doing to her for the sake of bringing in money? Have we been neglecting her? Abusing her, even?'

Cat feels all eyes upon her. She purrs, then licks her paws. Avoids meeting Abby or Emmy's eyes. Plays along. Where's Freya going with this? Might there be a world where she can continue her reading work part-time, have a weekly rest at The Purring Diva, look as gorgeous as Clary and Abby for their TV chats, and take a couple of days out in Freya's office each week to keep an eye on her rule keeping?

'Rule three: support each other.' Freya delves into her voluminous canary-yellow tote bag and pulls out her laptop. 'Have we been supporting Amantha? Have we been supporting her physical and mental wellbeing? Or has this all been about supporting each other by turning a blind eye to this gorgeous little puss-puss's wellbeing, keeping her slogging away at her readings to help save our jobs?'

'To be fair, Freya,' Abby's voice is parched, 'Amantha does communicate with us, well, with me, Emmy and Clary, and she always seems more than happy with the arrangement. You're right about the physical care. I'm mortified to realise that. Something we can easily address.'

'I'm confused, Freya.' Pixelated Serenity looms forward. 'I have yesterday's report in front of me, and I can see Amantha did her twelve tier-two bookings with you as her chaperone. And she's been fully engaged with readings all week – you are correct there, we are guilty of working her hard without a break – so when did she go to The Purring Diva, exactly?'

'Good question, which brings me to Exhibit B.' Freya opens her laptop and turns it to face Serenity. 'Abby, Emmy, can you come over here so we can all see this?'

Cat belly-crawls closer to the laptop, though rather in vain, because it's even fuzzier and more difficult to watch than Serenity on the big screen.

'Meet my next-door neighbour's ginger cat, Maxine.' A photo of Freya holding a cat not too dissimilar to Cat pops up on the laptop. 'Maxine took Amantha's place while she spent the day at The Purring Diva. She settled in happily, so long as I kept her supplied with my famous homemade nutbrown biscuits and plenty of cream.'

Cat squints and can just make out Maxine sitting in her reading room next to the pile of orange whorl journals. Her legs run hot and cold, and her throat parches and sears. She tries to move, but she's frozen.

'Here's her first client, Hayley.' Freya taps at her keyboard and Hoopla Giraffe, long neck and enormous hooped earrings, begins talking. *'Amantha is absolutely mesmerising. I watched her, as instructed, and straightaway I was transported to an ethereal realm where I met an angel. The angel was Amantha's spirit, right? It was as if she held my hand, poised my pen and guided my writing as the words and pictures appeared on the page, the messages I needed to hear appearing right before my eyes. I know what to do next now, and you know what, my stomach feels spacious and relaxed, and I'm breathing right down into my lower belly. It's like I've just discovered how to breathe. I feel so light.'*

'I've got footage from yesterday's other eleven clients,' Freya hits the 'pause' button and the screen freezes, 'all ecstatic about their experiences with Amantha, psychic reader. I can show you the rest later.'

'You passed Maxine off as Amantha?' Abby croaks. 'You ... you cheated people who paid three hundred pounds for a tier-two reading with Amantha?'

Cat's frozen screech ices her deepest bones. Freya cheated, again. And where was she, Cat, to keep her in line? To do her duty, to protect and guard the centre? Hoodwinked into a day's excursion to a beauty parlour! Lied to – lied to! Cheating, lying, betraying, evil moggy of a woman, parading as a loving, caring being with Cat's best interests at heart. And for what?

'I apologise for my wild, off-the-wall actions,' Freya lifts her chin, glowing red around her neck, 'but hear me out. I believe what I've demonstrated can help us all, Amantha included. Look, I'm open to learning that Amantha can talk to others and give valuable, accurate insight to her clients. I don't believe it, but I'm open to being proven wrong. I'm more partial to believing that Clary – and you, Abby and Emmy – are the psychic ones, unknowingly accessing your own inner wisdom through connecting with your instinctual energies, something that happens when we watch animals or immerse ourselves in nature.'

'It's possible.' Emmy nods slowly.

'And it's possible, no, I'll raise that to probable given yesterday's results,' Freya's skin colour cools, 'it's probable that when people have faith, faith enough to pay three hundred pounds for a fifteen-minute session, they release logic and doubt, the usual barriers to accessing their inner wisdom. Add nature into the mix – a cat – and add the instruction to focus on the cat, and they enter a meditative state, much like focusing on their breath in yoga. Within a minute or so, they're channelling their inner wisdom. Add another layer, the journals, pens and pencils, and you're in art-therapy territory. They can draw things they can't put words to, emotions, ideas, insights. Trust me, I studied all this for my social work degree and worked in the field professionally for six years.'

'So, what are you suggesting?' Abby, forget-me-knot eyes, reaches out to draw Cat towards her. 'That we stop offering psychic readings? That we cut off a stream of income that has enabled us to begin to establish a firmer foundation for our centre? That we drop Amantha from our branding? What, exactly?'

Freya closes her laptop. 'I can show you the other video testimonials later. I'm suggesting that we keep her in our branding because it's working well for us. And we keep offering her tier-one readings: either because she really is passing on messages or simply because it's a formula that seems to be working and is attracting money. We keep the TV appearances. But we bring in other cats for the tier-two readings, giving Amantha time off for her physical and mental wellbeing. Except we don't call them tier readings. We have psychic readings with Amantha two days a week, and we have 'cat meditations' – I'm sure Abby can think up a funkier name that works for marketing – three times a week, or more. That way, we can have several cats working reasonable hours, no hard cat-labour, as much income as bookings demand, and a bunch of healthy, happy cats. I'm more than keen to put my hand up to organise the cat meditations, supervise them – for a fee, naturally – even talk to the media about them, go on breakfast TV if you like, since they're always interested in an off-the-wall story. And to be transparent – though I appreciate that my undercover work yesterday was far from that – I would welcome the extra income from managing the cat meditations since, and again I'm just being honest here, my bookings have plummeted since Amantha's been the main psychic-reader attraction in this place.'

She could pee on Freya's laptop, but that would be dog eat dog, or cat eat cat, or Cat eat Catty Demon Lady. She could give away her psychic-reading work, take Freya up on a couple of days snoozing in her office in return for a weekly visit to The Purring Diva. Blood starts pumping again, a tingling rush to her heart. She leaps to her feet, screeches, digs her claws into the tabletop – her claw-print signature – and flies out the door. Rule four: leave your troubles at home. The centre is the only home she knows. Where to now?

Why is she in the dreaded daffodil bed? Why choose here to escape? Essence of snoozing daffodils, deep in the earth, taunts her nostrils. She's safe for now. What is it about this place, this very spot where she first read her right paw and understood that she was in her ninth life? Is this where she was born? Did someone bring her here?

'Back to the scene of the crime.' Pearl creeps up on her, making her jump.

'Oh, my beating heart, why did you do that? Half scare me to death?'

'You look very much alive to me, Cat.'

'The scene of the crime?'

'Ah, that's right, you don't remember, do you?'

'Remember what? My earliest memory is finding myself here and knowing, right down to my bones, that I need to get something right this life. That I need to follow the rules, stay in line and make sure everyone else does too. Like it was a clean start, and an opportunity – if I got it right – to graduate my ninth life and not have to go back to square one and who knows how many centuries more of an earthbound life.'

'And where are you up to with all that?' Pearl edges closer. 'Been getting it right?'

'I'm at square bonkers wit's end!' Anger spits her words, frustration frenzying her paws and claws at sods of earth. 'Wake up, you evil daffodils, you might as well come and get me, what's left of me. Useless, pathetic failure that I am.'

A swarm of bumble bees thunder in her ears, block her vision and sting her legs. Scarlet blood spurts, splattering the yellow daffodil petals towering above her. The searing heat of nearby flames, essence of rusty iron, a knife plunging into her heart, sneering coal-black-bearded face above her. 'Got you, you evil shapeshifting ginger-haired witch. Got you once and for all.'

Pearl is upon her, around her, holding her to their soft, warm chest, so close Cat can hear the rhythm of their heart, slowing, soothing, quietening. 'You're safe, Cat. You've just had one of your flashbacks. You're safe here with me.'

It's all Cat can do to breathe and watch a single bumble bee retreating, a tumble of crinkling tawny leaves in a sudden cooling breeze, the glint of a golden chrysalis rolling into view, its soft shell expanding, bursting, a tiny, moist butterfly emerging.

'Hello, little one.' Pearl blows softly onto the butterfly's wings.

'The flashback,' Cat gathers courage, 'was it to my first life, do you think, or one of my others?' She leans back into Pearl, secure in their sturdy support.

'It's the first-life flashbacks that can haunt us, Cat, and that haunting can continue through the second, third, all the way up to the ninth life if the wound remains unhealed.'

'The wound?' Cat watches the butterfly open its wings, preparing for flight, maybe not now, but sometime soon. 'Am I wounded?'

'How did you feel during that flashback?'

'Powerless. Helpless. Like I didn't have a leg to stand on.'

Pearl shifts to meet Cat eye to eye. 'Strange, the words we use to describe our feelings.'

'I didn't have a leg to stand on? Are you saying ... in my first life, was I missing a leg?'

'You're saying it, Cat, not I.'

'And what was that about a shapeshifting witch? Was I a witch?'

'That's something I can answer. No. No such thing. Witches can't become cats or change into any other form. They're people. Healers, medicine women, not broomstick-riding old hags that morph into cats or lizards. That's the stuff of fairytales and scared old men.'

'The guy that – did he kill me? The guy that killed me seemed pleased he had put an end to a ginger witch. Was I a ginger – I mean honey – cat in my first life, too? Did he mistake me for a ginger-haired witch?'

'Seems so.'

'And killed me in the daffodil patch?'

'Seems so. Explains why you're scared of daffodils.'

'Was scared. I'm suddenly feeling sad for the daffodils. They just happened to be there, bathing in spring's promise one moment, then next moment, they're covered in blood and flooded with my pain. It wasn't their fault at all. They were – are – beautiful. Another thing I've got completely wrong since I've been here, clearly.'

'Another thing?' Pearl lifts into wise-sphinx pose.

'Maybe, just maybe,' Cat shifts uncomfortably, feeling a hot flush rise and fall, 'maybe Freya's not so bad, either. She's an innocent, doesn't understand cats like us, wants to protect me from being put to work for financial gain. But then again, she cheats, wickedly.'

'And you don't?'

'Cheat? No way. I do my best to give people the wisdom, insight and guidance they need, to protect and guard them, to follow the rules, do the right thing.'

'And yet you read your clients' questions when they write in their journals, and you use that material in your messages. You speak of the people they mention in their questions, and what does that do? It raises your guru status and makes you look more psychic than you already are. Isn't that cheating?'

'One might use that word. I hadn't looked at it like that. But I'm not as bad as Freya. I don't lie and betray as she did when she told me my clients were cancelled and shunted me off to The Purring Diva so she could smuggle in another ginger and ...'

'And prove the truth that although you are psychic, people can connect with their own inner wisdom, and isn't that a wonderful thing? And save you from being a workcat, while giving you the grace and respect to continue your top-tier work? I'm not saying Freya's an angel. She cheats, and she did lie to you, but you cheat, and you betray all your clients by reading their questions when all they do is trust you.'

'She's not an angel, for sure,' Cat juts out her chin, raising her purr, 'she badmouths me ...'

'Like you badmouth her?'

'She tells me I'm just a cat ...'

'You tell her – only she doesn't hear you – that she's a, what is it? A Catty Demon Lady, or worse?'

'She ...' Cat searches for another misdemeanour she can attribute to Freya, but draws a blank.

'You peed on her brochures, and only this morning you contemplated peeing on her laptop.'

The tiny butterfly tries to lift from the drying remains of her chrysalis, but she's a little early. She needs more time in the sun.

'Like I said, I'm a useless, pathetic failure.' Cat lowers her chin and droops her ears, taking Pearl's observations on board.

'You're not a failure, Cat. You've followed your nose, listened to your bones, judged yourself severely for not being able to whip everyone into line, while at the same time acknowledging the enormity of the task you set yourself. You have tried your best, even if you have been a bit, shall we say, catty and judgemental of people for not following the rules from time to time.'

'I suppose. Now I think about it, where did the centre's rules come from, anyway? Who sets them? Who says what is the right thing to do in any circumstance?'

'Well,' Pearl takes a moment to consult their paws, 'you set your own psychic-reading rules, didn't you? And as for the centre's rules, I do believe that Milly's discovered something about those. Why don't you ask her?'

'I feel like an idiot.' Cat reaches out to friendly-box Pearl. 'I got sucked into all that psychic-reader-guru stuff, the fun trips to the TV studio in London, the glamour, the fame, the amount of money I made for the centre. I could have lived that life – Amantha's life, not mine – and ten thousand more like it, but what good does that do for anyone in the long run?'

'What good do you want to do, Cat?'

'I want to graduate this ninth life and do some good for the world by becoming a wise spirit mentor to an earthbound being, and it's only now that I'm beginning to understand what that means. It's not about giving people messages and telling them what to do, is it? I'm not even sure that it's about getting them to follow rules. It's more about guiding people to see what they can't see, helping them to make good decisions, helping them to do the right thing according to their hearts. Am I right?'

'You still need to be right?'

'Hmm. I never ask you how you are, Pearl. How are you?'

'At last! I am well, thank you. My mission finishes soon, and I'll tell you all about it then. Bit hush-hush for now.'

'Like a spy?'

'Not a spy, but I keep my ear to the ground, and right now I hear the rumble of heavy machinery and the scrape of chairs on the café patio. That's where you need to be, over there, with Milly and the others, watching Briar lift Reclining Woman with Child from the earth. And you still haven't solved the mystery of the Silver Crescent Nest. Today might well be your day.'

With sudden lightness of step, Cat canters over to the patio as Briar drives a giant tree-spade machine up from the main road and onto the lawn, a huffing, puffing dragon with a protruding bucket of a jaw sticking out front, gleaming metal notches for teeth.

∴

'Amantha!' Milly's arms are wide open. 'I haven't seen you for ages, and we've missed you over at Briar's. Clary's been the lucky one, getting to spend time with you during your readings. Quite the TV star now, aren't you?'

Milly's lovely essence of musk and bouncing halo of dark curls tugs at Cat's heart. Essence of life, this is what she has missed in all her dark, indoor reading hours.

'Hop up on my lap.' Clary brings a tray of coffees and pastries to the table, pulls out a chair and offers the emerald-green folds of her woollen coat. 'Can't sit in your basket today, it's filled with paperwork. Lap's better, anyway.'

Cat eyes the basket, once a comforting and comfortable nest, her throne as an art-class model, her sedate carriage across the lawn to Briar's, her guru-queen safe space for Open Day, her warm retreat during reading days when she tired of prancing and dancing. And once, in her first life, long, long ago, according to her vision, a place to sit and guard herbal treasures that stealthy visitors collected, lifting her up, dropping in silver coin and settling her back down. A silver-lined nest?

'Croissants!' Pixie strides over to the table, Anna close behind. 'Crescent-shaped croissants, theme for the day?'

Milly reaches for a chocolate croissant. 'You've heard some news on the grapevine, then?'

'Bits and pieces.' Anna chooses a marmalade pastry. 'But we're all ears for the full story this morning. Oh, Amantha, you're here, too. We are so honoured.'

Cat snuggles into Clary's coat, deeply reassuring essence of clay. A silver-lined nest? Crescent-shaped croissants? Silver

Crescent Nest? Not making sense. She eyes the basket again, relieved that it is filled with other stuff, that she is free to stretch her legs.

From nowhere, the distant smell of burning flesh, a young boy wielding a branding iron, and sudden, intense, searing pain. 'Burn, witch, burn!' His retreating steps, a halo of ginger curls lifting her up, pressing a bundle of aloe and honey into her numbing leg and placing her into a basket. Bed bound, basket bound, is she lame? Essence of herbs beneath her, the vision intensifies, work to do, guardian and protector of herbs and silver.

'Are you okay, Amantha?' Clary lifts her to her face. 'You were trembling. There, there, little one. Perhaps we've been overworking you. Just as well it's a day off for you today.'

Milly cracks her knuckles and stretches her arms above her head, a cluster of jade bangles drawing attention to her new tattoo: a crescent moon. 'Potted history catch-up.' She looks at Pixie and Anna. 'Saving all the big mysteries and reveals for my book, which you'll be able to read next year. But for now, we've read through most of Briar's family logbooks, and they're not what they seem. Yes, they record gardening details, when to plant, prune, fertilise and so on, but the first odd things I noticed were the crescent-moon symbols in the margins. At first, I assumed they recorded the times of the new moon, and related to gardening or planting rituals. But then I noticed there were too many of them, not one every twenty-eight days. They began in the early sixteen hundreds and were regularly recorded until the twenty-second of March sixteen fifty-six. They didn't appear after that.'

'March sixteen fifty-six.' Anna taps her fingers against her cheek. 'What was special about that year?'

'The logbooks record a fire. The lacemaker's cottage was burned to the ground.'

'The lacemaker? Did they make lace around these parts then?'

'The foundations of Briar's cottage go back to before that time, one of several cottages on this land, mostly to do with sheep farming. The landowners were the Gables, who lived some distance away. They bought and sold sheep and wool, and housed workers, including wool spinners, weavers and a lacemaker. There must have been a flax farm nearby, or they bought flax in to make the lace that would have sold to the gentry. All very normal and above board for this part of the country.'

'Except for the witches,' Pixie says, high on caffeine after her third espresso. 'Everyone around here knows there were witches.'

'Let's call them healers, herbalists, medicine women, apothecaries.' Milly checks her watch. 'Briar's all set to start lifting the topiary in twenty minutes, so I'll cut to the chase. Our elaborate code breaking, and several trips to the London Metropolitan Archives and the National Archives, led us to believe that the crescent-moon symbols related to the preparation of herbal remedies, made to order for both locals and – secretly – gentry. When we looked more closely at the logbooks, we found other symbols we believe relate to the types of remedies prepared: red raspberry leaf, rose, rosemary, even the crushed woodlice that our Amantha here prescribed for Hazel. Everything either grown in Briar's ancestors' cottage garden, or gathered further afield according to strict, secret rituals.'

'So, Briar's one of a long line of witch enablers.' Can't-sit-still Anna fiddles with her coffee spoon.

'Judging by the colour of his hair – you've no doubt noticed his ginger beard – they were more than that. We think the women of his family may have worked on the farm as healers. There's plenty of local folklore about ginger-haired witches and their ginger cats, stories about the witches shapeshifting into cats to hide or move about undercover.'

'Oh, Amantha,' Anna says, 'no wonder you're psychic. Who or what are you really, my dear?'

'Speaking of undercover.' Milly glances over to check on Briar's progress. The tree-spade monster sits in silence. Briar is walking the perimeter of the topiary, poking a long metal rod into the soil at intervals. 'We're thinking that the lacemaker's cottage was the apothecary – the old plans show plenty of room out the back where the remedies could have been prepared and stored – with the lacemaking business going on in the front of the building. Some of the symbols in the logbooks suggest the remedies were sewn into lace pockets.'

'I'll never look at lace in the same way again,' can't-keep-quiet Anna says.

'You'll never look at oranges the same way again, either,' Milly says, keen to get to the end of her potted history. 'Did you know there were orange trees right here in the village at that time?'

Pixie's face lights up. 'The gentry were experimenting with growing oranges indoors. I've always been fascinated by the orangeries they built, the architecture and their early culinary experiments with making marmalade. Studied it as a special subject for my architecture degree.'

'I didn't know you were an architect, Pixie,' Anna says, eyebrows quizzical.

'Story for another time.' Pixie splays her palms upwards with a shrug. 'But oranges here, on a sheep farm?'

'The logbooks record a gift of three orange trees in tubs, a pot of marmalade and – wait for it – a marmalade cat to catch mice, on the twenty-second of January sixteen fifty-four. The logbooks indicate the tubs were overwintered inside the lacemaker's cottage, confirming that it must have been a big cottage, certainly a good candidate for an apothecary. Anyway, the point of the story is, and we had a bit of code breaking to do, but as far as we could tell, they may have been a gift in return for herbal services rendered.'

'Let me guess.' Anna wriggles excitedly. 'Based on knowing about crushed woodlice through Hazel, and knowing, personally, as I do, that red raspberry leaf is a modern-day herbal support for childbirth, maybe even for preventing miscarriage, I bet the apothecary specialised in women's medicine, in pregnancy and childbirth, and I bet the orange trees, the marmalade and the marmalade cat were a gift for a successful delivery. I know myself that first-time mothers are so ecstatic after giving birth that they're keen to express their gratitude in the shape of hospital donations and extravagant gifts.'

'Right on track, Anna.' Milly taps the table with her forefinger. 'On one of our London trips, Clary and I traced the family history of the Gables. Isobel, who was one of Briar's ancestors, married William Gable, and she gave birth to Henry Gable – yes, the same Henry Gable who designed our Reclining Woman with Child topiary. Henry was born in early January sixteen fifty-four, only days before the gift of the orange trees. A bit more sleuthing and we discovered William and Isobel Gable had an orangery.'

'So,' Pixie says, 'since Isobel was one of Briar's ancestors, and presumably raised on the farm until she was whisked by marriage into higher society, she would have known about the witches – can I call them witches? It's more exciting. She would have known about the remedies, and perhaps she'd had a miscarriage, or a tricky pregnancy, and sent for the appropriate herbs. I wonder if William knew anything about it, or whether she kept it to herself.'

'I imagine the menfolk were kept in the dark,' Milly says, 'but I daresay other women of the gentry and perhaps even of the aristocracy sent their servants for remedies when required. Hiding the herbs in lace would help. You know, women being supplied by their lacemakers to keep them in fashion. No-one would have suspected anything.'

'But hang on a minute,' Anna shakes her head, 'I'm getting lost. We know from the brochures in the village information centre that Henry Gable designed the topiary in sixteen ninety-eight, when he would have been forty-four. Did he know about his connection to the village? When I look at Reclining Woman with Child, now that I know more about the local history, I'm seeing a mother leaning back in bed after giving birth. I'm seeing a memorial to the work of the witches – sorry, to the local medicine women who perhaps specialised in pregnancy and childbirth. I'm seeing the topiary with new eyes.'

'We're thinking the same, Anna.' Clary finally joins the conversation. 'Milly and Briar trawled through the logbook entries covering the design of the topiary. It was Henry who drew it on paper, and Isobel's brother, Sandy, known for his sandy-coloured hair, who planted the box hedge and over the years clipped it into shape. Anyway, we found what we think is a reference to a memorial buried underneath the topiary. The language was flowery, almost alchemical, but it suggested that a Silver Crescent Nest – now, we don't know what that is yet, a memorial of sorts, we suppose – has lain under the topiary for all this time, hidden away from prying eyes. Briar's ancestors were charged with maintaining the topiary, thereby protecting its underlying secret.'

'Which is why Briar is lifting the topiary today?' Pixie asks, brushing her fingers through her spiky pixie hair, her dangling crescent-moon silver earrings catching the sunlight.

'Briar was planning on lifting the topiary at some point, anyway,' Clary says. 'He wants to prune the roots, feels it won't survive another decade if it doesn't get the attention. He says it feels like a betrayal of his roots – pun not intended, but a good one, hey – a betrayal of the rules laid down in the logbooks, but time for action, nevertheless. When he and Milly surmised the possibility of a secret memorial, he decided to stop hesitating and get on with it. He's been digging trenches and taking measurements for a couple of weeks now and brought in some kind of echo-location device to see if he could detect anything solid in or under the root system. Looks like there's something directly under the topiary woman's heart. He's got the tree spade in to hold the topiary aloft in case the object gets caught up in the roots. Otherwise, the machine will lay the topiary on the tarpaulin you can see over there while Briar digs deeper.'

'One more titbit for you.' Milly leans forward onto her

elbows, somewhat conspiratorially. 'You know the centre's four rules, do no harm and so on? We found the same rules – word for word – in the back of one of Briar's logbooks, the one dated sixteen forty-four to forty-five. How's that?'

Cat's ears prick as Pixie gasps, 'So, what are we saying, that Serenity's a descendant of a witch, too? She doesn't have ginger hair.'

'Very funny, Pixie.' Clary lifts Cat closer to her chest. 'We asked Serenity about the origin of the centre's rules, and she said she found them written in the margin of a herbal remedy book dating back to the nineteen twenties that she found in Stacey's, the preloved bookshop in the village.'

'And to draw it all together, because I can see Briar's accomplices have arrived now,' Milly starts to gather her things to go over and watch the event, 'we believe that the rather odd rule four: leave your troubles at home is code for evacuation. The medicine women were aware of the dangers of being arrested and tried by the witch hunters, who were rampant at the time, and we believe – going by the symbols in the logbooks – that they had a secret getaway plan. Leave your troubles at home somehow encoded that plan, we think. Every time they recounted their rules, they would have been consoled by the thought of the plan and would have refreshed their memory of the steps they needed to take if the alarm was raised.'

'Sorry we can't all go over to watch,' Clary stands up, snuggling Cat under her arm, 'but Briar needs to focus, and has asked us to take photos of the excavation. You'll be able to see a bit from here, and we'll report back as soon as we can. So excited!'

Cat sails across the lawn in a billow of forest-green woollen coat, Clary's earthy clay essence, and Milly's musky perfume, underscored by essence of damp earth and the scent of sky-high anticipation. She'll soon know exactly what the Silver Crescent Nest is, and everything else she's heard so far fits perfectly with what she now knows, in her deepest bones, are her first-life visions.

The last puzzle piece is about to be revealed, and didn't Pearl say that the Silver Crescent Nest was the key to her graduation from this, her ninth life?

🐾

Cat stares into the deep clay ditch at Clary's feet, slices of grey, red, ochre and chestnut along its walls, some sliced roots from the brush box, a few earthworms wriggling in puddles of water at the bottom. Like a moat. Where has she seen a moat before? A moat circling, as far as she can tell, Reclining Woman with Child. An army of red spades, well, at least a dozen of them, stand sentry, each with its shovel embedded in the topiary side of the ditch wall, each with its handle leaning back towards Cat. The growl of the tree-spade machine starts up behind her.

'Stand well back.' Briar rides the jawed monster closer, as three soldiers – no, they must be gardeners – dressed in orange uniforms, start to push on the spades, gently lifting the topiary below its roots.

Cat calculates the position of Reclining Woman's heart as the grumbling dinosaur's jaw extends, wavers and finally slips in below her airborne roots, lifting her free from the ground where she has lain for more than three hundred years. She looks quite unperturbed, as serene as ever, gazing out towards Briar's cottage, although now from a higher perspective.

Briar silences the monster and jumps down from his saddle. 'Not too many roots damaged from lifting, but plenty of pruning work needed. She's in worse condition than I had thought. Milly, are you taking plenty of photos?'

Milly *click-click-clicks*.

Clary seems frozen to the spot, tightening her grip on Cat. 'Briar, there, in the root ball, is that a parcel sticking out? A bundle of leather?'

Briar pulls a pair of secateurs from his belt, clips away at the root ball, lifts out the black parcel, bowl-shaped, as big as his chest, and dissolves into shaking rivers of tears and bellows of laughter. 'Never in my wildest dreams did I imagine it was going to be as easy as that!'

Milly clicks more photos as Briar lays the parcel on the tarpaulin. 'Are you sure about this, Briar? It's not too late to bring in an expert.'

'Let's play innocent a little longer.' Briar sits back on his heels, catching his breath. 'Maybe it's illegal to unwrap it, maybe it's classified as national treasure, but for now, the story is that I've lifted the topiary to prune her roots, and we've found this parcel and I'm naively opening it. I'm too spooked, to be honest, by the warnings in the logbooks to bring anyone else in at this stage.'

The leather, spotted with the greens, reds and greys of moulds and fungi, judging by the smell, creaks and breaks as Briar tries to gently unfold it, despite its years hidden away from drying sun and winds. Too soon, it shatters into shards.

'We can stop here, Briar,' Milly gasps, 'bring in the authorities, get some expert help in preserving whatever this is.'

'I've come this far,' Briar responds, essence of sweat, fear and high excitement. 'Just one more step, then I promise, if it looks significant, we'll contact our local coroner, as you advised, and perhaps also check in with the Portable Antiquities Scheme. But for now, it might just be a bit of old leather packed with stones, for all we know.'

But it's not a bit of old leather packed with stones. What emerges is a stone statue of a cat and a tarnished silver cradle. Briar lifts the stone cat, as Milly crouches down to take more photos. 'It's got an inscription, Briar, can you make it out? The writing looks very small.'

Briar peers at the base of the statue, reading slowly, 'In memory of our Beloved Marmalade Cat, protector of our medicines and our souls, who courageously sacrificed her life, that we might be saved. Martha, Alice, Anne. Seville, Spain, September sixteen fifty-six.'

'She's got three legs, must have been lame.' Clary cranes her neck over Milly's shoulder. 'But a marmalade cat. I'm getting goosebumps. What's Spain got to do with this place?'

Cat breathes deep and slow, holding back the creeping edge of a vision.

Briar sweeps his hand across the dusty surface of the silver cradle. 'It's going to take an expert clean before we can read this, but look, it's covered in inscriptions and drawings. What are these, orange trees in tubs? And this, a cat sitting in a cradle, or a basket? And this, flames licking a cottage?'

'Looks like a list of names, too.' Clary almost tips Cat forward onto the cradle. 'Around the edge, are those crescent moons?'

'Are they crescent moons or are they cradles?' Milly breathes, head almost touching Clary's. 'Is that a baby in that one there in the corner?'

'September sixteen fifty-six.' Briar looks skywards. 'That's two years or so after the gift of the orange trees in tubs, and if my memory serves me, the year the lacemaker's cottage burned to the ground, according to the notes in the logbooks.'

'And forty-two years before Henry Gable designed the topiary, and Sandy began the work,' Milly adds, investigative researcher in full swing. 'Why did they wait all that time before erecting a memorial?'

'The logbooks said a Silver Crescent Nest was buried beneath the topiary.' Clary gently strokes Cat. 'This silver cradle is crescent shaped, crescent-moon shaped, see? It's a nest perhaps for the babies born through the medicine women's help, but look at it from a different angle. Isn't the message here that the silver crescent was a nest for a three-legged marmalade cat? Is this simply a memorial to the cat, and for the lives she apparently saved?'

Cat's world whorls and stumbles, expands and contracts,

fires and ices. Martha, Alice and Anne have been out since before dawn, harvesting herbs beyond the farm, leaving her, as always, in charge of the apothecary, the orange trees and the oil lamps keeping the temperature inside the cottage right for the trees. Her crescent-shaped basket is musky cosy, the smell of the citrus leaves a loving embrace while the women are out. There are no deliveries at this time of day, no-one expected on horseback to lift her and deposit silver coin in payment for their herbal remedy, so whose horses are these rumbling far away, drumming closer in her ears?

She listens to the pattern of the approaching hooves, and beyond that, the snorting of the horses, and beyond that, the intentions of their riders, a skill she has honed during a lifetime of being on guard, of distinguishing friend from foe. Her hair stands on end and her stomach retches: witch hunters in a beeline for the cottage. Her duty, what's her duty? All she can see is the need to signal the women, to let them know it's not safe to come home, to consider escape if they are to avoid being captured, trialled and killed for being witches. Her body makes the decision for her. She hauls herself, three-legged, from her basket, drags her belly to the closest oil lamp, nudges it until it tips over, flames rapidly devouring the nearest orange tree, and pulls herself along the flagstones and out the door, hot orange tongues licking at her hind legs, belly-squirming through the grass to the safety of the daffodil patch, where she can hide from the witch hunters who are almost upon her.

Surely the women will see the fire, imagine the witch hunters they constantly fear are trying to flush them out of the cottage. Surely, they'll enlist rule four, and they'll escape to safety. But deep down in her exhausted bones, Cat fears they'll misunderstand, that they'll already be running home to extinguish the fires, blaming a failed oil lamp or a clumsy three-legged cat. The horror of her action bites at her throat, strangling her lungs. She has broken rule one: do no harm. She has destroyed the very medicines that can help and heal, as per rule two. And in her endeavour to support each other, rule three, her action may have exposed them to danger. She can't engage rule four because she is the very essence of their troubles, failing to guard and protect their home. Her only hope, as the coal-black-bearded face above her drives his knife into her heart, sneering, 'Got you, you evil shapeshifting ginger-haired witch. Got you once and for all,' is that he truly believes the witch he sought was dead, and he would triumphantly gallop off with his henchmen before the women arrive home.

🐾

Pearl shimmers beside her. 'Tell me, then, what have you learned?'

Cat sits on the patio. Briar is watering Reclining Woman with Child, and Milly and Clary are comparing notes over a coffee, only they don't seem to notice her.

'When I left my first life,' Cat lifts her face to the blackbird flying overhead, 'I believed I had failed in my duties. All I had to do was guard and protect the apothecary and the orange trees. Instead, I destroyed them and died, never knowing whether Martha, Alice and Anne survived. Then when Briar uncovered the statue – of me – I learned the sisters had escaped to Seville, in Spain, and that they believed I sacrificed myself to save them.'

'A job well done, then?'

'Well done if measured by saving their souls. Not well done if measured by following the four rules, and that seems trite and stupid hearing myself put it like that now.'

'Following rules can be trite and stupid compared to saving souls?'

'So obvious now, isn't it? I've wasted so much time, this ninth life, judging people for not following rules, feeling the enormity of my mission, a mission I set myself, to get everything right this time. Getting everything right was never the point, was it?'

'It was quite an adventure, your ninth life, wasn't it?' Pearl's voice is more blackbird than cat, their essence more butterfly than feline.

'Was?'

'Look at your right paw, Cat.'

Cat tentatively raises her paw, but she already knows what she will see because she can feel her body lifting, flying alongside the blackbird.

'Why are you still with me, Pearl?'

Pearl's tail dissolves into a helix of orange butterflies, her belly into a mass of autumn leaves. 'We've always been with you, Cat, and always will be. You never guessed, did you? We were, are, and always will be your spirit mentor, just as you are about to become once we've helped to brush you up on a few techniques.'

'Clary and Milly can't see me, can they?'

'That was then, this is now.'

'I did so much wrong, in that ninth life. How did I manage to graduate?'

'You finally forgave yourself for breaking the rules in your first life. You understood that you did the right thing, not the rule thing, and doing the right thing trumps the rules at any time. You also got first-hand experience of what it's like to be a guru, and what it's like to be at the mercy of a guru, because being a mentor is a whole different kettle of fish to being a guru. Most of your work will be unseen, unacknowledged.'

'Freya never acknowledged my abilities, did she? Was that part of my training? To be at peace with the judgement of others?'

'Training is ongoing, it doesn't end with graduation. Neither does your story with Freya. You two are karmically bound. A story for another time, Cat.'

'I never got to hear what was written on the Silver Crescent Nest. Is a student spirit mentor permitted to be curious, Pearl?'

'It told the story of Martha, Alice and Anne Johnson's work. Yes, they were Johnsons, some of Briar's ancestors. Most of the story you now know. Henry Gable's mother, Isobel, gifted the medicine women with three orange trees in tubs, a pot of marmalade and a marmalade cat – you in your first life – in a crescent-moon-shaped basket with silver coin in a leather pouch, in thanks for the herbs they supplied that helped her bring her first son, Henry, to full term after several miscarriages. The crescent-moon basket was a symbolic reference to the women's work, to the moon and to birth. In later years, Isobel told Henry the story, and he decided to commemorate the work of the medicine women through the topiary and the deeper memorial buried safely within its roots. The names of the medicine women, some of the women they helped and some of the babies' names, were listed on the buried Silver Crescent Nest, along with the whereabouts of Martha, Alice and Anne. Memories of the witch trials were still too fresh, and stories of witch hunters still rife at the time to do anything other than bury the memorial for a future, more enlightened generation.'

'What happened to Martha, Alice and Anne? Why Seville?'

'Their leave-your-troubles-at-home rule was to go downriver to the coast, where one of their customers had promised safe getaway if they needed it. They were shipped to Seville, where they established a new healing sanctuary, nestled in an orange grove. Briar is planning to go to Seville sometime soon to trace their descendants, the relatives he never knew existed.'

'One thing, Pearl. How did they know I knocked down the oil lamp and burned the apothecary?'

'I believe a little bird told them, but that's not something you need to know. Your job is done.'

'Pearl? I did have fun, though, in my ninth life, looking back on it, deluded though I was about all the rule following.'

'We need the disguise of our mission – yours being to ensure people follow the rules – so that our lessons can take us by surprise.'

'Pearl? Am I still a cat?'

'You're as curious as a cat with nine lives.'

'But I've graduated from my ninth life. Am I a spirit cat?'

Pearl shapeshifts into a single fluttering butterfly, a silver-trailing snail, a many-branched oak tree heavy with acorns, an orange tree in a tub and a pearly, fluffy kitten. 'You can be whatever you want to be, but I shall probably always call you Cat.'

Acknowledgements

I finally let the muse into my heart. Or did I let the cat out of the bag? I had noticed my non-fiction writing growing more lyrical with each passing year until eventually, in early 2023, I acknowledged the call. It was time to write a novel, although I had no story in mind and no training in writing fiction. I signed up for an online course in novel writing through The Writers' Studio and danced between learning about structure and letting the muse direct my story. My tutor, Neasa Nic Dhómhnaill, kept me on my toes whenever I wanted to deviate from the course – or, truth be told, abandon it altogether – in favour of the story I wanted to tell. I also wanted to make Cat the protagonist and tell the story from her point of view. I'm forever grateful to Neasa for encouraging me to do this and guiding me in the finer points of such a quirky approach.

I would like to thank the random tabby cat who slinked her way into our garden in March 2023 while I was exercising in the kitchen, before pausing to stare at me through the window. I was listening to a podcast interview with a psychic medium whose messages from spirit seemed highly dubious. The moment the cat arrived, the idea for Ninth Life fell from the sky. I had never seen a cat in our garden. It was three weeks before the start of the online course, so her timing was perfect.

I am deeply thankful to my beautiful family and friends who were excited about my mission though somewhat baffled that I wanted to keep the story idea secret until I had finished the first draft. A huge thank you to my husband, Michael Collins, and son, Euan Gray, for doing first reader duty even though Ninth Life did not fall into either of their usual preferred genres. It was a delight to hear that Cat enticed both Michael and Euan into her tale. Thank you to you both for your excitement and constructive feedback.

I commissioned a full manuscript report through Curtis Brown Creative. They assigned Nicholas Blincoe to the task. Thank you, Nicholas, for your practical and insightful suggestions, for nailing the genre (I didn't know it was UpLit), and for acknowledging Cat's charm as an unusual protagonist.

Thank you to my editor, Alexandra Nahlous, for an immaculate copyedit, and for suggesting that Cat might have a future in my next work of fiction. Thank you, Alex, for sharpening my grammatical skills and keeping my tenses in line.

Thank you to Nada Backovic for your spectacular cover designs: it was hard to pick one from the range you created. They were all so eye-popping and clearly reflected your understanding of Cat's personality and the story she had to tell. Thank you too for your beautiful page design.

And, lastly, a big thank to you. If you're reading these acknowledgments, you've probably read the story. I hope it entertained you and made you smile.

Jane Teresa Anderson is a dream analyst, mentor, host of *The Dream Show with Jane Teresa Anderson* podcast, and author of seven non-fiction books on dreams and dreaming. Born and raised in England not far from the scene of Cat's ninth life, Jane now lives in Hobart, Tasmania.

Discover more at: JaneTeresa.com